Hide Me Sundown

By

Jay D. Heckman

ISBN: 1-4033-2194-9 (e-book)
ISBN: 1-4033-2195-7 (Paperback)

Library of Congress Control Number: 2002091395

This book is printed on acid free paper.

Printed in the United States of America
Bloomington, IN

1stBooks - rev. 01/23/03

Dedicated to
Doug and Roma Lea Heckman

Two people of that generation who lived those days of the Great Depression and World War II and became my parents.

A special thanks to

my wife Roselyn and her college roommate and sorority sister, Patsi Bale Cox

Chapter 1

Wednesday, July 25, 1945

Henry knelt on a hill over-looking Cheyenne, Wyoming in the dusk of late afternoon. He had been studying the town for some time trying to understand what to do next. In the bottom of the ravine, behind him, was parked a 1938 V-8 sedan, along with too many people to conceal in the open plains of Wyoming.

There was Josh Archer, a young draft dodger who had turned to crime on the run instead of life, or death, in the military. Josh didn't have much to lose, so he didn't spend much time caring about anyone else. His sensitivity for human feelings did not extend beyond his own arms. He could follow orders, with exceptions and appeared to be loyal to Henry. Josh's choices in life were becoming limited.

August Stauble was a second generation German-American and a first generation criminal from a hard working family. August was a big man and "might making right" came as a natural policy to him. Part of being a man was his physical presence over other men. He was smart about some things, but rash about others. His decision-making lacked the educated touch of a more successful man. He sought the good life with little thought of cost. Loyalty was a random thing to August.

Sammy Keller was the wild card in the deck. He could be explosively violent, yet a quiet, private man, who didn't drink or smoke, but was always wrong about more basic choices in life. No matter what he did in life, the results worked against him and someone else would come up with the prize. Any success Sammy had was tied to other people. He learned this after several years of failing the straight life. His temper always put him back where he started, with nothing.

Finally, there was the most unlikely of all in that ravine, Jean Lester. A bright, pretty brunette, Jean had little direction in life. She was one of four sisters in an upper-middle class family from Missouri. She had never lived-up to the expectations of her parents or the success of her sisters. Grabbing a chance to escape the oncoming burden of conforming came at age 23 when she met the man on the hill.

Henry Lapointe was deeply in love with Jean. He held these thoughts to himself as he surveyed the social distance between them. He carried this suppressed love with the knowledge it would probably never be returned to him. She was with him now and had even enthusiastically participated in the romance of their dating. But Henry always felt her eyes had been set on some indefinable love in the future. As heart breaking as that was for him, he quietly held hope that in the short time they would have together, she would change her mind and see in him the things he saw in her.

Henry Lapointe was a Canadian citizen who floated between Canada and the United States, taking what hc could from cach. Born in Quebec in 1913, his mother died of influenza when he was three. His father was unable to care for him with the demands of work so he was sent to the western province of Manitoba, near Winnipeg, to be raised by his mother's sister and her family. Never feeling he belonged,

Henry was constantly challenged by social rules and obligations. He found confidence in daring the boundaries that confined him. Pushing those boundaries had brought him success.

At age 13 he was tagging along with relatives and friends on journeys carrying Canadian made whiskey to the borders of the United States. Proving to be a lucrative occupation, the process of delivering prohibition liquor did not have a sense of illegality about it. It was an exciting adventure with people Henry knew well. In this atmosphere he felt he belonged, was happy and enjoyed his participation in outmaneuvering the law.

With the ending of Prohibition in the United States and the settling-in of the Great Depression over North America, young Lapointe found it impossible to get good work. He remained with the groups of men who were making money through a variety of illegal activities. It was a good schooling for Henry and his interest made him a good student. But the real money was to be made south of the boarder in the cities of the United States. For the next eight years he moved back and forth across the border selling his services to several different organized crime gangs. He maintained a degree of independence from the inner circles of the gangs. As a result, never rose in the ranks. But rising in the ranks was not his objective. He was developing a very self-confident stature without the anointment of power from lords of crime. He had patience and knew one day his time for wealth would come.

When Canada entered World War II in 1939, he became scarce for the Canadian government to locate. Staying in the United States, within an organized crime gang, he kept himself hidden from the intents of the Canadian Armed Forces. When the United States was drawn into the war in December of 1941, 28-year-old Henry Lapointe became invisible in a second country. Losing his identity in two countries, whose entire populations were dedicated to the war, was a daunting charade for a young, healthy appearing man. He sidestepped many accusing questions by creating new identities for himself, mainly as a U.S. Government employee whose "essential official" duties could counter prying inquiries about his not being in uniform. After years in western Canada, there was no longer a trace of his native French-Canadian accent. He became successful moving in and around the world of organized crime, making enough money to keep himself and his charade in good standing with legitimate society.

Early in 1945, he was working for a brewery in Kansas City, Missouri. Most of the job involved lawful deliveries of beer to the taverns and bars in the Kansas City area. However, the ownership of the brewery was secreted away behind the closed lips of local crime figures and thus certain requirements of the job involved deliveries of beer into a neighboring state. Henry was of value to the owners for several reasons. He was a good driver who kept his mouth shut, could be trusted to do what he was told and not go beyond lines drawn by the nature of their interest. He also did not display any signs of ambition within the organization, nor did he display any tendency for violence; both of which allowed his superiors to invest their self-preservation efforts against the other men.

Henry's weekly deliveries in the Kansas City area gained him acquaintances in each of the little bars and taverns on his route. Some of the spots were favorite hangouts of the men Henry was associated with. Here he had the luxury of a small social life with "friends."

Saturday, April 21, 1945

It was this night Henry met a young lady by the name of Jean Lester. She was quite different from the normal girls Henry would see at these small spots. Although she could project something akin to the surrounding crowd, her beauty and quick skilled expressions made it apparent to Henry that she had class. This intrigued him and led him to approach this member of the legitimate world, against his policy to maintain his distance.

She was sitting with a group of eight people all about the same age. Six girls and two male escorts. Of the six girls, she stood out, as would an adult on a playground. They were drinking beer at a table near the jukebox so they wouldn't miss a beat of the swing music, which was their social cement. Jean was focused on her group and the music, but occasionally surveyed the room and took in the ambiance of roughness. Henry sat at the bar with his two friends and his beer. His attention kept straying to the brunette. Now his head was propped against his left hand with the elbow firmly supported by the bar, his eyes focused on her. He pondered this young woman and questions without answers drifted through him. Who was she? Where does she come from? What is she doing here? Had he seen a more beautiful girl? Why has she captured his imagination?

One realization surfaced for him. He was observing this group in a brief stop over while out on a night on the town. They were here for the moment and this place could fill one's curiosity very quickly. He received a rare push from his emotions, which left other senses submerged by a very basic human need. When that party left, she would be gone and with her departure would come the killing of this rare presence of beauty. He knew he would survive the short-lived pain of that "kill". He had experienced that before. But this time he didn't have to let it happen. Couldn't he do something? At least make a gesture toward prolonging the moment? Before he had found answers to his self-imposed interrogation, he was walking toward the group…toward the girl.

He grabbed a chair in his last few strides, placed it backwards in the small vacant space to the girl's left and seated himself straddling it. The group's attention was immediately shifted to this intrusion and silence marked each individual's retreat into themselves, to analyze the nature of the unexpected.

His voice followed his smile, "It's not often that Freddy's Bar, here, is host to the college educated crowd, at least that's what I am guessing…that you are all of higher learning?" He left the question mark visible on his friendly expression.

Not knowing how to respond initially to the intrusion, the stranger's disarming smile opened a narrow corridor for a hesitant response. "Yes, we've all been to college." One of the young escorts answered.

Without allowing a moment to pass Henry enthusiastically jumped in, "I knew it, I just knew it!

In the tradition of hospitality, that is Freddy's Bar, I would like to buy the table a round of beers." At that, he turned to the bar and shouted over the music, "Hey Freddy, bring a round of beers over here!" His request was acknowledged by a wave from the bartender and sounds of approval from the beneficiaries. He turned back to the table, "Now, what is cause for tonight's celebration?"

With the party atmosphere mostly back intact, a blond across the table eagerly responded to the question. "It's Judy's birthday, she's 21 today!"

"And which one is Judy?" Henry inquired hoping the brunette next to him had not just turned twenty-one.

Further to the right another girl responded, "I'm Judy, it's my birthday."

Henry raised his glass, "A toast to Judy." Looking around the table with a smile he noted everyone had at least some beer in their glass with which to toast. "Welcome to the wonderful world of being 'of age' and all the good fortune and privileges that it so brings!"

All eight of the party raised their glasses toward his uttering their approval and additions to the toast. Freddy showed up at the table with a tray of full glasses distributing one to each of the guests. Henry reached for his wallet and was pulling out the appropriate number of bills to hand Freddy as he asked the table in general, "What does the rest of the night hold? Are you off on further adventures, or is this the last stop?"

One of the young men responded, "The night is still young so we've got a couple of more spots to hit before Cinderella has to be back to the palace."

"Well then, let me make the rest of your stay here a financial free one. The rest is on me." Henry raised his beer again and took a swallow with his smile still showing through the glass. The party responded well to his offer with vocal and non-vocal pronouncements of approval.

Henry's glance brought him the eyes of the brunette beside him. "And what's your name?" He made the inquiry quick and nonchalant so the display of interest in this particular person was not too noticeable. A pause ensued, so he let his right hand fall open in front of her in the gesture of a handshake and said, “I’m Henry and you’re…?”

She gave into his charm, took his hand and said “My name’s Jean.”

“Glad to meet you and your friends.” Henry gestured with a half sweep of his hand which held the beer glass. “Did you all go to college together?” Directing the question to Jean.

“We were all in college together at one time or another. But we have all graduated now.”

The rest of the table was a-buzz with conversation and the music was again the center of all activity as each person gave some physical movement timed with its rhythm. Henry had gained their temporary acceptance and each seemed comfortable with the “older” man, eight to ten years their senior, sitting-in on their party. He had crossed that boundary which separated these people from the unknown environs of the bar. They were here to expose their taste for the daring to the hostility believed to exist in this sort of place. Henry was their bridge over that gap. Their acceptance of him and, his of them, reflected in the patrons throughout the bar.

For Jean, Henry was more than that. Her attraction to the unknown was more than a lark. It was something that made her heart pound a little faster and her cheeks flush with the excitement of danger lurking just beyond reach. Henry was a part of this world and he offered an insight into it that she had heard about, but never experienced. A world where each individual had to rule his own domain, armed with acts of violence to preserve a little threshold on the edge of society. She was curious about this rough and unpredictable life and her new acquaintance was certainly part of it.

Jean was the fourth daughter of a prominent Kansas City businessman. Jean's father was a cattle buyer for a major meat packing company in Chicago. He had lived and worked in the Kansas City cattle market all of his adult life. He married the daughter of a large Missouri rancher and had raised the four girls in comfort, even during the desperate years of the Depression. Cattle from the plains states had dried-up with the dust bowl, which killed 600,000 square miles of farm and ranch land in six states. But demand for beef had not dried-up and he managed to keep providing his employer with "beef on the hoof" from the farms and ranches still able to keep two nickels together. His connections in the agricultural U.S. were prominent and he was well respected in the Kansas City community.

The Lesters' first three daughters were ready made for their parents hopes and wishes of raising beautiful, intelligent and talented young ladies; their social traits insuring a future of prosperity and happiness in well-to-do marriages. These were dreams of parents who had conquered tough times and were very proud of their success; without fully understanding the advantages they had over people with the same struggles and less wealth. Although money had been hard to come by for all, the Lesters were among the fortunate few whose monetary resources outlasted the Depression. While not being among the very wealthy, they enjoyed the obscurity of lesser wealth. They could isolate themselves from much of the world and not feel the burden of being targeted for their money. The isolation did have drawbacks. Losing track of the guideposts of genuine society lends one to start believing your ways are the only option. Their fourth daughter had been a victim of this drawback all of her life.

Jean was three years younger than her next oldest sister. The three older sisters were each a year apart. It seemed they were in different families. Jean was not a part of her close-knit sisters and thus, did not enjoy the overwhelming approval they received from her parents. While inheriting the beauty and intelligence of the family genes, Jean's thought pattern was in different realms and she viewed the world through eyes that reflected those thoughts. The family recognized her lack of talent in her early attempts at ballet, piano, vocal and other genteel pursuits. They simply labeled her as having no talent.

Jean learned from this form of neglect and it reinforced her feelings of independence from a family she loved, but could not belong to. Her mother and sisters could not understand why Jean couldn't fall right into step with the rest of the family. It was so easy for them. They termed the resulting turmoil unnecessary, viewing Jean as difficult and at fault. They never understood that prescribed talents were not what drove Jean. She had little idea of how to be their definition of a proper young lady. Her interests where self-developed from independent thinking and her enjoyments in life were enhanced by excitement and the touch of danger. These were the things which made-up her blood and commanded her attention from an early age.

Such excitement was beginning to register in Jean as she sat and listened to the man next to her talk. The appearance of being slightly older gave him legitimacy of experience. His plain talk and lack of originality in speaking reflected his background and its emphasis on action instead of words. The piercing bits of intelligence, which would spring forth once in a while, gave insight into his ability to step beyond his environmental influences. His attempts at charm were in fact, charming. There was no excusing his rugged good looks. Jean was fascinated. She thought she had found in him a voyeuristic window from which she could view reality in the social alleys and backwashes of life.

"Where do you work?" The question directed straight at her caught Jean by surprise and she hesitated not knowing whether to venture anything personal. Her pause suddenly seemed out of character. Did she realize where the line was drawn between viewing another's world and stepping into it?

"At Gibson's Department Store, downtown." She felt no strange departure. No fall from grace. It was a simple answer to a simple question.

"What do you do there?" Henry was now pursuing the reason he had come to the table.

"I'm a sales clerk in women's ready to wear…on the second floor." As he took a sip of beer, she entered the dialogue with more comfort. "Where do you work?"

"Oh, I'm a distributor for the Old City Brewery. I drive a truck and make sure places in town like Freddy's here…" motioning to the ceiling with his half empty glass, "are well stocked for the callings of thirsty customers, like all present." Again using his glass in a short sweep to indicate everyone in the bar.

"So you get around to all of the 'hot spots' in Kansas City?" she asked with a teasing smile.

"Oh yes, oh yes. I can take you out on a night on the town from one end to the other and be greeted by my first name in every bar." He said with a boast.

"I'm impressed. Not many people can make that statement. I'm sorry, your first name again is…?"

"Henry, Henry Lapointe." He missed her subtle, double jab at his ego.

One of the boys now rose from his place at the head of the table. "The night is moving on and so shall we. Another watering hole beckons."

The group starting rising and finishing their last swallows. Henry stood with them and asked Jean, "Would you mind if I came down to the department store some day and took you to lunch?"

Now she knew where the lines were, but this was still interesting and touched her sense of the daring. "Some Tuesday would be nice. That's the day my manager goes home for his lunch and I have a few more liberties with my lunch hour. Oh, if you come by, look like you're a customer and stay on the serious side. Some of the ladies I work with have old ideas about friendliness and customers."

The group was moving toward the door and Henry kept her lingering, "On Tuesdays I'm delivering on the east side of town. That makes it kind-a tough to get down town."

As she walked toward the door she played her trump in this little flirtation, "Suit yourself."

He watched her leave. She didn't look back. He stood there alone trying to understand what had happened. Did she cut him off, or did she leave the invitation open. Then he thought, "That's some dame. I believe I will 'suit myself'."

Thursday, April 26, 1945

Henry was working the downtown route. The weekends were heavily patronized in the down town bars, so Thursday's deliveries were big sales. Henry was looking for an opportunity to slip over to Gibson's Department Store, just to let Jean know he hadn't forgotten about the "some Tuesday" lunch. He worked for some very serious fellows. If you did your job and kept your nose clean and your mouth shut, you could make some very good money. Any perceived slacking-off was taken as loss of income. The men who owned the beer he was hauling had reputations about how they handled "scum" cutting into their revenue. The circumstances Henry was very much aware of, but he felt he had gotten enough good time in so that he could risk small indiscretions. Not enough to rock any boats, for his present position could open doors of opportunity. Little did he know he was approaching one of those doors.

At 11:30 A.M. he had just finished a delivery to Smokey's Bar. He asked Jake, the bartender, if he could leave his truck in the alley for a while to do some business down the street. With Jake's assurance, he walked quickly out of the back of the bar and turned down the alley. As he walked past his truck, he heard his name called…that is his nickname. Only one person regularly called him…" Frenchie! Hey Frenchie, wait a minute." The voice was too familiar.

It was Tuffs Bellenger, the "heavy" man for the beer company. Tuffs was the lead man used by the owners to carry out all of their less than legitimate mandates. Whether it was rough stuff, which earned Mr. Bellenger his nickname because of the enthusiasm with which the rough stuff was carried out, or his ability to organize the "ventures" of greater profit, Tuffs was a very valuable employee. No one messed with Tuffs.

As Tuffs walked quickly toward him, Henry turned with a polite greeting, "Hello Tuffs. What brings you down here so early in the morning?"

"Lookin' for you, Frenchie. We've got a run into Kansas scheduled for Saturday morning. Da boss wants you ta take it." Tuffs had walked right up to Henry displaying the normal "all business" manner, just inches from his face. Tuffs was always on the move and talked fast, very seldom repeating himself. He had a long list of assignments and was anxious to get the present one done so he could chase after the next.

"Sure Tuffs, I'll take it, but I thought this weekend wasn't mine."

"They got dis new kid break'n into da 'driving line' and da boss wants you there ta show him da ropes and keep him think'n right."

"Yeah, no problem. Where does it go?" Henry got the question in as Tuffs turned to leave.

"Wichita." Tuffs turned his big frame towards Henry as he walked backwards to get his final instructions in without wasting a movement. "Now you're gona have an early start so be at the brewery a seven a.m. sharp, ready to go." He pivoted in-stride, but yelled back over his shoulder. "No boozing it up tomorrow night. I don't want no screw-ups!"

"Don't worry, I'll be there. Oh, who's the new 'wheel'?" But it was too late. Tuffs had finished his business and nothing else was going to stop his progress toward the car waiting for him. He didn't look back again. Tuffs knew Henry would do what he was told; he just wanted him told. Now it was up to Henry to make sure things went right.

The assignment was on Henry's mind as he walked the rest of the way down the alley and out into the street. Dodging minimal traffic, he made his way to the other side, turned right and started the two-block journey to Gibson's Department Store.

He made the front door at a quarter of 12:00, entered and started searching for the first clues to Jean's location. The grand stairway answered all his questions and he took the stairs two at a time until he reached the second level. Once there, he slowly surveyed the floor until he spotted the familiar brunette behind a counter. She was folding scarves. He casually walked to her saying, "Hello Miss."

Her eyes reflected the surprise he had generated, yet she followed with a quick smile. "Hello, may I help you?"

Henry couldn't grasp his setting in this very female environment. He leaned over the counter and in a harsh whisper said, "I couldn't come last Tuesday, but next Tuesday is on. OK?"

Jean kept her attentive sales appearance in spite of his obvious failure and replied, "Yes, that will be fine."

With that, Henry quickly turned on a parting smile and walked briskly to the stairway. One glance back to Jean still showed his smile. He disappeared down the staircase. She had hoped he would come, but knew men seldom acted on their bravado. Now she was in a good mood. She felt the wonderful sense someone cared. It would carry her for the next five days until the lunch date.

Chapter 2

Saturday, April 28, 1945

Henry had arrived early at the brewery. He didn't own a car, but never worried much about transportation. If there weren't public buses or trolleys, he could count on a number of acquaintances to give him a ride. Usually he could get the loan of a car from a friend, or in some cases, the temporary responsibility of a truck from the brewery. Without a valid license, Henry was very careful with driving himself. He had a license all right, but it would not stand the test of a court appearance. If on brewery business, his "license" would not be an issue in court, as "lubrication" would be applied to the wheels of justice by brewery legal minds. This would avoid any unpleasant time away from brewery duties.

At this point in time, life was working out quite nicely for Henry. One never knew about the future and one hoped the past would not catch up. Beyond tomorrow, or next week, Henry had no long-range plans. In late April of 1945, the war in Europe was almost won. The papers announced the Russian army had surrounded Berlin. Speculation was all about the end of the war and when the boys were coming home. Yet there was always caution in these articles about the continuing war in the Pacific. Would the Yanks, who had survived the fighting in Europe, be shipped to the Far East to tempt fate again? The news from Europe had two edges for the families of servicemen.

To Henry and the social strata to which he belonged, the main subject of every day was 'business'. The war was something other people would deal with. His element lay outside the main social stream of the population. At 32, Henry still carried the stature and looks of a 25 year old. Questions about his participation in the fighting came without polite thought from citizens in daily life. Lies came easily and believable, with practice. Time spent with the delicate issue led him to portray himself as a government employee of this or that agency. With friends of special talent, he could sometimes back up his story with printed cards or I.D. and cease the questions immediately. Once people understood a reasonable, war essential explanation, they quickly bought into support of the war effort by not prying further.

Henry's peers did not have the creativity to follow his success, resorting to simple displays of what they really were to keep the public at bay. They depended on their employer to keep them hidden from the demands of the country. Henry was about to meet another one of these less creative persons. One who was new to bootlegging and all of the pitfalls such a life carried from both sides of the law. Josh Archer was in his early 20's and it showed. What he lacked in experience, he made up for in noise. Brash, without patience and making poor choices as a matter of a lack of attention, Josh was not the type of professional needed in the ranks of an illegal operation. But then, job applications were not a formality in the hiring process. The cruel nature of on-the-job training was an effective, after employment, screening tool. As far as military service, Josh just never reported. Coming from a broken home and the harsh street life of Detroit, it was easy for Josh to get 'lost' in the small bands of unorganized criminals. Minor arrests and short-term stays in smaller Midwestern jails, tagged his background with the word "petty". Now here he is, trying to make the leap into the bigger leagues.

Six-thirty in the morning was a busy time at the brewery. With a limited number of eligible men to employ, overtime was a common weekly occurrence in the endeavor to supply the liquid to quench the public's thirst. Missouri was a lucrative market for the brewery, but another market offered much more return for the delivery of beer. Kansas was a "dry" state. When the Federal government repealed Prohibition, Kansas, the birthplace of the prohibition movement, kept its laws against the manufacture and sale of alcoholic beverages within its borders. There were plenty of people in Kansas who liked to have a beer, especially in the Wichita area where the aircraft industry was pumping out military airplanes for the war. Many employees had come to Kansas for the work and brought their personal lifestyles with them in spite of the views of the Kansas Legislature. What leisure time they had available, was to be spent in the pursuit of the best time available. This would be Henry and Josh's mission, to take a truckload of beer to a "distributor" north of the city of Wichita. They were the vital link in the chain of supply and demand. The rules under which they operated were simple…don't get caught.

Henry was leaning against the dock when Tuffs came walking quickly toward him with a young man in tow. "Hey, Frenchie, good ta see ya!" Tuffs announced before he got to Henry. Of course he was glad to see him. Henry's presence meant this delivery was going to be successful. It made Tuffs' life easier. "This here's Archer. He's da new driver I was telling ya about. You gona show him da ropes so he don't screw up!"

Henry and Archer nodded acknowledgment to one another.

Tuffs put a big finger in Archer's face. "Now kid, what ever Henry here says to do, you do. I don't care if he tells ya ta jump in a river of shit and swim up stream…you do it! You can learn why later, when you're digging shit out of your ears!" Tuffs punctuated his lecture with a quick slap on the back of Archer's shoulder. Then he turned to Henry without waiting for the young man's reply. "Ok, Frenchie, you got the kid and the load. The return cargo goes to Skinny up there on the dock. He's gona do the settle'n up with ya when ya get back." Tuffs had used his pointing finger to establish Skinny Ferguson's presence on the dock above them. The gesture was an introduction for Archer as well as an empowerment of Skinny over everyone insight of Tuffs.

Reinforced with Tuffs' gesture, Skinny nodded to Henry, "Truck's loaded Henry. You can take 'er out."

Tuffs was already gone. Enough said, enough done.

Henry splashed out the last of his coffee onto the dirt, grabbed his thermos and a paper bag off the dock and moved to the driver's side of the truck. He motioned Archer around the other side. When the truck started rolling, they began a journey toward their destinies neither could foresee.

Henry drove out of the brewery grounds before he spoke. "What's your first name?"

"It's Josh. Never liked being called by my last name." The reply was a complaint.

"You ever drive a truck like this?" Henry continued with business.

"Yeah…I done some drive'n up in Detroit, where I'm from. In Detroit, sooner or later you get acquainted with about anything there is to drive." Josh was getting comfortable with the absence of the likes of Tuffs. He had only to deal with this Henry fellow and he could handle what he saw so far of this man.

"I'll do the driving down to Wichita. With this heavy load, it's no time to see how well you drive. On the way back, you've got the wheel. In the mean time, I'll tell you about what's goin' on and what you have to do to get it done right." He glanced toward Josh, just catching him finishing a yawn. "This too early for you?"

"Naw. I work nights on a construction crew down at the rail yards. We're replac'n every damned cross tie in the yard. We have to work at night when the traffic is the lightest. I been doin' this for some time."

"When did ya get off work?" Henry asked with some concern about getting this information now.

"We got off at four this morning. But don't you worry. I can hold my own. Like I say, I been doing this a long time and I know how to handle it." Josh was settling into the seat as he spoke and used the opportunity to sound tough to impress Henry.

They were two hours into the trip. Henry was sipping on a cup of coffee with one hand and steering the truck down a little used highway with the other. He looked over at Josh who was sound asleep on the passenger's side. He smiled at the thought of himself nine or ten years ago. How he was full of himself at that time, thinking he knew a lot more than he did. Here was a mirror, in the form of Josh.

"Hey, Josh…Josh…time to wake up now!"

His voice brought Josh out of a deep sleep. Josh opened his eyes and bolted up right in the seat. He connected were he was and what was happening. The flush in his face gave away his embarrassment.

Thoughts rushed to justify his failure, but did not find expression in words.

"Figured you needed the rest. I sure as hell would if I had worked till four in the morning." Henry's gracious words offered Josh, a way out. "If you're going to make these runs, you're going ta hav'ta find a different job."

"That's the rub Henry, I'm trying to get a job at the brewery so I can get out of that rail yard." Josh's sleepiness left him without the earlier brashness.

"I need you awake for the rest of the trip. So drink down some of this coffee and roll down your window. Ok?"

"Ok." Josh followed directions and knew his two hour lapse may have been forgiven this time, but it left him vulnerable to Henry. He was angry about the circumstance and wanted to get back to displaying the tough guy image. But how do you do that once you have displayed yourself as a fool?

"In about thirty minutes, we're gona come to a farmhouse. It's a ways out from town. I want you to know what to expect so nobody gets nervous during the transfer. These guys we're meetin' don't like the time they are exposed like sittin' ducks. If there is a perfect time to get caught, it's when we're high and dry transferring the load."

"What are the chances of getting caught?" Josh asked.

"Slim, but still you never know when some gung-ho deputy is going to take up one of these little visits as his personal road to local glory. That's why you always look for someone who's not invited."

"What'll we do if someone like that shows up?" The cockiness was gone from Josh. Instead of knowing all the answers, he had some questions.

Henry looked at Josh to make sure he was listening. "Mostly nothing. That is, if it's the law. If you run, they'll catch you, or worse use running as an excuse to shoot. Just stay put and don't give anyone any trouble. You keep your mouth shut and don't answer any questions at all. Kansas City will send a lawyer down to do our talking." Henry felt more detail was required. "If we go to a county jail, it won't be for long. If you do what I tell you, we'll have something to go back to K.C. for. But if you lose your head and blab about what this is, then there will be worse people comin' after you than the law. And you probably won't get back to Kansas City."

"You talkin' about Tuffs?"

"Not exactly Tuffs. These would be people that even Tuffs don't like to deal with. Not likable fellows at all."

"How will we know it's the law and not someone out to hijack the load?" Josh had some good thoughts when he wasn't trying to promote himself so hard.

"The cops come in yell'n. Other gangs come in shootin'. If you hear shootin', then all bets are off. It's every man for himself. Find a way back to Kansas City, then get ready to be apart of a war." Henry looked for Josh's reaction to the proposed violence. Josh seemed blank and there was no read in his face. Henry switched back to current affairs. "Watch when we get to this farm house. Most of the people there will be working stiffs, like us. They will do the unloading and handling of the trucks. There will be two or three other men who will do nothing more than just stand around and look mean. These guys are armed and will respond to any threats from other gangs. Don't bother talking to them, they know their jobs and won't put up with any interference. The only man we talk to and by 'we', I mean me, is the boss of this Wichita group. He's gun-a make sure of the delivery count and then he's the guy who will handle the payment."

"The last thing we do, after they're gone, is load the empty barrels they leave beside their truck. We leave a payment for the farmer and then get the hell back to K.C. Even on the trip back we've got to be careful about the law. No explanation is going to get around those empty kegs. All this clear to you?"

"Yeah, sounds simple." The education helped Josh gain an amount of self-image back. He felt like he knew all about it now and could start projecting himself again.

Henry picked up on this and needed to add to the lesson. "Ya know Josh? The best thing you can do in this business is not be stupid. When you learn that, then you are going to have a chance to survive a little longer." He wondered if anything had sunk in.

Henry made a left turn off the paved highway, onto a dirt road. Billows of light brown dust rose behind them as they made their way down the dry country road. The land was so flat around Wichita, the dust could be seen for miles. This was not unusual, even small coupes raised an impressive cloud in their wake. Had Josh looked back, he might have been uneasy about the large brown flag pointing to them like an accusing finger. Henry knew the men waiting for them would be watching for this cloud, or any other clouds, which may indicate unwanted visitors.

After three miles, they made a right turn and drove a quarter of a mile to a farm site, which was surrounded by Chinese elm trees and healthy evergreens. At the entrance to the driveway stood a lone man with a shotgun. As Henry made the slow left turn into the drive, the man stepped toward the truck. "What's your name?" He demanded.

"Henry." Was his reply.

"Who sent you?" The gruff untrusting man asked.

"The flower shop." It was not a smart answer. It was the verbal exchange necessary to get them by this unforgiving point of entry. Josh felt the threat and wondered why he hadn't been told about this secret stuff.

Before the man let them go, he asked a more practical question. "You see any other cars on the way in?"

"No, not a soul." The man motioned Henry to drive on, then returned to his serious appointment with the unexpected.

Henry drove to the big barn located at the south end of a group of farm buildings. He swung the truck around so the tail was pointed to the barn doors. The doors slid open by the efforts of two men from inside. Henry backed the truck through the opening into the darkness of the barn's interior. He obeyed the two men's hand signals and backed within three feet of another truck facing the opposite direction. Hand signals directed him to end this phase of the journey. As the front doors slid shut, darkness crept around the two trucks. Enough light from a few windows in the barn kept visibility to a functioning level, as Henry and Josh's eyes adjusted to the darkness.

A large voice came at Henry before he could see clearly. "Ya have any problems comin' down here?"

Henry knew it would be the boss of the outfit. As he pinched his eyes with his thumb and forefinger, moving them together toward his nose, he said, "No, not a bit."

"Good. Now lets see how many kegs we've got." The voice had turned to the business of unloading the truck, which also meant the pleasantries of a greeting had been fulfilled. Josh came around the truck and stood in a relaxed, "controlled" posture beside Henry. He wanted to display the look of a veteran, but he was the only one taken in by the ruse.

A five foot long steel plate was pushed from the back of the empty truck to bridge the open span between the trucks. Four men began dolling the heavy barrels across the bridge while the boss stood on the ground making special note of every keg. The kegs were brought across one at a time and each of the handlers was to report any keg that didn't have the right feel of weight to it. No such reports were volunteered, so at the end of the process the boss yelled out the question, “All da kegs heavy enough?” Four separate responses of “Yes sir!” gave him completion.

As the four men drew in the bridge and buttoned up the truck, the boss turned and walked to Henry. “Ok, fella, we got a good delivery here.” He handed Henry a thick white envelope and said, “Here’s the cash; I know it’s right, ‘cause I counted it myself. But you can count it if ya want.”

Henry said, “Well I appreciate your make’n sure it’s all here, but with my ass hanging out, I’ll take you up on your suggestion.” Henry started thumbing through the bills in the envelope. The big man gave a quick chuckle through his bite on an unlit cigar then nodded his departure. He turned to the supervision of the crew’s cleanup efforts and shouted orders for little things to be picked up, or tied down.

Henry finished counting the money, licked the envelope’s seal and pressed it shut with both of his thumbs. He held the white envelope up and gave a quick wave with it toward the boss. The man caught the movement of the white envelope in the dimness and raised a big open palm toward Henry. His business with Henry was finished. But for his crew, he still had the reins held tight. "Now you guys be careful with this here load gettin' it back ta town!" Nothing was heard from the cab of the truck. The man's voice boomed, "Ya hear?" With that, the "Yes sirs" were quick and sharp; making sure no further inquiry need be made of their attention to business.

Two loaders slid open the doors at the back of the barn, allowing sunlight to cascade into the barn. Two other men emerged from the darkness of each side of the barn and walked with the boss out of the doors to waiting cars. Henry and Josh stayed in place watching the small caravan pull out of sight.

Josh's posturing was gone, "Gees, I never saw those other two guys, those guys that came out last!" His voice was full of the recognition of the danger, which had passed.

"That's the way these things go, Archer. It's a good thing for you to know that everything you see is not everything there is." Henry walked past Josh carrying the envelope to the truck. He stepped up on the running board and reached into the cab. At the top of the driver's side backrest, he peeled back a hidden flap of leather, exposing a thin opening to the interior of the seatback. He retrieved a yellow envelope from the hiding place and stored the white one under the flap. Stepping down from the truck he raised the yellow envelope to Josh as he crossed in front of him. "It's important to leave the farmer something for the use of his barn. Remember, the farmer gets the yellow one, not the white one. Showing up back at Kansas City with no white envelope, means kissing your ass good-bye." He had a big smile for Josh as he finished the elementary lesson, regulating Josh's place as still the novice.

He carried the yellow envelope to a small box attached to one of the main support pillars along the center isle of the barn. The box was on the dark side of the pillar and had a little paddle lock hanging from the bottom. A mail slit was in the top and that is where Henry dropped the yellow envelope.

He then pointed Josh to the other side of the isle and said, "Now let's get to work!"

Empty kegs lined the east side of the barn. Henry grabbed one and swung it up on the back of the empty truck. He climbed after it and carried it to the front, then walked back to the open end. Looking at Josh from his lofty perch he said, "Now start getting the rest of them up here."

Josh nodded. He could see he was going to get this end of the "stick" every time it was available. He had been quite impressed with the whole business and was willing to do the grunt labor as his contribution to smoothness and coordination of the whole affair. He was sweating and his arms ached by the time he swung the last keg up to Henry. Henry was also drenched as he jumped down from the truck and secured the opening for the trip back. "Ok, Josh, it's your turn to drive. Back it out the open doors and keep me in your mirrors."

Josh was behind the wheel watching Henry's directions until the truck cleared the open doors. The path was open for his larger roll in the second half of the journey. Henry climbed in on the passenger's side and both men wiped at the sweat clinging to their exposed skin using handkerchiefs and sleeves. They were now out in the late April sun again and a breeze aided them in removing the discomfort of the heavy sweat. It was a welcome change from the stuffy, smelly interior of the barn.

Henry reached down to the floor between them to retrieve a gallon glass jug wrapped in wet burlap. He and Josh took turns drinking the surprisingly cool water. A sack of sandwiches was also retrieved. Josh was delighted with the thought that had gone into this little part of the plan, so welcome in its timing.

The truck was rolling northeast as they ate and took in the cool water. They were both enjoying the wind sweeping through the vented cab and open windows. Josh was doing well behind the wheel, but driving the truck was not a large accomplishment. Without knowing it, Josh had passed Henry's test when he backed the truck out of the barn. Henry had noted all, from the sound of the clutch engaging to Josh's attentiveness to the mirrors and the hand signals. As a driver, Josh was acceptable, but what was going to be his reaction to the discipline and the authority that awaited him in this profession?

Josh spoke above the wind in the cab, "Man, that was really something! Everything went down with no hitches. Everybody doing the thing they were supposed to and then, whoosh, they were gone."

"Yeah, well that's the way it has to be. We got no room for screwing-up. People get hurt when somebody screws-up." He looked at Josh to make sure he understood all this didn't happen by accident. Planning was the main ingredient in everything they did.

Josh took the look from Henry and carried beyond its intent, "You put this all together?"

"No, no, no…I've been doin' this sort-a thing since I was thirteen. I know a lot about what to do and what not to do, but they don't leave it up to me to put it together. I just gotta make sure I do my part right. Sometimes I'll see something that ain't right on a job and I'll tell Skinny. Sometimes they make changes, sometimes they don't, but I haven't seen nothing bad enough yet to pull off a job. These guys know what they're doin'."

"How much money have I got behind me?" Josh asked with an eager smile. The question was not appropriate, but Josh didn't know that.

Henry was silent for a few seconds and then figured "what the hell", he knew how much there was, so why not? "You've got about four grand between your shoulder blades."

"Wow-wee, four grand! I ain't never seen that much money in one pile before." Josh carried a big open grin as he half turned to view the "bundle" through the seat behind him. "You mean those boys in Wichita can make money off that beer after they pay that much for it?"

"Yeah. They break it down into gallon jugs and quart jars and sells them for $20 to $60 a pop. People will pay that to get their beer. There are a lot-a people working in the aircraft factories that aren't from Kansas and are used to having a beer when they want. They get good wages and there's not a lot of things to spend it on. Bootleg beer is well worth it to them."

Josh's excitement over the money carried him on. "Hey! You ever think about heading this truck south with that kind-a money sittin' here?"

Josh's inexperience was taking over, so Henry needed to put him in school again. "You walk with Kansas City's money and you're going to wake up dead, real soon." He looked at Josh and calmly continued. "They don't sit by and let that happen. Anyone, and I do mean ANYONE, who walks with even a single dollar of their money, is going to be hunted down and killed like an animal. I've seen it happen. Some fool thinks he can hide and the next thing you hear is they found him crumpled up in a trunk somewhere. No sir, a million won't do you any good if you're dead!"

"They really do that?" Josh was still in school.

"Oh yeah! They don't think twice about wasting some guy to keep everyone else in line. No, you and I will take our $150 and be happy with that. That's not bad money for these times."

"Well then, when do guys like you and I get into the big money?" Josh asked the question that exists in every man's mind in this business. Henry noted how quickly Josh had brought forth the big question. There was no patience in the boy.

Henry thought for a while trying to decide how far to take this. It was a question he had dwelt on for years. His long developed thoughts on the matter were private and were best kept that way. But Josh's impatience had struck a note in him, which had made him think about how long he was going to keep these thoughts to himself. Long enough to never do anything about them? He started exploring those thoughts out loud, as if a thought never expressed had no value. "There's going to come a time when it's right; when it's not Kansas City, or Chicago, or St. Louis money. When it's there for the taking and I will know it. Everything will line up and chances will be good to get away clean."

"You think that's gun-a happen?" Josh was captivated by Henry's serious tone.

"Oh yeah. It's gun-a be there. A lot of money is floating around this country. Someone's bound to get careless with a big stack of it. I know it happens. All I have to do is be there when it does." Henry starred ahead as he spoke, building that fantasy in his head.

There was a long pause between them. Josh became uncomfortable with his own thoughts. He rubbed his hand across his mouth and slowly ventured into this apparent moment of opportunity. "Henry…do people rob trains any more?"

"Trains?" The thought fell heavily against Henry's experience. "Hell no! You can't get at trains these days. How you gona stop a train. It takes damn near a mile or more for a train to stop itself. Hell, it'll just run you down and leave it to someone else to scoop you up and put you in a bucket. There's so many people riding trains these days, what if you could stop one. You'd have hundreds of people all around and most of them would be soldiers. No, the days of robbing trains went with the old west."

"Well I'm not talking about a train that's movin'. What if that train is stopped in the back of a train yard?" Josh had been carrying his own thoughts around.

This sounded different to Henry. The newness caught his curiosity. “What kind of train?”

“Well, it’s a train that carries money shipments for the Federal Reserve Bank in Kansas City.” Josh seemed to know more about this than his experience should have allowed.

Looking for the hook in the bait, Henry asked, “Where did you learn about this kind-a train?”

“There’s this Yard Bull, where I work at nights…his name is Eldon Appleby. Ya know my job at the railroad yard?” He looked for and received a nod from Henry. “Well, this guy is with the yard police and works the night shift the same as me. He got to talking to me on my lunch times and breaks just to pass the time at first. Then I noticed the more we talked, the more edge he seemed to have in his voice about his work with the railroad. We got to be friends. Then one night I asked him about a train that was all alone in the back of the yard, with big flood lights around it and people all over there like it was the President or someone sneakin’ into town. Old Eldon said it was a train carrying a shipment of money for the Federal Reserve Bank, in the millions of dollars."

Henry cut in, "Whoa, right there. You just defined a situation I told you couldn't be had. Ain't nobody gun-a to walk in there and take that kind-a money!"

"I know Henry! That's not the train I'm talkin' about. Old Eldon has been working for the railroad all his life and there are certain people who keep him from betterin' himself in his job. Turns out that edge in his voice is pure hatred for some of them people. He goes on to tell me about another train that comes in there with less money and less fuss. He says sometimes, as people in the Midwest spend their money around the country, especially with the army's big training camp at Fort Leonardwood, the paper money supply gets low at the local Federal Reserve Bank. Then a special shipment is made from one of the other Federal Reserves and is brought in the same way, by train. Only with these trains, there is not the millions of dollars involved, maybe two hundred thousand, or more. They don't spend the money to beef up security like on the big trains. Eldon hinted that a few tough guys could knock over the whole train without no problem."

It registered with Henry right away. There were, of course, huge gaps in the information, but on the surface, everything Josh was saying was making sense. It was logical that too much attention would be paid to the big shipments and too little to the routine small shipments. "Would this Eldon guy be interested in meeting with us?"

"I don't know, I'll ask him." Josh replied.

"First, ask him what he would think of someone coming into his yard and knocking off a train. If you get a good response from him, then ask if he would like to meet with you and I to discuss it further." Henry remained in thought about this idea for the rest of the trip back. He responded to Josh's excited statements with nods and affirmative grunts, but his mind was on the possibilities.

The trip back was uneventful. They turned the truck and the cash into Skinny. He gave them their cut and the two men parted acknowledging that they had the beginnings of a partnership founded in the business of this train.

Tuesday, May 1, 1945

With all that was going through Henry's mind, he had not forgotten about the pretty brunette. Matter of fact, he had trouble trying not to think of her. He had pulled off his eastern city route to keep his lunch date. He parked the truck in the alley behind Smokey's Bar again and stuck his head in the back door to clear it with Jake. He got the OK for the truck to be there for the noon hour. Then he lit out down the alley and across the street headed for Gibson's Department Store. In the main entrance and up the flight of stairs, taking the stairs two at a time. He entered the Ladies' Ready to Wear. The sight of Jean was very pleasing to him. She looked like she had put on some extra polish for this day. Henry wondered if he might be a little shoddy looking to be seen with her. He walked to her and said, "Hi."

She spoke to him with glances going left and right to understand her current privacy, "I'll meet you out front as soon as I can get free."

Without further words, Henry retraced his steps, trying to look nonchalant as he walked down the stairs this time. It would seem when two people have an eye for one another; nothing they do to disguise the fact can overcome the obviousness of their actions to other people. In such cases, the two infatuated people are the only ones who don't know the transparency of their efforts.

Soon, Jean came walking out of the main entrance. They walked two blocks to a luncheon café. They got a table in a corner and Henry took the seat facing the interior of the café with his back to the wall, as was his custom. He wanted to observe who was coming and going so he could control conversation against the panorama of moving people.

They began their conversation with polite inquiries and statements, yet each most wanted to talk on a more personal basis. They wanted to explore the reasons they were here, seated across from each other and give answers to those internal forces which had made each divert from their normal path in life. They felt the press of time in this short, one-hour of opportunity. Henry asked first, "Jean, tell me something about you."

"Nooo…" she drew the word out to take control and accented it with a smile. "A girl just doesn't tell about herself like that! No, I'm here to find out about you. You interest me, but maybe that is all you should know about me, until I know more about you."

"About me?" The question was weak; because Henry knew the key to any relationship with this attractive young woman lay with her judgment of him and not the reverse. "Where do you want me to begin?"

"Well, the lunch hour is not standing still, so between eating and talking, I would hope to be a little wiser about you when we leave." She said this with her continued smile, which was both disarming and inviting. As Henry struggled with a starting point, Jean added, "First of all, why aren't you in the army or navy or something?"

Henry was willing to talk, because he really didn't have any dark secrets. His life had been governed by the discipline of not talking about himself. As he shifted and glanced away from their table, he knew it was time to either trust her or forget her. He looked back at her smile and made his decision. "Yeah, Ok." He slowly reached for the explanations, which he had not ventured to explore for himself. "One thing I know for sure, the army and I would not get along. When the war broke and people started rushing to sign into the army, I had a different mind on the matter. Not that I didn't want the Nazi's stopped, it's just that I wouldn't have been able to do anything about them from the brig. Had I gone to the army, in no time, I would have been popping some officer for the smallest of reasons and I'd have been hauled off for the rest of the war. Because I was older, they didn't come after me for enlistment, so I just didn't step forward. Before long I was in the States working. Never went back."

"The States? Where are you from?" Jean asked with surprise.

"Canada. Now that's not so far off is it?" he said responding to the surprise he saw from her. "French Canadian, actually. I was born in Quebec, but was raised by my aunt in Western Canada after my mother died. My dad couldn't take care of me so off I went at three years old. My Aunt Elizabeth had four children of her own. The whole family was as good to me as if I was theirs, but I always knew I had my own mother and father…" His voice trailed off as he considered what he had said and realized he had always governed his life on the fact that he actually belonged somewhere else, but lived in a current geography, all brought about by the untimely death of one woman, his mother.

His serious pause was interrupted by the waitress coming by with their order. It was a good time for an interruption. Henry's pause was taken up by her duties at their table. When she left, he gave a self-conscious glance at his surroundings and then his eyes came back to Jean. She had the look of deep interest, so he realized what he was saying was not foolish and he had a genuine audience. He relaxed and went on. "We had a good life, out in Winnipeg, but the family never had much money to speak of. The three boys and I got into everything boys get into and then some. Aunt Elizabeth had quite a time keeping us under control. Uncle George was a big good-hearted man with a streak of orneriness all his own. Sometimes I wonder who was the bigger worry to Aunt Elizabeth, us four boys, or Uncle George." Henry gave a slight chuckle as a dozen memories flashed by. His eyes were fixed on the glass in front of him as he continued speaking from this newly found platform.

"Life seemed to revolve around looking for something to do. Most times I ended up doing things most folks wouldn't approve of. But that's what boys do best, I suppose." Again he chuckled at the flashes of memory, but choose not to verbalize any of them. "My Uncle and his brothers got to runnin' whiskey down to Minnesota during Prohibition. They were making money and having a good time. Most folks didn't pay too much attention to runnin' whiskey. Guess they seemed to think drinking whiskey wasn't all that bad, so someone had to sell it."

"When I was about thirteen, Uncle George started taking me and one of my cousins with him on these runs. To us it was real excitin', a great adventure each time. To the men, the money they could make became the main interest, but to us the adventure never quit. I got acquainted with all kinds of people doin' this. As I grew older I stuck around and stayed with the 'delivery' business. I moved down to the States, the Chicago and Detroit area and always seemed to find work driving a truckload of beer, booze, or other highly prized goods of the less virtuous."

Jean's interest called for participation, "You mean you were working for mobsters in those cities?"

Henry's eyes came up and his look went past Jean to see if anyone had responded to her use of the word "mobsters". No reaction was evident, so his eyes rested back on Jean. He held his hand palm down over the table and gave a gentle patting motion as he softly spoke to Jean, "Hold it down a little. People leap to conclusions when they hear talk like that." Talking about his employers was an uncomfortable and risky venture. "The people I work for don't like being talked about. They get very serious, very fast about that sort of thing, so have a little understanding, ok?"

"It's your story, Henry, all I'm trying to do is understand what you are talking about when you don't talk about it." She justified her position, but loved hearing about the very subject he wanted to stay away from.

"Well, for right now, just make some assumptions and sometime when we're alone, I can get into details." He cautioned.

"What makes you think we are going to be alone?" she responded with a satisfying smile.

He smiled back at her defiance, but recognized her interest in his profession. "Oh we'll be alone sometime, cause you're gun-a want to hear about these details. May I continue?"

She motioned with a horizontal, twirling finger, for him to continue while her lips were busy with the duty of sipping her cola through a straw. She was maintaining a teasing aloofness to keep a light air to this short time together.

"I've been on both sides of the legal line in the selling and distributing of spirits..."

"How deeply do you get into the mob?" she interrupted.

Still on the subject he wanted to stay away from, he noted her determination and the flash of beauty in her eyes as she anticipated his response. He tilted his head, to display to her he was viewing her from a different angle, then with a slight smile he resolved to form the words, which would settle the issue at hand. "Look, organizations like the ones I work for are closed societies. You either are born into them, or you are invited in. Invitations are very hard to come by, but that's ok with me, cause I'm not up to what you got to do to get an invite." He raised his finger to keep her from asking the obvious question and then continued. "I'm on the fringes. A guy who drives a truck and takes orders and keeps his nose clean. I like being there 'cause, ONE, it keeps me from getting into big trouble and TWO, it gives me more options in my life than if I was on the inside." He took a bite of his sandwich.

She took the opportunity. "ONE, what 'big trouble' and TWO, what 'options' are you talking about?"

He looked at her while he was chewing. This game of words was enjoyable, mostly because of the personality, which was flowing from his luncheon partner. He smiled as he started again, knowing she was going to keep asking until he could provide a good answer. "A guy like me, who's just on the fringes of this thing, makes good money, but I don't have to do any of the heavy stuff. You know, like, gun work, or kicking people in the gut. They just depend on me to get their merchandise delivered and that's all they expect. If they come asking for more, I play dumb and they get the idea I'm not worth trusting with the rough end of the business. That keeps me out of prison. Also keeps me from getting my tail shot off. As far as options go, if I'm deeper in the organization, I got no options. I either do what I'm told or I suffer the consequences. Now, if an opportunity comes along, either 'legit' or not so 'legit', I can move on without anyone getting overly concerned."

"And have you taken advantage of any opportunities so far?" She challenged.

A quick rush of blood shot through Henry's face as he absorbed what he thought was and insult. He hesitated to regain his thoughts and then dismissed her intent as having any malice. He liked being with her and was getting an education on her personality. There was a quick jabbing punch behind that smile, as if he was facing a boxing opponent whom he could not strike and could only avoid absorbing sharp blows by being one step ahead of each thrust.

"I guess I've just got longer term greed than most people. Short-term greed makes you do things without being completely ready for what could happen. That could lead to disaster.

I can wait for an opportunity that's going to be on as many of my terms as possible." He just realized that her questions had brought out answers he himself had not had before now. He was pleased with her and what she had been asking. Then again…

"You ever shot anyone?" she continued on her quest.

Whoa, change of direction, reassemble, think about this one…what was the question again? Oh yeah, "Shot anyone? Naw. I carry a 'piece', but that's just because you never know what you're gun-a to run into. I only fired it a couple of times. Once getting out of an ambush." His statements were coming in spurts as the thoughts occurred in his head. He looked at her to see if he was making sense. He could see the question on her face about the ambush. He continued without her needing to ask. "We were driving three truck loads of booze into Minneapolis a few years back, when another gang decided they were gun-a knock us off and take the booze. They started firing from ambush too early; I guess they got too nervous to wait until we were in point blank range. The guy riding 'shotgun' for me stepped out on the running board and started firing back with this Browning automatic rifle he had. I was trying to back out of there and while I waited for the trucks behind me to get out of the way, I started firing my .45 from the window. It seemed like forever before we could move, but I only had time to fire one clip and we were outta there. No one got a scratch, not even the guys we were shooting at, cause we never heard anything about someone dying or nothing. Not one of the best efforts on behalf of a criminal intent, but it was darned exciting for a while. Other than that, I haven't been in any real serious stuff."

Jean was captivated by the thoughts of the shootout and what it must have been like to be in Henry's place at that time. She regained the present by looking at her watch. Time was running short. "Where do you go from here? What does the rest of you life look like?"

He took a deep breath and sighed as his eyes became fixed on his empty soda glass. "Well…I don't know. Always figured something would come along, but ya know, the times are changin' and I'm not sure what is out there now."

Her philosophy took over as she started making movements indicating it was time to go. "If you sit around waiting for something to happen, chances are it won't. Sounds to me like you ought to get up and make something happen." This came flooding out of her quite naturally and matter-of-factly.

His jaw set as he took offense, then as he watched her preparing to leave, the words sunk in. She was right. He had always taken what came his way. Everything he was and everything he had, had been presented to him from circumstance. He depended on other people to provide him with what his life is. He was 32 now and had just gotten by. But what were other people going to do to give him the future he wanted? Nothing. She was right.

In his awkward moment, he started to verbalize his recent plan in-progress, "There's something that could happen…" He was interrupted by a sudden burst of voices from the front of the café. Several people gathered at the counter with the cook and the waitress flanking a radio on a shelf. Everyone seemed to be talking and the cook was motioning for silence so he could hear the news better. The energy level continued to rise, so it must be big news.

Henry and Jean walked toward the crowd. Henry reached into his pocket for the money to pay the bill and caught the waitress's attention. He lifted his head toward the radio and asked, "What's the news?"

The waitress had an open smile, which was doing double duty chewing gum. She was delighted for the opportunity to broadcast what she had heard, "The Russians, they're takin' Berlin! That means Germany is kaput! The war is going to be over any time now!"

Henry thanked her as he paid and escorted Jean out of the café. They walked together toward the department store and Henry turned and looked back toward the café. People were spilling out of the door headed in separate ways, each with an eagerness that was reminiscent of Christmas morning. Jean and Henry walked together both locked in their own thoughts. They shared some small talk, but neither displayed the enthusiasm expressed by their fellow diners. Henry did not walk into the store with her, but asked if she would have dinner with him on Saturday night. She agreed, gave him her phone number and asked him to call her to make their plans. With polite good-byes they parted at the entrance.

Jean had a curious feeling as she entered the familiar surroundings of Gibson's Department Store. The world was foreign to her now. She heard the buzz in the air as news of the impending collapse of Germany spread inside the store. As she walked up the stairs to her post, she met Gertrude Cline coming the other way. Gertrude had always been one of the snippiest fellow sales ladies on the floor. Jean had never had a kind thought for her. Now Gertrude came across the stairs and embraced Jean with a big smile and an even bigger hug.

"Did you hear? Did you hear? The war is going to be over! That means my Johnny is going to come home now. He's not going to die!! He's going to come home!!"

The sudden understanding of why Gertrude had always been so sour stunned Jean. Jean managed a "Yes...yes, I heard...", before Gertrude was off down the rest of the stairs abandoning her sales position as well as her inhibitions.

Jean continued up to the second floor and went around the couther to her sales position. She put her handbag and scarf under the counter and looked up to assume her duties. The world was indeed changing.

She stared at the empty room with unseeing eyes as thoughts of her burden gained advantage within her.

More than half her life had been spent with great clouds of anxiety hanging over her society. There were memories of the Great Depression and the pressure she felt radiating from her parents and her friends' parents as bad news flowed in on everyone's personal life. The long years of enduring the fear of the unknown brought by the Depression were followed by a new kind of fear. War had started in Europe in 1939. One could not easily trade the fears of the departed Depression for this new kind of terror in the world.

Jean's parents, like all the other adults in the country, had endured fifteen straight years of this struggle; a struggle which dominated their daily lives. Her parents and people like Gertrude Cline had each dealt with that struggle in their own limited ways and with their own individual, God-given characters. Now those fifteen years were coming to an end. Gertrude's change was dramatic, but how would Jean's parents change.

As a teen and young adult growing up in those fifteen years, Jean had followed her own inclinations of the better side of life. She sought fun and excitement and avoided the unpleasantness of a responsibility to the world, which her parents faced. Boys, cigarettes, alcohol, good times and laughs were the things Jean armed herself with. People like Gertrude didn't have that option in their lives. Gertrude's son, Johnny was called to war and the pressure of living with the anticipation of her son's death was an unthinkable trial. Sons, brothers, husbands, fathers, had gone to war and in their absence, millions of people lived with the same trial Gertrude endured. But Jean retained only herself. She had carefully structured her life to avoid the worries of her parent's generation.

She had gotten her first jolt of life's reality about three weeks ago, when the only President she could remember, died. Franklin Roosevelt had always been there. She trusted her world with Mr. Roosevelt in the White House. Now he was gone and the war was ending. Her parents were now going to experience a freedom they had not had in fifteen long years. They would use that freedom to make life bow to their wishes. What would be their demands on her to conform to their idea of who Jean Lester would be?

She knew what she wanted from life. She also knew her parents had not accepted her claims of life on her terms. Change was coming and Jean was in its path.

Chapter 3

Saturday, May 5, 1945

He was sleeping, but not soundly. A dream had invaded Henry and it was a menacing creation of his mind. In the dream, his foe was a barely visible face. A face Henry did not know. It was a threatening vision. The factual based part of Henry's brain was in control. The emotional confrontation had been created by the part of Henry's brain, which was based in fantasy. The fantasy base had enlisted Henry's will to ally against the image and a struggle was ensuing within him to destroy the projected threat. Henry's attempts to physically attack the image were held in check by the logic-based components of his brain. Henry's arms remained at his side while the torturous struggle of his will fought to gain the tools to lash out and destroy the enemy, so close to doing him harm. Frustration mounted as his helplessness made him intensify his efforts. Outwardly, evidence of the anguish created by the various facets of his mind was present in his muffled moans, physical thrashing and a resulting heavy sweat.

Suddenly, his right arm came free. The alliance of fantasy and will had overcome the powerful logic resident in the mind. He swung his fist as hard as he could at the face. The strike passed through the image of the face. The face did not exist in the same dimension as his right arm. In that instant, Henry's conscious mind took control and he realized the image was created by a dream. But, the momentum of his swing continued through the air and made contact with the bedside lamp, which did exist in his dimension. The resulting crash accelerated his journey to becoming fully awake. His mind raced to reconstruct and review what had happened to restore his fears and calm his aggressive outburst. He sat up on the edge of the bed as he went through the completion of this process. Shaken and unsteady, he slowly rose and retrieved the lamp from the floor. He placed it back on the stand and tried the switch. The light bulb had been a casualty of his strike.

Sweat covered his body and no air moved within his room. He walked to the open window, knelt down and crossed his arms on the sill. A small breeze brushed him as it moved by the open window. Henry leaned the upper part of his body out to catch as much of its cooling effect as he could. It was a welcome addition to his recovery. He was grateful for the effect it was having.

The further he moved from the frustrations of his dream, the closer he moved toward the frustrations of his reality, the turmoil within him. He felt lost and trapped and didn't have answers, answers that could calm him as the cool breeze had done. Questions started flowing again as he restructured the recent decisions he had made in his life. He had started his long awaited journey to the 'big score'. Instructing Josh to arrange a meeting between the two of them and this Mr. Eldon Appleby, he had taken the first unsteady steps into an uncertain future. This not only carried a great amount of personal risk to his freedom, but to his very life. Was it going to be right? Had all of his thoughts been proper in coming to this decision?

Should he stop it now, or would there be little harm in seeing it unfold a bit more? Doubt gripped him as the questions passed by.

What time is it? His meeting was at 6:00 a.m., at the Blue Moon Diner, on the north side of Kansas City. It was a casual truck stop on Highway 40 that stayed open all night. Not the best of spots, in not the best part of town, but it would provide the seclusion in public that Henry was seeking in this meeting. Josh and Mr. Appleby would be coming there after their night's work.

He turned toward the bed stand, which supported the recently assaulted lamp. There, beside the lamp, was the white face of his alarm clock, but from across the room, he couldn't make out the location of the hands. He gave-up the comfort of the window to satisfy his knowledge of time. It was 12:30 a.m.

He sat down on the bed with his eyes still on the clock's hands. It was too early to be awake, yet could he go back to sleep. His mind worked, but his troubled thoughts were all that it could produce. Depression was adjusting its grip on his being. Henry had reached another low point in his life. He had known this feeling before.

At first, the sound did not get past Henry's thoughts. But it was there for his ears.

Slowly he became aware of the faint sound announcing its presence to him. He raised his eyes to the open window. There it was again. He could hear it more clearly now. His attention was now focused on the sound and all other thoughts were being shed as he embraced the sound of a train whistle in the far distance of the night. His mind and body were transported to his youth, when the fears of life surrounded and assaulted him in his quest to end his day in sleep. It was the train whistles in the night that would come to his rescue. The assurance that he wasn't alone, that life was going on in its normality out there while bringing thoughts of normality into the restless imaginings of a little boy. For that boy, the safety of sleep was very near to the sounds of the train whistles.

The same still held true for the man. Sleep came before the sound had faded away.

Henry was early for his meeting with Josh and Mr. Appleby. He sat at the counter in the Blue Moon Diner, waiting for his chance at a secluded booth. He sipped coffee as he eyed the progress of two men in a corner booth. Soon their telltale signs of leaving grew to fruition as they rose to make their way to the cash register. Henry moved immediately to claim his rights to the security of the corner before others had a chance. He squeezed past the two men and occupied the un-cleared table with his back to the wall. He commanded an unobstructed view of the rest of the diner. It was busy for 6:00 a.m., but most entirely made up of truckers intent on their own business and their own problems. He was satisfied with what he saw.

As the table was cleared by an unconcerned waitress, Henry informed her there would be two more and that he would like another cup of coffee. Her response indicated appreciation for information that he was not going to occupy a booth by himself. Soon, the two men came into the diner. After a short standing search, Josh directed his companion toward the corner booth. Josh was followed by a ruffled, gruff looking man whose scowl told of his displeasure. Henry gave a quick thought about that scowl being a permanent part of the man's face. The man was big and looked to be in his late fifties. His whole nature, from his clothes to his attitude, identified a physical type who used his brawn before his brain.

Josh slid in opposite Henry and Appleby turned and surveyed the diner before he sat down next to Josh. Appleby looked Henry over, then again turned his head back to the interior of the diner for assurance. If he was satisfied, the scowl remained to show otherwise. Josh was looking back and forth between his two new 'friends' waiting for someone to start the meeting he was so anxious to be apart of. No words were spoken.

Henry raised his hand to get the waitress's attention. Appleby turned to confirm the intent of Henry's motion. The waitress responded with her order pad as Appleby turned back to Henry. "Breakfast, Mr. A.?" Henry asked in a tone of complete disarmed politeness.

It might have been imagination, or not, but Henry thought the scowl softened just for a moment. "Yeah."

Came Appleby's answer, then gave a patterned order to the waitress, probably the same order he had placed for breakfast every time. Josh followed with his order and when the waitress turned to Henry, he just motioned that coffee was fine.

"Mr. A., our mutual friend, here" a quick nod toward Josh, "says there may be a way to gain financially by visiting your neighborhood." Appleby knew what was being said, or asked, and spent a moment reflecting on the significance of the moment at hand. He noted Henry did not use his name. His host was serious and this was playing out on a professional level.

"I…have…access to certain information, which for the right kind-a people, could make such a visit very rewarding." The old man cautiously formed his words on the pattern set by Henry's statement. The two men continued this exchange of words, neither asking for a restatement, but each involved at the same level.

Josh sat there listening, but most of what was being said left him a step behind. He had expected a meeting where everyone would talk in a straight, forward manner with his involvement a necessary and major component. Because he had missed out from the first beat, his only ploy now was to act like he understood everything to validate his presence.

Henry was speaking. "From what I gather, there is a target, in the low six figures, previously circulated, which comes into your neighborhood on an unscheduled basis."

"That's right." Mr. A. conceded.

"Do you think a team of three, or maybe four, could take the target?" Henry asked.

"With the right people and my help…it can be done." Mr. A's reply was sure.

"What would your take be?" Henry asked.

"About 10 to 12 g's. I'll show you how to get in and how to get out. The rest is up to you." He lifted a big pointing finger at Henry. "And let you know this, if you screw it up, I ain't never seen you before. As a matter of fact, it will be my duty to track down your sorry ass and see to it that you pay for screwin' up. You understand what I'm sayn', fella? Any attempt to bring me into this thing is goin-a come down hard on you!"

Henry looked into his coffee cup as he absorbed Appleby's threat. He had to rethink this, because he could see Appleby had no intention of detaching himself from his position with the railroad police, no matter how this thing came down.

"Mr. A." Henry paused. "It's important for me to know as much about what I am proposing ***we*** do as I can. I know who you are and can appreciate why you want to remain apart from this. But what puzzles me right now is why you are sitting here with us in the first place? No disrespect intended, but your asking to have my side of the fence and your side of the fence at the same time. What's your story?"

The waitress interrupted with the delivery of breakfast. Her timing gave Appleby opportunity to form a reply, if he indeed was going to reply. For Josh the interruption was a major break in the most fascinating discussion he had ever been privy to. The stop in the flow of information was driving him nuts. Henry and Eldon remained calm during the delivery and when she left, Eldon began to salt and pepper his food and then put his fork to use. Between bites, he would now and then look at Henry with the intimidating glance of a cop. By the time he finished his plate and wiped his chin, he was ready to talk. Josh felt he was sitting in the wrong place. No way out from what was about to happen.

Appleby began, "Young fella, how long you been a workin' man?" Without waiting for an answer, he continued. "You probably have 15 years in…maybe more, maybe less. Well I've been work'n for this railroad since I was fourteen years old. That's forty-five years." He took a drink of water and waded his napkin up and let it drop on the empty plate. "Now, what I am today is a good ol' Yard Bull. The same job I had twenty-five years ago. In those twenty-five years I've taken every opportunity that come along to better myself, but the Railroad don't see it that way. They think I'm not good enough to be any more'n what I am."

"Fifteen years ago they needed to hire more men to cover the transient problem in the Yard. They needed experienced Captains to head up the watches and control the crazy things that were goin' on during the Depression. They wouldn't even consider me for a Captain. Then there were two more times in the Thirties where I applied for an open Captain's position. Each time they passed me by. They would go get someone from back east and put their skinny little asses in control of me. Skinny little pups, who don't know one end of the Yard from the other." A slight smile straightened his scowl as he remembered with a chuckle, "One of them pups got his self killed by a 'Bo' one night. Sure caused a ruckus up on top for a while and I thought sure they would wise up and look to a man like me to get things right. But they didn't. Didn't even look my way."

Eldon looked at Henry with earnest intent. "Now ***I*** can take it, ya see. If it was just me taken' that crap I could take it like everything else that has been dished my way. It was my wife that I was tryin' to better myself for. Everything I done was to get that woman something good in life and to make her proud that she had me as her husband. For thirty-nine years I tried to give that woman a better life, but the Railroad wouldn't let me. Six years ago, the doctors told my wife she had the cancer. I spent what we had and borrowed the rest to do what I could for her. I watched her die for a year. I kept thinkin', 'if I had been a Captian, if I had been somebody, then the Railroad would have made sure she got better care than I gave her'. Hell, with the best of care, she might-a beat that stuff and lived. The boys in the Yard took up a collection to see that she got buried the way she ought to. Now that was right nice and for that I am grateful. But you know, the Railroad never even sent a card. Things like that a man don't forget or forgive."

After a silence, which lasted too long for Josh, Eldon continued. "Now you want to know about sides of a fence? This side is yours and this side is mine. The way I look at it, there is no fence for me any more. Here is an opportunity to get as much as I can back from the Railroad. Payment for what they owe me. That's why I'm going to help you for a fee. The only way I can keep you in line is to let you know, you screw up and I don't get my pay…I can do something about it."

Silence followed as his stare fixed on Henry. Josh sat there frozen by Eldon's words.

His jaw was slightly a-gap and he had not touched his food. His fork was still at the ready as it had been when he food was hot.

Eldon sat back and changed his tone. "Now, I know the Railroad is going to cut me loose before I can retire. They've already done that to two fellows on the force. Little excuse, no reason. One day I'll go to work and the Captain will call me in and tell me the Railroad doesn't require my services any more. Young fella…I'm not gun-a let that happen, not after everything else. No sir, you are gun-a be my retirement plan, one way or the other."

Henry's eyebrows raised and the corners of his mouth pulled down as he acknowledged Eldon's well spelled out intents. "Interesting, Mr. A. I was figurin' you to be my retirement plan."

With that, Appleby's scowl broadened into an open smile and he began to chuckle. It was his own private enjoyment and was not intended as an invitation for anyone else to join him. Josh looked back and forth at the two men, not knowing whether to laugh with Appleby or remain calm like Henry.

"Ok, Mr. A., let's start this with our present understanding and see how far it goes."

Then Henry looked at Josh, "Josh, I've got to get in that Yard and see what it's all about. Get me on with your crew for a few night's work so I can figure things out."

Josh blinked but failed to respond. Mr. Appleby broke in, "Naw…ya don't wanna do that. You get on that crew and someone will be watching you all the time to make sure you put in a good shift's work. Look, my patrol area covers from the Union Station on the east side, south and all the way around to the west side. It amazes me to think the Railroad believes they have security with one man covering that much space. Now, in the southeast corner of the Yard is an old creamery warehouse. You can enter through that building on my shift. I'll have some clothes in there for you so you can look like you belong in the Yard.

Now about thirty per cent of the work force on them trains is women. They're the most likely one's to ask you what you're doin'. The men generally won't give ya any trouble; they leave it to me to keep things sorted out. So my advise is ta stay clear of everyone and you won't have any problems. I'll have a map with the clothes. It will show you where they park the target when it comes."

"When do I go in?" Asked Henry, amazed that so much detail had come on such short notice.

"Monday night. The sooner the better." With that Mr. Appleby got up to leave.

"When should we meet again?" Henry asked, feeling he had lost control.

"Wednesday morning, for breakfast again, only I'll pick where we eat. This place ain't much on food. Josh, here, will let ya know where." With that the gruff old man walked away.

Henry and Josh looked at each other. Henry smiled at all that had taken place and said, "Ya know what? I think that old man's been waitin' for us to come along."

Josh could only manage a weak, "Uh-huh." His unused fork was still at the ready.

Henry arrived at Jean's apartment in a borrowed car. Even though his mind was full of the experiences of the morning, he was looking forward to seeing the intoxicating brunette, who held so many mysteries of her own. He had been instructed, by Jean, to remain in the car and just honk the horn when he arrived. She roomed with three other girls and the less exposure he got at this time, the better. The notion fit well with Henry, so he honked.

Soon she appeared on the porch and made an energetic advance on the passenger's door of the car. Her smile could be seen from a distance as an announcement of her good mood. She climbed in the passenger's side and they said their hellos. Small talk started as the car responded to its driver's enthusiasm.

Henry had made reservations at Smith's Steakhouse, one of the best in Kansas City. People went there for the food, not the ambiance, as all good Midwesterners would prefer. They were seated promptly, ordered drinks and settled in for a pleasant evening.

As the small talk eroded, Henry assumed his turn at resolving questions about Jean, "How many brothers and sisters do you have?"

"No brothers, but three older sisters." She still displayed the evening's delight. Henry didn't know it, but his very first inquiry had struck the center of Jean's vulnerable foundation in life.

"What are their names?" he followed with the natural question.

"Well, there's Helen, she's the oldest, at thirty. She's married to an attorney here in Kansas City. Then there is Marlene, she's 28 and married to a doctor who is just starting his practice at the University of Kansas Medical Center. Judith is 26 and married to an attorney also, although he is with the Army's Judge Advocate's Office in Washington, D.C."

"So he's the only one of the husbands who's in the service?"

"Yep, but he'll never go overseas. The Army has enough legal work for him to do here that he'll never have to carry a gun. Isn't it funny that the Army would have legal problems during a war? You'd think they would just brush all that stuff aside until the war ends." She observed.

"Never thought about it much myself. But I do know I'd need a lawyer before a gun in any Army. Sounds like your three sisters are pretty well off." Henry said.

"Oh yeah, they all got their man. Mother and Dad couldn't be happier." Her mood took one step down.

"So, do you have a lawyer or doctor in your future?" he continued on the theme.

"I'm not the type. A life like that just doesn't interest me."

"That's strange…I would guess that's the kind of life you live now." Henry's statement was his first to cross her well-guarded lines of defense.

Jean looked at him and knew he didn't understand. She hesitated about going into any kind of explanation. She liked him and felt their relationship deserved explanations if it was to continue. Even so, by creating words for him she might verbalize truths that she must face. She had never done that before.

Slowly, she started into the search for words that would satisfy both sides of her dilemma. "I suppose you are right. I seem to be talking one way and acting another. Maybe having a well-to-do family gives license to such reckless behavior. That sounds like me, but there's more to it." She gathered her thoughts and then spoke again, "I love my family and I know they are good, gracious people. They have very strong beliefs about how life should be lived. For some reason, I don't think they are right. Because they are so staunch in their beliefs, I have to put on an act around them, just to avoid trouble." She had uncovered one of those truths her intent had been to avoid. Strangely, she felt more relief than burden, as she realized she was never herself around her family. This was the reason.

Henry, also a benefactor of her explanation, saw the mix of emotions crisscross her face and asked, "Are you OK?"

She came back to the surface and responded to his question, "Of course I'm OK. I just realized something about myself that I had never understood before." She continued verbally exploring this thought more for her benefit, than his. "All these years I thought there was something wrong with me, because that's what my family thinks. But there's nothing wrong; there is just a difference."

She looked up at him and knew he didn't have a clue about what she was saying, so she took a quick breath and both arms came up above the table as she continued the examination for herself and possibly Henry too. "All these years I would get angry at the way things would always go wrong for me, but so right for my sisters. Mother and Dad always telling me I'm in trouble for this or that; how I make wrong decisions and can't do anything right. They think I'm flawed because I'm different from my sisters. But I'm not flawed…I'm just different! It's not my fault I'm different, is it?" she asked the question, but was on a roll, so no time was allowed for Henry to answer. "It's not a crime either! Come to think of it, it's probably more unlikely that my three sisters would turn out so much alike as they did. You would think at least one of them would have some thought patterns which would stray beyond the branches of the family tree?"

Her lower lip came under the grasp of her front teeth as she went deep into thoughts of her life and her family. The way things had occurred; the reasons behind their occurrence. Henry watched her. He could see her inner struggle. He could also see her beauty. She was heart-warmingly lovely. Her lower lip was released from the bite and she gathered herself with a big sigh. Her eyes were fixed on her water glass in forsake of her sense of sight.

Henry found words to use in this time where no words seemed due, "You speak with a great deal of intelligence."

Her eyebrows raised to acknowledge his compliment, but her eyes remained on the glass of water.

He continued. "I don't necessarily mean the school-kind of intelligence you can get from a book. I'm talkin' about the kind few people have, naturally.

I listen to you talk and it makes sense to me. I haven't been around too many people who do that."

"Thanks," she said as her eyes lifted to his, "I haven't been around too many people who would take the time to listen."

He raised his glass in a toast, "Well, in some ways, we might be two-of-a-kind."

She returned his salute with her water glass and said, "Lord have mercy!"

Their dinner was pleasant, with the quiet secure atmosphere making them both comfortable. The wine was good, but the companionship was better. Neither wanted to wander from this fragile, enchanted space in time.

The after dinner conversation gradually brought them back to the world around them.

Henry brought reality back with a step toward a subject that was always there, "News from Europe says the Germans are going to surrender. They say Hitler is dead."

"Yes, that's what I've read. The papers say the war is over, it just hasn't been made official yet." She responded to the subject, but neither one of them carried the enthusiasm such news would generate between any other two people.

He spoke of thoughts, which had been accompanying him for months, "I think when the Americans start coming home, it's gun-a be tough for me to keep my job, or to get another job here in the States."

"Oh, how come?" Her intelligence seemed to fall short around subjects of the war.

"I've been thinking about this for a while. It seems to me that with all those soldiers becoming civilians, jobs are going to go to the boys who have been fighting. Being Canadian and in this country illegally, I don't think there is any way I can stay without the protection of an employer like the one I got."

"You're here illegally?" She had zeroed in on one word.

"Oh yes, competing for American jobs is frowned upon by your government. They've looked the other way during the war. I think now, Uncle Sam is going to have the time and the reason to clear out people like me."

"So are you going back to Canada?"

"I'm not too welcome up there either."

"What are you going to do?"

"The way I see it, there's one ticket that will get you anywhere you want to go in this world and people will leave you alone. That ticket is the American dollar. If you have enough of them, people tend to have memory lapses and it makes things a might more do-able."

"You talk like you're going to rob a bank." She said in jest.

"No…not a bank. Sometime this summer I'm gun-a get enough money to go anywhere I want." It was said so he glanced around to see if anyone overheard. His survey brought him to a surprised Jean.

"Are you serious?" She asked in amazement.

"Yes, I am serious. My days in the saddle are numbered with this war ending. I have to do something, I'm running out of options." He braced for her reaction and feared he should not have gone into this.

"You are going to hurt someone just to get some money?"

"With the way I think this is going to come down, the only thing I'm going to hurt is a stuffy old ego here or there." He said to assure her.

"You can't guarantee that!" She replied with a biting truth.

"No, that's a fact. There's no guarantee that ***I*** won't be the one who doesn't come out of it. But, like I said, I'm out of options." He didn't sound flexible on the subject.

She grew quiet. More thoughts were now streaming behind her eyes. The signs she gave where of an evening coming to a close. He followed her queues, paid the check and escorted her from the restaurant.

"Can I see you again?" he asked.

"I don't know. I'm a little mixed-up right now." She was searching for her feelings on this new information about Henry. Or was it new information.

She guessed at his character from the beginning and his descriptions of his occupation had left nothing in doubt. But now it was coming to touch her and she wondered why this had caused her to be confused instead of flatly refusing to see him again. Why?

Henry drove her back to her apartment in silence. He stopped the car, put it out of gear and let it idle while he turned to her. "Jean, people like you and people like me aren't meant to be together. It just isn't done. I'm trouble and I know it. I can't be no other way. There's something I have to do if I'm gun-a have any shot at life…and I'm gun-a do it. I'm not asking you to be a part of that, or my life. I'd just like to be around you a little more before I'm gone. Now I don't know what you're gun-a do, but I'll go by what you say. If you want to see me again, leave a message for me at the Old City Brewery. If I don't hear from you, I'll understand and that will be that."

She nodded her head up and down and reached for the door handle. As she stood up, he spoke again. This time with a little urgency in his voice, as if this was a moment in his life that was vanishing and he realized it would be gone. "Jean, I've never been in love before, so I don't know much about it. But it seems to me…I'm in love with you."

She stood there for that moment and then closed the door.

Monday, May 7, 1945

It was eleven o'clock at night. Henry drove his borrowed car to a neighborhood southeast of the Union Station train terminal. In driving the area, he had found the old creamery building Mr. Appleby had told him about. Two blocks away, he parked his car in an area that was mostly warehouses and garages. Nobody was in sight as Henry left the car and started walking toward the creamery. Across the street from the building, he was able to study it with the aide of the street lamps. The main entrance and the office area were to his right. The docking doors were directly across from him and this is where his interest focused.

Three docks were side by side with their huge doors four feet off the ground to allow trucks to back up to them with their cargo beds even with the docks.

The doors were boarded over and sealed with cross-timbers. The next feature was a concrete ramp, wide enough to accommodate two trucks, leading up to another set of huge boarded doors. But this door had a small walk-through door built in its large vertical panel. This was to be Henry's entrance to the building.

He watched the area for a moment and then trotted across the street and up the ramp. The huge door was recessed into the building allowing Henry the security of shadows in which to examine the small door more closely. A padlock was the only devise denying entry. He pulled a short iron bar from the side of his trousers, leveraged it through the inverted U of the padlock and against the edge of the hinge. He lifted hard on the bar, fearing all the time it would slip from its precarious position and damage his fingers in the ensuing folly. He shuddered at the thought of the pain he knew was possible, but continued to push harder for the sake of other gains. It seemed like nothing but his premonition would occur when, WHAM!

The old, rusted padlock had given up with enough complaint to send echoes down the empty street.

Henry froze as the sound rang in his ears. Thoughts of discovery ran their natural course. Reassured, he removed the broken lock and retrieved a replacement from his left pocket. He pushed the door open and entered. After a quick security check, he hung the replacement onto the bracket and locked it. He then closed the door giving the appearance to the outside that the door was still secured by a lock.

He turned to the inside of the creamery. Little light entered the building as most of the windows had been painted over. A few panes were broken and some light from the street nudged the darkness around him. He pulled a flashlight from his right pocket and shined it on the floor ahead of him. He was careful not to raise the light too high, keeping the light purposeful and his presence undiscovered. A steady search of the area revealed a sight totally out of character with his surroundings. There on the floor was a small stack of neatly folded clothes, with a white piece of paper lying on top. He knelt down and examined the paper. It was a hand drawn map of the train yard with various notes and listings identifying landmarks for his journey. A large fat arrow pointed into the side of a set of tracks on the west side of the yard. It was identified as his target.

After a short time of studying the map, Henry felt he knew what to do, once he was out in the yard. All of the tracks were running North and South and widened in the yard like prongs of a fork. The yard was big, but he wouldn't know just how big until he was out there. He dressed in the denim coveralls and a flannel shirt, putting these on over his own clothes. He tied a dark kerchief around his neck and donned an engineer's cap. He walked to the west side of the building where there were several sets of dock doors facing into the train yard. Henry soon found one with a walk through just like the one he had used to enter. This door was secured by an iron bar on the inside. Henry lifted the bar out of its brackets and cleared his way into the yard. He stepped through the door onto a very thin ledge. Pulling the door closed behind him, he noted left and right for his position so he could find this door on his return. Next, he surveyed the ground five feet below for the safety of his jump. There was a narrow strip of weedy ground before the set of tracks, which once served the creamery. Turning sideways, Henry bent down and placed one hand on the concrete ledge, then leaped the distance to the ground. He stayed knelt there and looked around for the direction to take. He knew he had to move North and West, across two service roads, which paralleled the many sets of tracks. The third service road is what he would be seeking.

Henry moved, following his plan based on the brief education from the map. There were clusters of floodlights on tall poles spaced throughout the yard, but their separation provided dark areas in which he traveled. Trains were moving in various parts of the yard. Other noises of a busy night at work were beginning to reach him the deeper he moved into the yard. After crossing several sets of tracks, he came to the first service road, which was used by vehicles on business within the yard. There were planked crossovers now and again to permit those vehicles to transverse the tracks in an East and West direction. Henry crawled under several standing trains as he moved west. Only once did he encounter a moving train. He had held his position under another as it passed. He looked for people, but only saw one lantern swinging in the distance indicating the presence of a railroad employee.

He crossed over the second service road and soon came to the third. He was getting close to the west side of the yard and thought there would be only a few sets of tracks left before the huge light stands which marked the western edge of the yard. Nearly all of the light stands were dark. He couldn't risk using the flashlight, so he was mentally noting everything he could.

About a half mile north of him, he saw a concentration of lights closer to the ground and heard the sound of diesel generators keeping those lights lit. "That must be where Josh is working." He thought with his eyes on the lighted area as he walked. He was comforted by thinking of someone he knew being in this place with him.

As he picked up his foot for his next step, it caught on something solid, but soft to his boot. The momentum of his walk carried him on, but his boot remained caught on the object. He went down hard, as the unexpected fall left him barely enough time to get his hands out in front of him. They caught the cinders along the railway bed first and the sharp pain of torn flesh shot up both arms. His attention went immediately to his hands as he cupped them inward toward his chest and rolled over on his back. Using his elbows, he sat up not risking use of his injured hands until he could examine the damage. He slowly rubbed them together and felt the small, embedded pieces of cinder give way. It was a painful process, but his disgust at his blunder was now overcoming the injury to his hands. He shook them to get the feeling back into his numbed palms as he looked to discover what had felled him.

There, in the shadows of the boxcar next to him, he could see the outline of what looked like a person lying on the ground. Once he realized that's what the form was, panic started to overcome him. Who was this? Had he gotten caught? And a hundred other thoughts crowded their way through the narrow time frame of a few seconds. He got to his feet disregarding his wounded hands and stared down at the person. It was human, laying face down, head away from the tracks. But the form ended at the waist. There was no more form after that. How could that be? Again he verified that what he was looking at was human, but only half of the body was there.

Horrified, Henry began to run east across the tracks and under trains with but one desire…to get away from the sight, which was fueling his flight with adrenaline. Finally he could stop and he leaned against a freight car. He remained in its shadow as he gasped for air and looked back in the direction he had come. The pain in his hands returned. He rubbed them together and against his coveralls to get more of the grit out and seek relief from the pain. He looked around and wondered where he was. He had lost his position as he ran from the shocking sight, still haunting his memory. He walked to the end of the boxcar; the last one coupled to this line of cars and rounded it to move east.

As he cleared the opposite side of the boxcar, he walked into the open area between the tracks. He was again startled by an intrusion. "Hey!" Too numb from all that had happened, he stood in place as three people came toward him. The middle figure spoke again. He recognized the voice as female, "What you doin' there fella?" Henry didn't reply but just struggled with his labored efforts to breath. They were dressed as he was, two women and a noticeably taller man. But it was the woman in the middle who kept making demands. "Do you know what you're doin'?"

Henry made a defenseless reply, "No…I…"

She cut him off with her impatience, "What the hell, are you lost?"

It seemed like a good explanation to Henry so he just nodded.

"Are you new here?" She kept at him, but kept her distance at the same time.

"Yes, I just started." Henry found his voice.

The woman shined the beam of a flashlight up and down her discovery. "Damned, if you aren't a sorry sight. What the hell have you been doin', crawlin' under these trains? That's a good way to get yourself killed. You just get back from overseas?" She ran all of her lines together not allowing Henry opportunity to respond. Henry figured the less he said, the better. He responded with a nod.

Her disgust manifested itself in an apparent washing of her hands of this green "employee". "See Kate, I told you!" She dropped the beam of her flashlight and concerned herself with her female companion. "They're bringin' these boys home now and the Railroad is hiring them. It won't be long and you and I will be asked to leave! ASKED to LEAVE?" She repeated herself as she and Kate moved on by Henry. "Hell, I make it sound as if we're going to have a choice in the matter!" She never gave Henry another look.

The man stepped to Henry, "Don't pay her no mind young man, she don't mean any harm. Just her way of fighting something that can't be fought. Now you go down to one of those crossovers…down there" he continued, lifting his arm with a pointing finger into the distance, "and work your way back to the superintendent's office where you started from.

They may give you a little grief, but just take it and get back to work. You'll be OK." He nodded a smile to Henry.

"Cal! You comin' or are you going to get lost with that new kid?" Her voice retained its aggression.

Cal looked in the direction of the two women and softly responded to her inquiry for the benefit of the 'new kid'. "Wish I could, Mary. Wish I could." He gave Henry a kind pat on the shoulder and then was on his way to catch up with the two women.

Henry watched them go and as soon as they were comfortably away from him, he set out in the other direction. His caution returned. He slowly worked his way back to the creamery. He moved through the creamery locking it with his key this time and then trotted the two blocks to the car. Once inside, he took a deep breath and tried to settle himself against all that had occurred. He looked at his hands and thought about the body he had seen in the yard. "Shit!" The word was directed at himself and summed up his entire efforts toward this planned leap to wealth.

Wednesday, May 9, 1945

Six thirty-four, a.m. By prearrangement, Henry picked Josh up on a corner near Josh's apartment. "Where are we supposed to meet Appleby?" Henry asked as soon as Josh cleared the door getting into the car.

"I've got directions written down…here." Josh located a wrinkled piece of paper in his pocket and gave it to Henry. It contained a crudely drawn map and a street address.

"This doesn't look like an area for a diner. It looks like a residential area." Henry was irritated and upset at all the events in his recent life and another kink in his plans was no help. He was not receptive to any social graces, to say the least.

Josh came back with a 'don't worry' attitude. "Eldon said it was a house at the end of the street…there." Pointing at his artistic rendition of Mr. Appleby's directions. "It's a two story gray house, with a white porch." He sensed Henry's displeasure with his friend, Mr. Appleby but did not understand

Henry's reasons. "We're just going to this house to meet with him about the plan. What's the big deal?"

"Well it don't sound right to me." Henry continued his displeasure. "I thought we were gun-a meet at a diner or café, you know, someplace public. Not some house tucked away in a little corner. I don't like it."

"What's wrong with it? We haven't broken any laws yet. Nobody has any warrants out on us. Seems to me, we can get some privacy and some straight talk about this job." Josh saw his ticket as Mr. Appleby, whether Henry was in or out.

Henry absorbed the back talk from the younger man and thought about it. "You're right, Josh. It's no big deal. I just don't like someone else holding the deck on my deal."

"Appleby's got something to gain here too and it's damned important to him. He won't steer us wrong." Josh was capitalizing on his break through with Henry.

Henry heard all of this from Josh and, except for the last statement, figured it was right.

Henry gave Josh a ‘sizing-you-up’ look and said, “Since when did you get so smart?”

Josh felt it was time to bring the three of them back on the same track; so a little patronization was in order. “Hangn’ round you Henry! Anybody’s gona get smarter doin’ that!” A big smile served these last words and Josh knew he had contributed something of value to this partnership.

He couldn’t read Henry as well as he thought he could, but his youthful energy was an ingredient the other two men didn’t have and sometimes that worked.

A few seconds passed and Josh felt it was ok to change the subject and get onto some really big news. “Hey, did ya hear about that ‘Bo’ that got killed in the Yard Monday night?”

Henry looked at him trying not to display his intimate knowledge of the news. But this was more information about what had occurred and Henry was anxious to get anything on it. Josh continued, eager to tell another person about one of life’s morbid occurrences. “Man, he got cut right in-half by a train! We wanted to go down there and look at him, but the old supervisor wouldn't let nobody off to go look. When we got off work, there wasn't nothin' to see but some blood still there. Everything else was cleaned up. Can you imagine that, seein' a guy that was cut in-two?" Josh's enthusiasm was misplaced, but youth could do that also.

Henry could imagine that. "You say he was a Ho Bo?"

"Yeah, I saw Mr. Appleby and he told me it was a 'Bo' that got caught under a train. He didn't know much more about it, but I bet he's got the whole story today! Man, that is somethin'!"

"I think we're gun-a get a lot of answers from Mr. Appleby today." Henry was relieved to hear a little about what had happened that night. He was now looking forward to this meeting.

The two exchanged opinions about the map and which road it was actually telling them to take. Finally they were on the street before they could agree that it was the street. The clues from the map testified to this being the correct street, although there was no street sign to confirm the matter. At the end of the street, a steep hill rose from the road's end. The hill was overgrown with tumbleweeds and lack of attention. The neighborhood, in general, was a reflection of the hill. The house was indeed gray, but the paint had been applied so long ago the original color had weathered to the simple bland description. The porch was white, sort of, but not much else could be said for it. Henry and Josh crossed it to the door. Mr. Appleby answered their knock.

"Mornin' boys." He said rater flatly, greeting them with the same sour face Henry had seen at their first meeting. "Come on in, I got breakfast a-cookin." The gruff man did not match with cooking. Henry wondered what other sides Mr. Appleby had yet to display.

The aroma of fried potatoes, eggs and bacon blended into the smells of the old house as they followed Mr. Appleby into the kitchen. Mr. Appleby continued. "I told you we could do better than that Blue Moon place. Now sit down here and I'll have this ready in a minute."

"This your place Mr. Appleby?" Henry asked as he continued to dwell on the anomaly that his host appeared to be.

"Nope." Appleby replied without looking away from his duties at the stove. "This place belongs to my wife's brother. He moved outa here a year ago and went to Arkansas to get into some kind-a fishin' business. He hasn't been able to sell the place, so he has me keep an eye on it for him." Appleby seemed to soften and appeared to enjoy his duty as a cook.

"You find out anything more about that 'Bo' that got killed the other night?" Josh asked as he bit into a piece of toast already prepared for them. Josh was again excited to talk more about the morbid subject.

"Yeah, he was an old 'Bo' by the name of 'Red Sky' Murphy. I've known him for years. He used to be in the merchant marine and traveled the seven seas working freighters most all his life. When he didn't have a ship, he would ride the rails with the rest of the 'Bo's'.

He wasn't a 'Bo', yet he was. He was made for the solitary life like the rest of them. He came through

Kansas City quite a bit." Appleby started serving his breakfast to his guests. "I met old 'Red Sky' the first time we arrested him for trespassin' a long time ago. The only 'Bo' I ever knew who had a bank account. He had the money for the fine wired in from a bank in Oakland, California, so we let him go. From then on we didn't bother him. We liked him and had respect for the man as a worker riding the rails on his time off. The Railroad wouldn't of liked it, but when ever we saw 'Red' in the Yard, we looked the other way."

"Why'd they call him 'Red Sky'?" Josh asked between bites.

"He was a sailor Archer, like I said. You know that sailing stuff…***red sky*** in morning, sailor take warning…and a bunch of other talk us land locked fellas don't know about. It was an easy 'tag' for him." Appleby showed a little impatience for a dumb question, but quickly softened his tone for his ally, Josh.

"Tell me," Henry could hold his thoughts no longer, "how is it that this 'Red Sky' fellow gets himself killed where he did?"

Appleby let a big smile come about on his face. It was the first Henry had seen from the man and thought Appleby was going to laugh. But the knowing smile stayed there as he played with his questioner. "I wondered if you met up with old 'Red' Monday night."

"Met up with him? Hell, I fell over him…or what was left of him!" The level of Henry's tone rose as he spoke, irritated at Appleby's apparent fun at his expense. "Christ, how come he was there?"

Appleby continued his mastery of the moment and calmly and authoritatively explained. "Coincidence, young man, just pure coincidence." Appleby looked Henry straight in the eyes to make sure he was taking this as the truth. Then he supplied further information.

"About four or five times a year we find one of these guys in the Yard. It happens in every Yard across the United States. Who knows what kind of slip they make, or miss time a leap, or just plain fall off the train…but it happens. For us in the Yard, it happens too often. It bothers all of us quite a bit to see something like that. But if it happens enough, you find a way to live with it. And I've seen too much of it." He paused to reflect and dismiss the emotion he just stirred up. "I was sorry to see it was old 'Red' though. Never thought it would happen to him."

Henry believed what had been said and dismissed any notion of the place of the dead man and the fat arrow on the map having any connection. He stared to find a base on which he and Appleby could work together. The gruff old man had an interior in spite of his attempts to display otherwise.

They got down to business talking about the target train and roughing out details about the whole plan from entry to exit. As they talked Mr. Appleby continued his command of the meeting, even as he cleared the table, washed the dishes and pans and put every thing away. Neither Josh nor Henry made notice of Appleby's mastery over the meeting and his kitchen with the same ease at the same time. Had Henry understood, he would have found this useful to his future decisions. But being so distracted by the development of the plan, it didn't even occur to him to thank Appleby for the meal until he was on the porch.

He turned back before the door was closed and said, "Thanks for the breakfast, it was better than the Blue Moon!"

"Well young man, I've had a lot of practice." Mr. Appleby closed the door and Henry responded to Josh's pleas to hurry-up, cause he needed some sleep.

From this meeting, Henry had the entire structure of the hold-up in his mind. He would continue to go over and over what was to be done and when it had to be done. His contact with Mr. Appleby would cease here. Their future dialog would be conducted through their now indispensable partner, Josh. As unlikely as the three were to ever be socially linked in their lives, the unholy nature of their ambitions made them mutually dependent upon one another.

Henry committed himself now. Only an absolute fact of impending failure would dissuade him from going for his once-in-a-lifetime shot.

Chapter 4

May, 1945

Germany had surrendered to the Allies the day before Henry and Josh had their breakfast meeting with Appleby. The war in Europe was over. GI's were starting to return from the European Theater, though not in large numbers, yet. It was a very special but uncertain time for everyone. The elation of surviving the hell of war in Europe was soon encroached upon by the reality of a very brutal war still going on in the Pacific. To make it through the European battlefields only to be sent to face death in the Pacific was almost too much to expect from the American soldier and his family.

Conversely, Henry felt the on coming peace was encroaching upon his life. His hiding place was being searched-out by all of the joyous people moving the war to its close. Their fulfillment was going to be his dissolution. He was even more convinced his personal salvation lay in enough money to raise him above the suppression, which was surely coming.

The train was his only chance.

Daily, Henry thought about the plan. Incorporating what he had seen, with information relayed to him by Josh. Josh had complained he wanted to quit his job with the railroad. He was tired of the hard work during the night and the way it prevented him from doing more jobs with the brewery. Josh's impatients kept him living for the moment, even with involvement in the longer-term plan of the robbery. Henry told him to hang on and keep his eyes and ears open. Josh's position in the Yard was valuable and Henry said it would pay off in the end. Appleby had sent word, through Josh, that he expected a train carrying previously circulated bills to come in this summer. Henry assured Josh, as soon as they could fix the date, he would have a schedule for Josh quitting so as to place time between the two events of Josh's leaving and the 'hit'. This would not eliminate suspicion falling toward Josh, but it might delay it long enough for them to clear the country.

Henry wanted two more men to enlist in the effort. He was very particular, wanting reliable, experienced men who were not currently deeply involved with a gang. Needing the help and having to solicit from experienced criminals did not appear to be mutually beneficial to the 'plan' and its successful execution. The lure of money was the first thing Henry would use to keep them in line and following his orders. Beyond the robbery, he would have only his word of leading them in a clean get-away to keep the collection of thieves and, who knows what else, together as a unit.

Henry had three men in mind whom he would enlist without hesitation. Only one was currently in the Kansas City area this summer. A second he learned was in jail in Texas and the where a bouts of the third was unknown. August Stauble was the man Henry had located in Kansas City. Henry had known him off and on for the past nine years. August followed the same kind of jobs Henry had and, on occasion, the two had driven together. August's parents had immigrated to the United States from Germany, after the turn of the century. They had settled in a German community in Western Kansas and August spent his youth speaking only German. As his perimeters expanded in his early teens, the Americanization process gave him command of the English language, although a German accent remained. It was his accent that held him back, in all parts of American society, but August pressed on as best he could in spite of the discrimination against him.

August was energized by Henry's offer to be part of this group, which was going to dare to lift its members into a different class of people in one bold stroke. His pride was enhanced by Henry's seeking him out and, in exchange, his loyalty and obedience were committed. Like Josh, August was asked to keep working at his present job in a cement factory, until Henry would give him the word.

August brought another man to Henry's attention. A construction worker whose specialty was building forms for the laying of concrete. August first became acquainted with Sammy Keller when they were paired together by a loan sharking thug, to do collections. August and Sammy got along and were soon working together in all endeavors of dirty work required by the criminal element in Kansas City. Sammy was a quiet man, considered an odd bird, even among his undesirable peers. His ability to quickly drop his regard for his fellow man made him a valuable agent to the underworld. August and Sammy became friends because of the mutual treatment they received from others. They worked well as a team because of August's large intimidating 'muscle' and Sammy's nasty temper, which he would employ to carry out any standing threats. Although they both worked with concrete, their main ties were after working hours.

Henry met with August and Sammy to assess Sammy's acceptability. Henry found a small framed calm man who did not reflect his reputation for violence. Although he believed what he had heard, he also believed August's presence would have a controlling influence in both inhibiting and/or directing Sammy's use of violence. Sammy was accepted and instructed in the same manner as Josh and August had been.

The little team was complete. Henry felt need for no more and found purpose in his three choices. He grew more confident as he blended the three personalities into his plan. A common thread ran through all four men...all four lived on that small ledge between legitimate society and the criminal world. None had found real success with either.

Henry had saved about $4,200 over the war years. This would be his seed money to obtain the list of items needed for the job. Interestingly enough, he had kept the money in a bank and now withdrew the entire amount and closed the account. The largest budget item on the list was the get-a-way car. No ordinary car would do. To get what he wanted he went to a man named Lucas Berry. Luke owned and operated his own mechanics garage next to his house on a small farm just south of the city. Luke was a successful man even though he had only a few clients. He was the mechanic of choice for the Brewery owners and other similar "businessmen" in the area. He worked on Brewery trucks when something special was needed to enhance their performance and reliability in the profitable business of bootlegging. He was also called upon when the fleet of regular mechanics could not overcome a repair problem. Luke also rebuilt cars for people who might need to fend off bullets, or out run the people who might be shooting those bullets. Luke was an artist in automobiles.

Luke had another valuable trait…he could be trusted. Henry went to Luke with two requests. The first was to acquire a V-8 sedan and bring the car into perfect running order. This would include filing away all serial numbers on the car, installing a good engine, tires, fan belts, radiator, suspension system, drive shafts and axils. Henry also wanted a custom gas tank installed, which would hold more than half again as much fuel. The second request was to take charge of most of Henry's $4,200. Luke was to use the funds to buy and re-outfit the car. The remainder would be kept for Henry, minus the fee Luke would charge. There was no question about this arrangement on Henry's part. He knew the right sum would be there when he asked for its return.

Some of the money was used for other purchases. Among these were three more .45 caliber semiautomatic hand guns and ammunition. The weapon was plentiful on the black market as this was the official handgun of the United States Army. Nearly all officers in the field carried one. The Army chose this weapon because it was a large caliber, heavy hitting weapon at close range. One well-aimed shot from its nine cartridge clip would stop an opponent and, if not kill him, it would take him out of the fight. For Henry, the most important aspect of the gun was its reputation. The thick, rectangular barrel was unmistakable. Law enforcement agents knew the gun well and the effects of being hit by one of its rounds. If people didn't have personal experience with the gun, looking down the business end of this barrel told them all they needed to know. The gun commanded respect.

Henry was counting on the appearance of the weapon to be all that was necessary. He had used it in that fashion a couple of times and knew its power to freeze people who suddenly had it introduced to his side of a dispute. This gun, as well as any gun, could make him nervous. When he carried it or handled it, the butterflies could flirt with his stomach. He knew it could dramatically change a life, or end it, with the simple application of pressure on the trigger.

Monday, May 28, 1945

Henry got back to the Brewery from his route just before quitting time. He backed the truck up to the dock where Skinny Ferguson's dock gang would unload the empty kegs Henry had collected that day. He headed for the Supervisor's office to check out and exchanged greetings and small talk with other drivers. In the office he was finishing his paper work when he heard the dispatcher call his name. "Hey, Henry, there's a note for ya here. Some dame wants ya ta call her!"

Henry suffered through the catcalls and rude remarks that such an announcement was bound to provoke, as he waded toward the announcer holding the note. That was the normal fate of any man in the room who would find a female calling for him at the brewery, even if it was his wife. He looked at the very satisfied, smiling dispatcher and said, "Thanks, I appreciate the discreetness you have in delivering messages." He patted the smiling man's cheek as he took the note.

"Think nothing of it." The man replied. "I'm here to please."

Henry motioned to the group of grinning drivers with his note in hand and said, "And I'm sure the pleasure is all theirs."

Again the laughter rose as Henry smiled his way out of the office taking no offense at the light moment at his expense.

As he walked toward the street and the bus stop, he unfolded the note. He believed it was going to be from Jean. Who else would it be? In spite of his sureness, he was still delighted to confirm the note was from her. In the dispatcher's scribble, the note read: "Call me at 7." The dispatcher had signed it "Gene". Henry chuckled at the mistake while wishing he could use the gender slip to get back at the man behind the desk. But he knew it would only backfire on him, as he would hand the man a ready-made counter-punch. No, he would take his medicine and because Jean had called him, the ribbing did not matter.

A little before seven o'clock, Henry made his way from his apartment across the street to the drug store on the corner. He had Jean's number and hoped the phone booth would be empty so his call would be timely. It was and he was. On the second ring a woman's voice said "Hello?"

"Is Jean there?" Henry asked the voice.

"This is Jean, don't you know my voice Henry?" Jean had been waiting.

"I do now." He didn't know exactly what to say. "Your voice just sounded differently to me." He had no idea why.

"How do I sound now?" She asked.

"Oh, it sounds like you alright. No question. I'm glad you asked me to call." He was delighted to be talking with her again.

"Well there are a couple of questions I want to ask you." Jean got down to business. "Now don't get mad at me, just answer with the truth, O.K.?"

Not knowing what would be asked, hanging-up was dismissed as an option, so Henry agreed.

"The last time I saw you, you said you were in love with me. Why did you say that?"

Henry never even suspected this would be the subject. He remembered what he had said, but never expected to be called on to explain his words. He was embarrassed by such a private moment being re-played in the light of a more public setting. He closed the phone both door. With eyebrows lifted, Henry took a deep breath and exhaled it through relaxed lips. The audible rush of air accompanied by the slight lip flutter carried through the phone lines. Henry began, "Wow!"

"Now tell me the truth, Henry." She restated her condition.

"I don't think I have the time to make up an answer to that question." He paused as he restructured that night and his emotions. "I guess I felt that was the last time I was going to see you. I wanted to let you know something about how I felt." There was silence on the other end, so he continued. "If I would have left that night and never saw you again, I would have regretted not saying something to let you know."

"Are you in love with me?" Jean asked.

Henry's eyebrows arose again while thoughts auditioned for his mind and he tried to form the words that would display the most accurate effort of truth. "Like I said that night, I've never been in love before so I'm not sure what it is or what it's supposed to feel like. I do know the way I feel about you is special. I guess time will tell me whether it's love or not."

There was silence again on the other end. Henry steadied his nerves with a heavy sigh and waited this time for Jean to respond. "If I hadn't left a message for you to call, would you have let it go at that?"

Here was an easy question. "Yes…yes I would have. If that was the way you wanted it, that is the way it was going to be. Hell, a girl like you and a guy like me…man…we're not only from different sides of the tracks, we're from different sides of the border!"

She understood his description of the social gap between them and how it existed as an issue, whether spoken or unspoken. "Ya know, I've dated a lot of boys and too many times I've heard them talk about love. It seems I just get started with a fella and he brings out this love stuff. I don't know why they want to do that, but I'm told they either want to get married or get lucky! I could never tell which of the two they meant."

"I see your point." Henry conceded.

"You gave me a lot to think about that night and I didn't need that comment as a parting shot." She didn't sound angry, but what was she saying?

He arrived at the conclusion that this was her 'parting shot' before she went on with her life. His emotions sank and his thoughts returned to the former state of this being over. "Jean, I can assure you I had neither in mind. All I wanted to do was let you know something before you were gone. That's all."

There was silence again. Henry felt the conversation and the relationship were at an end. He waited for her 'good-bye'.

A new tone in her voice emerged. "What are you doin' Thursday, you know, Decoration Day?"

Henry was caught off guard by this abrupt change. "Thursday? Ah…I guess I'm not working that day, I didn't even know it was a holiday."

"Good! I don't have to work either. Why don't you pick me up about 11 o'clock in the morning and we can go on a picnic. You can teach me how to drive your Brewery truck."

"I can be there, but I probably can't have one of the trucks." His spirits were cautiously lifted. "I'll figure something out."

"I bet you will." She teased him. "Good-bye."

"Good-bye." Then he heard the click, which seemed all to soon.

He had a big smile on his face as he exited the phone booth, made a polite nod to the waitress behind the counter and then, deep in his own thoughts, walked out of the door. The waitress, with her customer sitting in front of her, watched him leave. The customer said, "He seemed to perk up a bit after that phone call."

She replied, "Yeah, maybe I ought to get that number from him. I wouldn't mind getting a little perky now and again!" They laughed at their little joke, but Henry didn't hear the friendly banter. He walked across the street taking a swing in the air at an imaginary foe and voiced a very enthusiastic "Yes!"

Thursday, May 31, 1945 Decoration Day (Memorial Day)

Henry pulled up in front of Jean's apartment and sounded the horn. This time he got out and went part way up the walk to wait for her. Soon, she came bounding out of the front door onto the porch, with a picnic basket, in hand, taking the swings of her cadence. She had seen Henry, but it wasn't until she reached the bottom of the steps that she realized what he had driven to her apartment. It was a dump truck, complete with dirt, dents and scars from service to the "Bennett Cement Co.", whose name barely remained on the door of the cab.

She stopped dead in her gallop and screamed with surprise. She started laughing so hard she had to put the picnic basket down and place her hands on her knees as she doubled over. Tears were soon streaming from her eyes and she protested through her appreciation of this absurdity, "You didn't!"

Henry raised one arm with uplifted palm and presented her the dump truck. "My Lady, your carriage awaits." He looked toward the "carriage" and back at her with a big grin.

"Where did you get that?" Jean asked as she recovered from the effect.

Henry walked toward her, "Well I know it ain't no beer truck, but I guarantee you that when you learn to drive this beauty, there won't be a beer truck in Kansas City that you can't handle!" Mock pride still intact.

He picked up the picnic basket and extended his arm, as would a proper escort. She took his arm and walked with him to the truck. She wiped her eyes as she asked, "Don't you care about my reputation?"

"I do indeed. This here's the best dump truck I could get my hands on! I think it reflects the dignity and…ah…charm of the occasion." He stood there for a moment, erect in pride of his accomplishment, then quickly twisted his upper body so his face came in front of hers, "Don't you?"

She started laughing at his gesture as she allowed him to open the passenger door for her. He helped her up the step and into the cab. He had to slam the door twice to get it secured. While he walked around to the other side, two of Jean's roommates were on the porch to see what all the noise was about. They issued a few catcalls at Jean as laughter rang across the yard. Jean leaned her head back with one hand covering her eyes, then she tilted forward and out of the window with her arms and head hanging straight down, pantomiming "Dying of Shame!"

Henry started the big truck moving and she recovered from her posture of 'death' and waved an enthusiastic good-bye to her friends on the porch. The big truck rumbled and bounced down the street.

Henry drove to the Berry farm south of town. He had arranged to have the picnic in Luke's pasture down by the creek on the property. After entering through a fenced gate, he followed a rutted path down to the creek. Both he and Jean were bounced and jarred by the rough little path. She enjoyed every minute of the adventure.

They ate the lunch and drank Henry's beer under the big cottonwoods beside the creek. They laughed, joked and spent their time in light, entertaining conversation. They both enjoyed the other's company.

Then it was time for the driving lesson. Jean got behind the wheel as they spent a solid hour getting her to use the clutch and the accelerator in symphony. The gears ground away providing the counter melody to Henry and Jean's duet of laughter: a crescendo blending with every mistake.

She wanted to lift the bed of the truck to see how it worked. Henry directed her through the steps. Once it was up, he told her she would have to figure out how to get it down. There they were, slowing driving around in that pasture with the bed all the way up, trading barbs and mock insults and having the time of their lives.

She drove the truck out of the gate when it was time for Henry to take over. He put the bed down for the drive back. He stopped in front of her apartment and said, “You look like you enjoyed the ride!”

“I did and thank you! My jaws are aching from laughing.” Then she reached over with her right hand and grabbed Henry’s neck. She followed with her red lips and gave his smiling face her kiss. She intentionally left the lipstick on his lips and hopped out of the cab. After slamming the door twice, she waved and ran up the walk and into the apartment.

Henry tasted the lipstick, but wouldn’t wipe it off. Her kiss consumed his soul. He kept clinging to the memory of her lips touching his. He moved the truck out on the street and headed for August Stauble’s place to return it. By the time the truck would be returned, the lipstick would be gone, but not the memory of that kiss. His life would always have that moment.

Sunday, June 17, 1945

Jean and Henry continued to date during June. They went to movies, danced to swing bands, had dinner dates and spent as much of their spare time as they could together. They were to celebrate Jean’s 24th

birthday on this Sunday, June 17th. When Henry asked what she wanted for a gift, she said she wanted to learn how to shoot a gun. Surprised, Henry set about to grant her wish. He arranged to take her back to the creek on Lucas Berry's farm. He would teach her to shoot his .45 pistol, this time without the borrowed dump truck.

They celebrated with a picnic lunch again. Afterward, Henry went to the car and brought back a cardboard box, which rattled and clanked as he carried it. As he passed Jean he paused and tilted it forward so she could see the contents. The box was full of empty beer bottles with his .45 laying on top of them. He proceeded to the creek and Jean stood up in anticipation of the coming experience.

The trunk of a large cottonwood had been felled across the creek to act as a bridge. The bark was long since gone, so the footing was sure. Henry carefully walked across carrying his box of 'targets'. On the other side, a high dirt bank rose from the creek to form a perfect shooting range. Henry sat the box down and started transferring bottles to various spots on the dirt bank, sometimes leveling a small shelf with his hands for a place to set a bottle. He had enough targets and returned to the box for his .45.

Jean watched him as she munched on what was left of a batch of chocolate chip cookies, a standard in her picnic baskets. Henry had taken two steps way for the box when he suddenly jumped what appeared to Jean to be four feet straight into the air and let out a yell that definitely announced something was wrong. Jean's attention fixed on Henry as she saw him scramble backwards up the bank and then begin shooting into the ground in front of him. BAMM. BAMM. BAMM, BAMM, BAMM, BAMM. The .45 spoke with a tremendous clap which astonished Jean. This was the first time she had experienced gunfire. Henry let out a string of oaths, which overlapped some inaudible phrases as he came sprinting back across the tree trunk without missing a step. At the end of the trunk he wasn't done running. He launched himself into the air, but was not prepared for the distance he was carried and discovered in mid-air his flight from fear was coming to an abrupt end. His feet hit the friendly side of the creek bank and his momentum took him forward and down to his knees and hands, the smoking .45 still in his right hand. There he remained, breathing heavily as the adrenalin raged through his body.

Jean hurried to him very concerned with what she had just witnessed, "What happened? What was it?"

Henry's breathing was deep and fast as he managed to express a word between his body' efforts for oxygen, "Snake!"

"What?" Jean asked, trying to connect everything she had see with his breathless one word reply.

He was a bit put out by having to explain and simply said again, "Snake."

"Well, what kind of snake was it?" It was making sense to her now.

He looked up at her with an unbelieving expression, wondering why she was asking this question at this time. His answer, "Big!"

She fell to her knees in laughter. Her laugh was infectious. Soon Henry rolled over on his back and began laughing at what he must have looked like in his hectic scramble and run from the snake.

She caught her breath to ask him, “Did you kill it?”

Still caught in his silly adventure he replied, “If I didn’t kill it, I scared it to death!”

They continued to laugh at this strange event, while he punctuated his last statement with, “I hate snakes!”

“No kidding! If that tree trunk hadn’t been there, I think you would have still made it across without getting wet!” Her energy was up now. She got to her feet and made a quick search of the area and came up with a sturdy stick about three feet long, with a short ‘v’ at its end. “Let’s see what kind of snake it is.” She announced as she started across the trunk armed with her ‘weapon’.

He hollered after her, “Are you nuts? Didn’t you hear me? There’s a snake over there…A BIG ONE!”

She looked back and smiled as she continued on her way. She approached the area where she had seen Henry ‘levitate’, reached down with the stick and leveraged it under the body of the dead reptile. As she held it up for display, she gave Henry a play-by-play.

"You're right, he is a big one! About four feet I'd say. He's a bull snake…very harmless. They are actually a good snake, they keep the rodent and pest population down and actually kill other more threatening snakes."

She started toward the bridge with Henry's battle trophy when he spoke up, "Jean, what are you doing. Don't bring that thing over here! I'm warning you!" Then in desperate jest he carried his will further, "Ya know they allow a man to shoot a woman in this state if she comes at him with a snake!"

"Is that right?" Jean was having fun with Henry's phobia, but had stopped on the bridge.

"That's right!" Henry said, feeling he was winning his struggle of words to keep the snake on the other bank. He pointed a finger at her and waved it up and down in a gesture to throw the snake away. "You look it up in the law books, no jury would convict me if you bring that thing over here!"

"Well, we wouldn't want more blood on your hands on my birthday, would we?" and with that she gave the snake a toss into the brush where it would be out of their way for good.

Henry was relieved as he watched her cross back over. He said again to soften the humorous blow to the facade of manhood, “I hate snakes, ya know!”

As she hopped down from the trunk, she answered a question he had not asked yet, “I had a job in college taking care of the lab animals in the biology department. I got to learn all about snakes and found them very interesting. I even went out with grad students to catch them.”

From his point of view, Henry asked, “On purpose?”

“Sure, silly. It was quite exciting, especially when we went after the rattlesnakes!”

Henry shuttered at the thought, waved his hand to say, “that’s enough” and slowly picked himself off the ground. She had a big smile, as if the fun they had just had was all apart of her birthday present. Henry saw how beautiful she was and logged another memory for his life.

He took the opportunity to show her how to dismantle the .45 and clean it and reassemble it. The gun needed attention after he had drug it through the dirt on his hands and knees. She still got tickled at the flashback thoughts of his run. He would stop the lesson to admonish her for making fun of him, only to end up laughing at himself in agreement.

He taught her to shoot the powerful gun that day. She did very well, taking the big kick in stride, just as she had the snake. Henry never re-crossed the creek.

Chapter 5

Friday, June 29, 1945

Henry and Jean had returned from the movies and were parked in front of her apartment. The humidity was high and along with a slight cooling of the evening air, contributed to the inside of the car windows being fogged over. The main source of the fog was from a level of passion. Jean had Henry pinned against the driver's door with his head just below the window. It was terribly uncomfortable for Henry, but who would complain? Jean was kissing him and breathing hard. The attention he was receiving was something more important than the growing temporary paralysis in his shoulders.

With his arms around her in the aggressive nature of her passion, he read the moment as appropriate. His right hand moved across her back and around her rib cage. There he received an answer to his probing inquiry. Her right arm came down forcefully against his hand stopping its progress. At the same time she vocalized a surprised "umph" with her lips still pressed against his. Her strength was such, he could not pull his hand away in retreat.

He started to rise up as a reaction to her drawing a line. Words of apology started forming in his head. She released his hand and he grabbed for the back of the seat to lift himself the rest of the way up. But she kept her weight and her lips against him. Then she took both hands and grasped his collar at the throat. She pulled on him and gave him three quick kisses, then let out a playful laugh as she pushed him back and used the same motion to sit upright in her seat.

Henry was a little confused. He felt an apology was needed. She immediately started working her hands through her hair and beginning the rituals of departure. She retrieved her handbag from the floor and began sorting though it for the needed items.

He fumbled for his apology. "I'm…sorry for…"

Jean quickly leaned toward him and pressed her index finger to his lips. "Henry, now there's no need to say a word. This is all part of what goes on in a parked car at night. I'm a big girl and can take care of myself." She continued with her grooming. "There are things that I feel just like you do, but I don't think either one of us is ready for that right now. I know I won't until the time is right, however, I'm not so sure about you!"

He felt a little sheepish and took her casual ribbing as a sign not to go on about it. He admired her stance. "I've never been around someone like you. You're quite a girl!"

"It's just a practical thing Henry. I've seen girls get pregnant while they are dating a guy and I've seen what that can do to your life. If you're not ready for that to happen, then you simply don't get carried away." She stopped putting on lipstick. She sighed as she looked at him. "That's all it's about, OK?"

"OK." Henry was relieved that he hadn't done something she didn't understand. His personal code of conduct did not include forcing himself on a woman, any woman. He had simply misread the signs. Correctly reading Jean's signs was going to be an issue of confusion for him for quite awhile.

She leaned over to him again and said, "Give me a call this weekend." She gave him a quick kiss, leaving some of her freshly applied lipstick as her trademark, then out of the passenger's side she went. She stopped with her hand ready to close the door. Henry noted a shift in her mood. She slowly sat back down with her feet remaining out of the car. She was in thought, then spoke. "When you go through with your plans, will I know when you are leaving, or will you just be gone someday without a word?"

"I'm afraid with the way it's going to come down, I'll be gone before you know it. As for you and I, you call the shots. I'm going to do this thing because I'm running out of a future. Hurting you is not part of the plan. I don't want to stop seeing you, but I will if that's what you think is best." He was prepared for the result.

She thought for a short while longer as she gazed up the sidewalk to her apartment. Then she repeated, "Give me a call this weekend. Goodnight."

"Goodnight." He said softly and watched her walk toward the house. He thought to himself, "she's even beautiful walking away! I hope that's not how I'm going to remember her." He started the car and pulled into the street. As he picked up speed, he was deep in thought. She had presented a small wedge of awareness in his life he had not known as an adult. She represented one of two realities to him, which were directly opposed to each other. His great attraction to her and his planned illegal act. Facing those two realities in the same thought process made him feel sick to his stomach. His faith in his future had its questions. With a girl like her, he had no future. With his plan, he had a future. Could he have her and his plan?

Saturday, June 30, 1945

A knock sounded at his door and woke him from a deep sleep. Accompanying the knock was a voice he recognized, but couldn't identify at this stage of his awakening. He looked at the clock. It was 5:12 am. The knock and the voice sounded again. It was Josh. Henry went to the door without turning on a light and opened it to Josh.

"You still asleep Henry?" Josh's opening line.

Henry was not amused. He walked back to his bed, sat down and turned on the lamp. Josh was talking, but it was just noise. Henry asked him to stop, pull over a chair and begin again. Josh did as he was asked and pulled a chair up backwards to Henry and straddled it. In the light, his face was beaming. "The train's comin' in!"

"The train, what train?" Henry still wasn't up to the explanation. Before Josh could utter another word, it hit him and he jumped at the question, "When?"

"Mr. Appleby told me last night the train we want is comin' in on the night of Friday, July 20th." He watched Henry's face as the silent calculations went on. Not content without a reaction, Josh continued. "Its supposed to come in on those tracks you scouted, just like we planned." More was available. "At eleven o'clock on that Friday night!"

Josh now waited with a smile of anticipation. He had exhausted all of his information.

Henry brushed both hands through his hair. "Let me see, Friday the twentieth…that's…that's three weeks from last night. Good! Good! That gives us time to be ready." Now his mind was alert and he was in the swing of his plans as he started arranging them in chronological importance. "OK, Josh, let's get Sammy and August together...say at Freddy's Bar tonight. Tell them to be there at seven o'clock sharp. We've got to go over the entire plan now and then refine it over the next three weeks. Can you do that?"

"Yeah, I can do that, but when can I quit my job?" Josh had his priorities too.

"You decide Josh. Any time now is ok. But drop the information you are movin' to Texas or Florida or some other place south, understand?"

"Yeah, no problem." Josh said with delight in anticipation of the freedom from that job.

He carried the chair back to the wall on his way out, turned in the open doorway and said, "Tonight...Freddy's, at seven." He disappeared behind the closing door and Henry heard him clap his hands together, once, in delight.

Henry sat there thinking in the light of the lamp. Events were now set in motion. He felt there was no turning back. There was only preparation and then the robbery. The seriousness of what he was doing could now be felt. He wiped the sweat from his brow and then continued down and across his face with both hands as if this would remove the discomfort of reality.

A sound came through the quiet of the early morning. Henry looked to his open window. There it was again, a train whistle.

Henry arrived at the bar ahead of the appointed time. He spoke to Freddy, behind the bar, to get the use of one of the back rooms from seven until eight-thirty. Henry would have to move out at that time because Freddy's Saturday night poker games would be starting then.

Henry assured him he would be clear of the room. Nothing was said to Freddy about what the room was going to be used for. Freddy didn't ask. What was important in this place was paying cash and staying in line.

Henry asked that a bucket of ice with six beers and two soft drinks be sent back when Freddy had the time.

Then Henry took a beer from the bar and went to the second room on the left in the back of the bar.

Shortly, Josh came walking in. He had a somber look on his face, the tale of woe. One of the barkeeps followed Josh in with the bucket Henry had ordered. As Josh reached for one of the beers, Henry asked, "What's the matter with you? At five this mornin' you seemed pretty pleased with yourself. Now you don't look so good."

"Yeah." Josh took a pull on the bottle. "I got a call from the foreman at work. He told me the Railroad called a halt to the repair work today. Everyone is laid-off as of today."

"Well you were gun-a quit anyway, what's the big deal?" Henry reached over and gave him a playful shove.

"That's the point!" Josh's voice was strong and clear. "I wanted to tell them where to stick that dirty job and they do this before I have the chance. Damn, I was really look'n forward to tellin' that guy he wasn't gon-a tell me what to do any more! The next thing I know, he's tellin' me what to do for the last time! Man, I don't get no breaks!"

"Look at it this way Josh, you may not have got the satisfaction of quitting on him, but the 50 or 60 men being laid off that job are gun-a work in our favor." Josh didn't react to Henry's statement, but Henry continued, "When we pull this thing off, they are gun-a know right away that someone on the inside of that Yard had a hand in it. Fifty more suspects to track down and question after three week's absence is gun-a have the Feds runnin' all over."

Henry raised his beer as a salute and waited for Josh's approval of this different way to look at the turn of events. A smile etched its way across Josh's lips and he clanged his bottle against Henry's. They both drank with a smile.

Sammy and August arrived together. After the greetings and the news about Josh losing his job, the closed-door meeting began. August spoke early, "So dat train is gona come, is it?"

"Yes it is Auggie. They've got it scheduled to be here on the night of July 20th. That's a Friday night, at eleven o'clock." Henry began the meeting.

August and Sammy exchanged smiles then August continued, "So vot do ve do?"

Henry brought a serious tone to his next words, both to get their complete attention and to avoid any more preliminary questions. "I've been thinkin' about this for two months. I know how it has to be done. I know what each of us has to do to get this thing pulled off without a hitch. I want each of you to agree to do it my way. If you can't, it stops here." He waited for approval then asked each man individually, "Josh?" "Sammy?" "Auggie?" He received an affirmative answer from each. "What we will do is hit this train fast and aggressively, leaving everyone alive and unhurt. After we pay our informant, we split the take four ways evenly. Then we are gun-a stick together and go to Canada where I can have each of us issued new identities 'till this blows over. Gentlemen, I want a clean, lucrative get-a-way."

August spoke again, “Ve think you know vot you are doing.” He got Sammy and Josh to collaborate with nods.

“OK, here’s what we have. The train will be carrying from 150 to 250 g’s of previously circulated currency. Because it’s been in circulation, the bills are not in serial number order and are not documented on this shipment. That means the money can’t be traced. They can, however, track any fool who starts spending money like it was free. Remember what I am saying, all of it is important.”

“We are gun-a base our hit from a vacant warehouse in the southeast corner of the Rail Yard. I will have a car, clothes and weapons for you to use. Bring one suitcase of stuff you want to keep with you and get rid of the rest of your belongings. If you have weapons of your own, get rid of them too. I’ve got a .45 for each of you. If you need to learn about this weapon, let me know and I’ll get one to you early.”

“We’ll be dressed in black and will move into the Yard from the warehouse. We’ll work our way to any cars on the tracks next to where the train is gun-a stop.

While we are moving in the Yard, each of us has to stay alert so we won't be seen. We stay in the shadows and we only move when it's clear. If we get spotted early, it's over. We bail and that means no money for anyone."

"A truck, not an armored car, is coming to pick up the shipment."

"How do you know?" was Sammy's first entry into plan. His question was asked with a calm but demanding voice. As Sammy took a drink from his soda, Henry made a mental note to watch for a sign of his commitment to the work.

"They will only use the armored cars on big shipments of money. With the war, they are short on parts for these cars and can barely keep them running. They will be using an Army 'duce and a half' truck for this shipment."

"There will be three guards; two up front and one in the back. A fourth man will be on the train. It will be a normal mail car and the fourth man will be a postal employee who is a regular on the Railroad. The truck will back up to the open train door to collect the bags of bills. We won't have long to move on them. It will only take a few minutes to load about seven bags onto the truck and then button up to leave. We've got to hit them in those early minuets."

"The driver and 'shotgun' will station themselves on the ground at the back of the truck and will guard the entrances from either side of the truck. The mail clerk and the man in the truck will load the bags. The driver and 'shotgun' will move back to the cab when everything is secure and off they go."

"What will they have, 'tommy's'?" Sammy asked. The Thompson machine gun was a favorite weapon for Federal Agents. Its rapid killing power was a well-recognized deterrent.

Henry could still hear the demand in Sammy's voice, but this time he felt Sammy's question was a contribution to the general knowledge of the other men. "No, they are gun-a be armed with 12 gauge, pump action shotguns. Again, this is a small operation for them and the smallness runs all the way through it. The guards will be standing with their backs to the train, because that's the direction they expect trouble.

We are gun-a come from under the train and hit them from behind. Sammy, you and I will take one guard and Auggie and Josh the other. We want to get them down and disarmed as fast as we can. Then with Sammy and Auggie holding them, Josh and I will go up into the car as soon as we can. Once we have control, we'll get everyone up in the car and handcuff them to the inside. We take all of the bags on the truck and drive out of the Yard, as they would have done. Sammy will be dropped off at the warehouse on the way out and he'll have the outside door ready for us when we circle back around with the truck."

"Taking those two guards by hand and not letting them get a shot off sounds tricky Henry. Maybe we shouldn't try to be so polite." Sammy said.

"Here's what I know." Henry was digging into all his preliminary detail work to match the points Sammy was bringing up. "These guards are not going to be Marines. They are what is left over after all the fighters have gone overseas. We take them quick and we take them hard and that will take the fight right out of them."

"How rough you want to be?" Sammy had first hand experience and did not like Henry's superficial statements about what it took to 'take the fight out' of a man.

"We do what is necessary, but if we are smart and fast, surprise is going to do most of the work for us. If we have to club one of them around, we do it." Henry looked at each of the three men and could see they didn't think he knew what he was talking about.

He sat up in his chair and leaned over the table. "I want each of you to know something right now. We're goin' in there with loaded .45's, but I don't want anyone using his gun. If it comes down to kill or be killed, then you done something wrong. I don't want it to come down to that. This is why we are gun-a go over this plan until each of you has the knowledge to carry your part off without firing a shot!"

The three men started grumbling at the thought of Henry's plan. It had not made sense to any of them as yet. Henry tried again. This time in a common take it or leave it tone. "Listen. We are pulling off a robbery and that's gun-a cause a stir. But the amount of money is not big enough for them to drop everything to track us down. If we were takin' a million or two, the newspapers would pick up on those big round zeros and pound on the Feds until someone is caught. A couple of hundred grand is going to be bad, but it doesn't have the same publicity value of a million, so the Feds aren't gun-a have the pressure to go all out on the case."

"We want to get the money and make a clean get-a-way, otherwise there is no reason to go on from here. The amount of money is perfect. The security is lax. We know everything about them and they know nothing about us. Everything works in our favor except one thing. If we kill a guard, then the Feds are gun-a come at us with everything they have. They will not rest until we have all fried in the electric chair. Now that is what I am talking about and that is the difference between us being free with the money, or on death row."

He had their attention now, hoping they understood. "You kill a cop and there's not a sundown that can hide you!"

Silence ruled the room. It was broken by Josh, "Why don't we wait and take the truck on it's way out?"

"Remember when we were in Wichita with that load of beer?" Henry asked in reply.

"Yeah." Josh said waiting for the point.

"When you and I had that truck movin', we were pretty secure. We had the advantage on the move. As soon as we stopped and we're tied up unloading, we were sittin' ducks. The same thing here. They are gun-a be most exposed when they are backed up to that train. That's the time we hit 'em!"

Josh remembered the day and his surprise when the two unseen men came from the shadows. He could now feel what Henry was talking about. He pushed out his lower lip and nodded to visually concede the point.

Henry went on. "I've got the car for us that's gun-a take us straight to Canada, through Minnesota. We are gun-a lay as low as we can when we are on the move. Once we are in Canada, I have some connections to keep us out of sight and get us some new identities. We will slowly exchange our U.S. dollars for Canadian. Then when this all blows over, we're free to go our separate ways. You know as well as I, if the Feds get one of us, it's only a matter of time before they make him an offer he can't refuse. That will be it for the rest of us. So we've got to stick together on this."

"It's a thin line we gotta walk to beat this all the way. But if we're smart, if we're patient, we have the chance to do it."

Each man nodded.

"Quit your jobs as you can. Give reasons of better opportunities further south or east or west. Start getting rid of the stuff you have that isn't goin' along." Henry was bringing the meeting to its close. "One thing I've got to say. Not a word of any part of this to anyone! I mean no one! We all work for people and with people who would sell us out for a five-dollar bill. If the bosses get wind that we are the ones fouling their nest, you and I are gun-a disappear the hard way."

"Any questions?" Henry looked at his watch. It was ten after eight.

August asked, “Are ve gona meet again?”

“Yes, we’re gun-a meet several times so each one of us can be solid before we go into that Yard.” Henry paused. “July 20th gentlemen, get ready.”

They drank down their last swallows with small talk and then it was time to give-up the room. The three men left, but Henry sat down at the bar for another beer. He was tense as thoughts crowded their way in on his comfort. “What about Sammy? What about Josh for that matter?” Time passed, as Henry was absentmindedly peeling the label from his beer bottle. Suddenly he was shocked by the boisterous sound of his nickname. “Hey Frenchie, what ya doin’?” It was Tuffs Bellenger.

A heavy hand came down on his shoulder as Tuffs gripped him from shoulder to shoulder with just one arm. The other arm came down on the bar in front of Henry. Henry not only felt surrounded, he physically was surrounded. He looked Tuffs in the face and caught a glimpse of a larger man out of the corner of his eye. Tuffs’s ever present ‘shadow’.

"Just havin' a beer Tuffs. What you doin' running around this neighborhood?" He hoped he sounded calm, but his heart was pounding.

"I got a card game here tonight…you wanna join in?" Tuffs was relaxed and smiling.

Henry knew the offer was polite and not intended to be taken. "No thanks, I was getin' ready to go. 'Sides I'm not in your league Tuffs, unless tonight's game is nickel-dime?"

Tuffs laughed at the thought. He leaned into Henry as if to share some private wisdom, "De only thing nickel-dime that is gona go on in there is the advice I'm gona get on how to play poker!" Tuffs laughed hard at his joke and glanced back at the big 'shadow' to get his patronizing gesture, which was the closest the big man ever got to a smile.

He motioned for the barkeep to get Henry another beer, which Henry would not refuse, then released him from his 'hug'. He rested both elbows on the bar and said, "I'm glad I ran into you tonight, Frenchie. I've got a shipment for you ta take over to Lawrence, Kansas next Friday. Don't worry about your day route, Skinny will get that taken care of. It's gona be a small load with no returns, but it's very important to us that it's handled right."

Henry understood all that was unsaid. "Sure Tuffs, who's my second 'wheel'?"

"Don't have no one yet." A slight frown came to his face at the thought of business matters on his poker night.

"How 'bout Josh?" Henry was trying to get this resolved.

"Nah, not him. The kid sleeps on the drive and I'm not goin' for that anymore." The frown stayed.

"I heard today that he quit that night job of his, so he should be OK." Henry wondered if he hadn't gotten too 'chummy' about Josh.

Tuffs raised up as the barkeep brought Henry's beer. Tuffs wanted to return to his good mood and finish this business stuff. "Tell you what, you get someone to go with you and just take care of it. I'm gona play some cards now." He slapped Henry lightly on the back and was immediately greeted by one of his fellow players just passing behind him.

"Vic! You ready to play some cards?" The passerby said to Tuffs.

"Hey Gino! Good ta see ya," Tuffs arm went around Gino as it had been around Henry as the two of them walked toward the hall. "I'm ready to take your money, that's what I'm ready ta do!"

The light banter continued down the hall. Henry felt released as Tuffs wasn't giving him another thought. Henry looked over his shoulder and saw the 'shadow' take a strategic seat at the side of the entrance to the hall. Henry turned back to his beer, drank down another swallow, flipped a couple of bills onto the bar and then casually walked out.

Sunday, July 1, 1945

In the phone booth at the corner drug store, Henry counted the third ring of his call and began to wonder if Jean was home. Before he finished the thought, he heard "Hello?"

Caught off guard he wasn't sure who had answered, so he ventured, "Jean?"

"Yes. Is that you Henry?"

"Yeah, I didn't recognize your voice again." He was trying to explain.

"Oh, that was my 'in case it's mother' voice. I never know when it's going to be her on the line. You know how mother's are?" Then Jean caught herself in regret at her casual remark.

"Yeah, I know." Henry said quickly more concerned about the drop he heard in Jean's voice as she finished her comment. He went on with a better topic. "You wanna go out this week?"

She was thankful for the release, "I've got just the plan. Wednesday is the Fourth so you and I are going to pack an evening picnic basket and go to the park. The Municipal Band is having a concert and we can stay for the fireworks. I haven't seen fireworks in years." She was full of life.

"The Fourth of July? I'm from the other side of that little disagreement between the Colonies and England!" He was poking fun at her good nature. "And picnics, is that all you do?"

"I'm a YANK, HANK! I wouldn't have it any other way!" She disposed of his proud French-

Canadian name for her Yankee slang as she upped the ante on poking fun.

"OK, COOKIE, let's go on another picnic!" He said with a chuckle.

"Cookie?" She didn't expect Henry to sling the slang.

"Yeah, every time you bring a picnic basket, half of it is chocolate chip cookies!"

"Well, if you are going to complain, you won't get any!" She was getting into this one-upmanship.

"That's nothing new!" He threw her a curve.

She was almost speechless. "Ohhh…you dirty minded pervert, if you weren't so damned handsome, I wouldn't be seen with you again!" Mixing insult with flattery in the same brush stroke left Henry without a reply. She took it as a sign of victory and she loved it.

"Pick me up at six on Wednesday and don't be late, we want to get a good spot for our blanket."

He saw the opportunity to sting her again, but he just couldn't be crude any more to this amazingly bright, beautiful, intelligent woman. She read the pause and quickly added, "Don't you dare say it!"

"You are something else! I won't be late. Goodbye." He had a pronounced smile on the inside as well as the outside.

He heard her goodbye and hung up the phone. He stood there with his hand still on the receiver in its cradle, thinking about her words. Did she really think he was handsome, or was she throwing baloney for the pure enjoyment of tormenting him? Then he came to a different conclusion. "She probably said that so I would stand here and think about her after she had hung up." Exactly what he was doing. He gave the groan of a "Rube" who couldn't find the pea under any of the carnival walnut shells. He joined her in laughing at his expense and left the phone booth shaking his head, but still with his big smile.

The waitress, behind the soda bar, leaned over to her customer, "I still want to get that number from him. I have a feelin' there's a lot more to this than just getting' giddy!" The customer smiled as they both watch the young man walk out.

Wednesday, July 4, 1945

Henry stopped in front of Jean's apartment. This time he didn't have to honk. As he looked toward the house, Jean was already walking toward him with the picnic basket. Her gait was not its usual. The basket did not swing with the gaiety he was used to seeing. She got in the car and Henry saw her somber expression.

"Something wrong?" He was naturally concerned.

"Yes." She said softly; then added, "I don't want to talk about it now. Wait 'till we get to the park."

Henry said no more, but as he drove, he would glance at her. If she responded to his glance, he would give her a slight smile of support.

They were in time to get a fairly good spot, on top of a grassy hill over looking the band shell. Big American Elms were lined up along the top of the hill, providing the shade so valued by the incoming public. Henry and Jean spread their blanket to claim their spot and examined the view of the concert area below them. They unpacked the basket and began to eat, still in silence. Henry felt the strangeness of no spoken words on a picnic, but waited patiently for Jean to choose the time. As she ate, her eyes would wander the tree line on the other side of the band shell, looking, but not seeing. She was within her self now.

"I think I'm going to leave Kansas City." Jean calmly lifted the ban.

"Where are you goin'?" Henry felt his cue to participate.

"California. I think that is where I need to go." Jean was exploring, still unsure of commitment to her words.

"Why California?" Henry followed her lead.

"I was reading about California in a magazine. Do you know it has the highest point in the United States and the lowest too? It's got rivers and oceans, mountains and deserts, farms and volcanoes. You know, there are trees out there that are three hundred feet tall? I'd like to stand at the base of one of them and see how tall that is. There are a lot of things I want to see." She looked right at Henry. "Henry, I've never seen an ocean! I want to wade out into the Pacific and see if it's really salty, like they say it is!"

"You know what else I want to do?" Jean's enthusiasm picked up.

Henry shook his head to reply.

"I want to ride every roller coaster I can find. I want to fly in an airplane and see what the earth looks like from up there. I even want to learn to fly myself. I want to climb up the side of a volcano and look down inside. There are so many things I want to do. I can start doing them in California. I think now is the time to go." She was looking away again as she finished.

Henry didn't know the words to say, so he kept his silence.

Jean's head dropped and her eyes focused on the grass in front of her. "I went to mother and dad's for dinner, Sunday. Mother was in a strange mood, but I didn't pay much attention until after dinner. She herded me into the sitting room and told me she received a letter from Jonathan Riley Woods, II." She pronounced the name with a mock grandiose roll of her tongue.

Her theatrics invited Henry's question. "Who's this Woods guy?"

"He was THE heart throb of every freshman girl at the University of Missouri. When I started school there, he was a senior, 'The Big Man on Campus'! He's from a banking family in St. Louis. He was a good-looking, straight 'A' student who was captain of the debate team and the swimming team. He was also top man in the ROTC program. All I heard for the first semester were all these freshman girls cooing at the thought of him."

"When I began my second semester, he asked me out. I didn't even think he knew I existed. It was a pretty heady experience and I did enjoy the fast times he and his friends had. By the end of the school year, the novelty of Jonathan Riley had worn off. He was one of the most egotistical, inconsiderate men I had ever met. I found out why he was only dating freshman girls; no upper class girl would put up with him. It was money and politics that kept him a circle of adoring friends."

"I wanted to call it off and get on with my life that summer, but he was so involved with himself that he never listened to me. He kept calling and talking to me like we were still an item. It was the strangest thing to go through. I transferred to the University of Kansas to get away from him. It helped, but he never gave up. Then he joined the army and with help from the office of a little known Missouri Senator, the Honorable Harry S. Truman, he got to become an officer in the 'Washington Army'. Last I heard, he had made the rank of major in England, supplying the various general headquarters in Europe with all their earthly needs."

She looked again at Henry. "He was a big success were ever he went, even though nobody could stand him. That is Jonathan Riley Woods, II."

"Mother was set on 'Riley' and me getting married and raising a bunch of 'Riley, III's'. She never got away from that, I guess. She and Riley corresponded all the time he was in England, but I was never involved so I didn't concern myself with what they were doing."

"But then she got his letter last week. He is coming home in a couple of months and he announced in his letter that he would marry me and accept an offer from the Truman Administration to be Assistant to the Truman Campaign Treasurer. He thinks my political science degree will be a nice touch to his rising star in the ranks of the Democratic Party."

"Sounds like a 'pat' hand Jean." Henry stated for a light moment.

Jean drew her knees up under her chin and wrapped her arms around her legs. She tilted her head sideways on her knees and stuck out her tongue at Henry. She followed that with a quick smile and relaxed a little, allowing the brief moment of humor to give her a better mental platform from which to continue.

"Mother declared this 'wonderful' news to me and said how glad she was to have Jonathan come into our family. I was dumbfounded! I told her I had no intention, AT ALL, of marrying Riley and she could forget about it right now! She went on, insisting on the advantages of being his wife, thinking she had the logic to suddenly make me see the light. Henry, I just had enough of this for too long. I stood up and yelled at her, 'You're the one he's been writing to; YOU marry him!'"

Her eyes teared as she completed the story. "Before I knew it, she slapped me across the face harder than I've ever been slapped before. Then she ordered me out of HER house and out of her sight." She paused as she relived the terrible moment and put her face down on her knees wanting the memory to disappear. "Dad came into the room as I ran out, but he couldn't do anything. I think she would have thrown him out too."

Henry moved from his sitting position to his side supported by one elbow. Not knowing what to do, he picked at the grass at the edge of the blanket and thought about what she might be going through. "Man, that's rough Jean. I'm sorry that happened to you."

She put her chin up on her knees again as her teary eyes looked straight ahead. "Yeah, me too." She sniffed and released her hands to wipe the tears away. She moved her legs into a cross-legged position and she took a deep breath. "So, you can see, it's time for me to go look into some volcanoes now."

Jean and Henry talked more about what had happened then slowly ventured off onto other subjects. By the time the band was playing, Jean's spirits had been lifted enough that she could enjoy the concert. Henry was sitting with his back against a tree while Jean kicked her shoes off and settled her back against his chest. With his arms around her, they listened to the band play the patriotic notes of Sousa. He could smell the fragrance of her hair just under his chin. He leaned into her hair and kissed her on her head. She looked up at him with a smile then turned back to the music.

After the concert, they laid side by side on the blanket where the hill started sloping away. They both had their hands behind their heads, which gave them the perfect angle to view the fireworks going off over the lake, just to the side and behind the band shell. In the darkness the magnificent explosions burst momentary beauty on the two young people. Jean was very enthusiastic about seeing fireworks again after such a long time. Instead of removing a hand to point to a particular pretty burst, she would raise her right leg and point with her bare foot, toes extended toward the vanishing glare. She felt as if she could touch them. Each new illumination was greeted with her vocal approval. Henry followed her gesturing foot to each explosion of light and absorbed the beauty of this young lady, who made the fire works secondary in his eyes.

They were walking back to the car with their picnic trappings in tow, when Henry got an idea. "What you doin' Friday?"

"Working." Her blunt reply. It was always a workday.

"Can you take the day off, call in sick or something?" He had the air of excitement in his voice, which did not escape her.

"I guess I could call in sick, I never have before. Why? What do you have in mind?"

"I've got a haul to make to Lawrence, Kansas and I would like you to ride 'shotgun' for me!"

"Shotgun?" She laughed at the thought of wielding a shotgun from the window of a moving truck.

"Yeah, ride in the passenger's seat and keep me company."

"You mean I don't actually need a shotgun?" She was still laughing.

"Naw, but maybe you could drive the truck on the way back."

That settled the question for her. "Why not? I'm not going to be working at Gibson's too much longer and it would be good to see KU again."

Henry had his second "wheel", following Tuffs instructions to get who he wanted.

Friday, July 6, 1945

Jean had taken a taxi, early in the morning, to a truck stop on the west side of Kansas City. Henry had arranged to pick her up on the way, with his truckload of beer. They traveled into Kansas passing the time with laughter and teasing. The trip was uneventful. Henry met his contacts at a warehouse on the east side of Lawrence and the unloading took place. Jean remained in the truck.

As they completed the transfer, Henry settled up with the cash and got back into the truck. He kept out ten twenty-dollar bills as prearranged with Skinny. He placed the rest in the hiding place in the seat back. He extended five of the twenties to Jean.

"What's that?" She was surprised by the gesture.

"This is your share."

"No thanks, you keep it. I don't want any part of that money!"

"I'll keep it for you." Henry stuck the twenties into his shirt pocket and moved the truck out.

Jean talked him into driving through the campus at the University. This time of year it was practically deserted. Jean enjoyed the sights again while pointing out the buildings and significant landmarks of the campus where she had spent three years. As they made their way back to the highway, Jean asked, "Are you going to let me drive?"

Henry knew it was coming. He had intended to, but hadn't reached that point yet. "Yeah, why not?"

Jean was at the wheel of the empty truck, having a ball driving down the highway.

She was doing OK.

Henry felt the time was right. "You goin' to California?"

"Yep! As soon as I can." She kept her eyes on the road and the fun continued for her.

"Do you want to make a side trip to Canada first?" Henry presented his invitation.

"What?"

"Two weeks from tonight, I start my trip. There will be four of us going straight north into Canada. I'm asking you…before you go looking for volcanoes, to come to Canada with me."

"Why?' She was evasive.

He sighed and looked down the road. He reached down to the floor and picked up his gallon glass jug with its soaked burlap wrapping and took a swig of the cool water. He offered the jug to Jean, but she held up her hand in refusal. The jug and the truck would be too much to handle.

He answered. "I'm not ready to be without you."

"Oh." She said as she continued to look at the road.

There was silence between them as she thought. The white stripes on the highway past by in rythmatic sequence while Henry wondered what she would say.

"Henry, what you are going to do is dangerous for everyone concerned. I can't be a part of something that hurts someone. My God Henry, what if you guys kill someone?"

"Jean, what if no one gets hurt. No shots are fired. Just a clean, quick grab and we leave some men tied up, but unharmed. Would you go then?" He sounded sure.

"You can't guarantee that!" She thought it fantasy.

"No, I can't guarantee nothin'. If something did happen, I wouldn't want you anywhere near us. But if this thing goes as clean as I think it will, then I would like to have you spend awhile with me in Canada." He heard no objection, so he pressed on. "Look, if that evening, you take a taxi to the Riverview Motor Lodge, north of town, we can stop there and pick you up on our way. If something goes wrong…if I even suspect someone has gotten hurt in the deal, I won't stop to get you. The next day you could be on your way to California and you'll never see me again. But, if we pull it off without a hitch…will you go with me?"

"Let me think about it." She found the offer interesting, but still feared the unknown.

"No. Tell me now. If the answer is yes, I want you to prepare for that day starting now. If the answer is no, then I'm the one who has to start preparing now." He was serious and left no flexibility in the options he laid out.

Silence again was master over the big truck's engine and the wind flushing through the cab. Henry waited.

Up ahead, they saw a pickup truck on the side of the road. It seemed to be loaded with all of a family's earthly possessions. As they passed, a tired looking man in coveralls raised his face to look at the two people in the truck. His mouth started to open to say something, but the might of the passing truck left him ignored. Jean saw on the other side of the pickup a thin woman in a cotton print dress, with an infant in her arms and two toddlers at her side. Steam was pouring from the open hood of the pickup. The entire scene spoke more eloquently than the tired man could have.

Jean applied the brakes and pulled the truck to the side of the road. Before the truck had come to a stop, she flashed a question to Henry, “You still have my hundred bucks?”

“Yeah. Why?” He was still concerned about the truck.

She stuck out her hand and beckoned forth the money with waving fingers. Henry retrieved the funds from his shirt pocket and handed them over. She jumped from the cab and went running back toward the stranded family. Henry had to scramble to reach and secure the emergency brake bringing the final roll of the truck to an abrupt halt. He surveyed the status of the truck and did notice that she had taken it out of gear. He was amazed at their good fortune in not wreaking the ‘Company’s’ truck. He then got down out of the truck to see what she was up to.

She was standing in front of the tired man and was talking with him. She thrust something into his hands and turned to run back. Then she stopped and addressed him again. He and she had a small exchange of words from her more distant position. Then she turned and was again on her run back to the truck. Henry moved quickly around to the driver's side and intercepted her with a pointing finger on his out-stretched arm. He was banishing her to the passenger's side of the truck. Again behind the wheel, Henry moved the truck back onto the highway. He looked at Jean then the road, then in the rear view mirrors, then back at Jean. "Did you give'm that money?"

She was still breathless from the excitement of her dash. "Yes and do you know what?

He said they only had three dollars and fourteen cents left in their pockets." She beamed. She grabbed the glass jug from the floor, took a less than dainty swig of the welcome water, sat it back down between her legs and smiled triumphantly at Henry.

Then she announced. "Henry, I'll be at that motor lodge like you said. I would like to see Canada." The rush of adrenaline had spoken to her and she had answered. Henry extended his right hand and they shook on the pact they had made.

Monday, July 16, 1945

One this morning, in the New Mexico desert, the lives of everyone on the planet would change. Before dawn, a different 'dawn' erupted on the desert floor, which signaled a new age in the history of man. It was the brightest man made light ever produced. Scientists, who were involved, stated the reflection of that light could be seen on the moon, 240,000 miles away. The experiment had been called 'Trinity' and its success would be a tightly held secret. The first atomic bomb had been exploded.

Chapter 6

Friday, July 20, 1945

The black sedan wound its way through the warehouse district on the southeast side of the Railroad Yard. Henry was at the wheel. Josh was in the front seat and Sammy and August were in the back. As Henry rounded the corner in front of the creamery, he reached under the dash and flicked a toggle switch. This was a special feature Lucas had installed for him. It cut the brake lights, so he could not be seen stopping at night. He watched the side mirror as he applied the brakes and no red glare was detected. He came to a stop in front of the creamery ramp and nodded to Sammy. Sammy sprung from the car as Henry moved on to circle the block and give Sammy time to unlock the door at the top of the ramp.

As they finished the last leg of circling the block they were driving west, toward the creamery. In the sky, a few miles beyond the building, they could see a huge thunderstorm approaching. It sporadically signaled its intrusion with stabbing flashes of lightning.

Sammy was sliding one side of the accordion doors open while Henry drove up the ramp. Henry slipped the car in the narrow opening and then Sammy closed and secured the door.

Henry opened the trunk and pulled out four bundles. Each man proceeded to pull clothes from his bundle and put them on over his existing clothing. The shirts were black flannel and the coveralls were also black. Each man had a black leather aviator's cap, which included the goggles. They blackened their faces with charcoal and lastly, pulled on black gloves. Each man secured a .45 semiautomatic pistol and hand cuffs in his coveralls.

Henry carried the only flashlight and turned it on to check his watch. It was nine twenty-four, p.m. "Are you ready?" He asked his three partners. Each responded in a positive whisper. "Any questions? Do each of you know what you're gun-a do?" Again they answered in the affirmative and Henry knew the moment was here.

For Henry, butterflies flew from his belly to his brain. His hands were shaking and he only hoped the three couldn't see this. He spoke in short bursts to keep his voice from cracking with nervousness. As he lead them to the outlet door, his legs grew weak and he didn't know if they were going to support him. He took a deep breath and led the way.

One by one, the men made the five-foot jump to the ground. Sammy was the last and stood on the thin ledge as he closed the door and secured it before jumping down. All four were crouched on the ground, black on black in the shadows. Henry glanced up at the coming storm and wondered what roll it would play tonight. He didn't like its unplanned presence.

Again he took a deep breath and started through the shadows following the path he had taken the night he met 'Red Sky' Murphy. The thought made him shudder, but they were in motion now and he felt better. They wound their way around and under train cars, taking special precaution to examine any open ground for Railroad personnel. Within twenty minutes, they had made their way to the spot Henry felt was directly west of where the target would stop. All four crawled under the cars on the tracks next to the open set of tracks, then settled down to wait.

Henry looked at his watch without the flashlight, but could not make out the time. "Oh well," he thought, "the time doesn't matter. When the train gets here, it'll be time."

As they lay under the cars, a big gust of wind rolled through the Yard. Dirt and debris were picked up in its crest and fought for release as the leading edge of the storm displayed its arrival. Shortly, big individual drops of rain would splat on the ground. Like the quickening pace of popcorn popping, the drops multiplied until an undeniable down pour was in progress.

The four held their positions for a long while. Thoughts of things gone wrong were entering their minds. No one protested as yet, but they would shift occasionally to avoid the rain as it moved through the Yard. They waited and, as time passed, their attention focused on the event of the storm. They were shaken by the loud blast of a train whistle. The train engine was only fifty yards away. It had arrived with an unbelievable lack of notice. Their tension grew as they watched it pass and then the following cars slowly came to a jerking stop. Only one car on the train was lit with interior lights. That had to be their target. They were two cars too far north, so they crawled south, still under the cars of their train until they were directly opposite the target.

Henry brought the three close to him and tried to talk above the pounding of the rain. "Don't use your goggles, you won't be able to see in the rain. If you can, poke the glass out of them so they can keep you disguised. We'll wait until the truck starts backing up to the train.

Josh, you and August on the left…Sammy and I on the right. Understand?" They nodded as they busied themselves with poking the lenses from their goggles. They separated into their two teams. Henry couldn't get his lenses out. The goggles kept slipping in his wet gloves. Sammy started to help him, but then the shine of headlights under the train took their attention away from the goggles. The truck swung quickly away, then backed up to the opposite side of the train. Henry had sat there watching the truck and realized things were moving fast. They should have been across the space by now. He discarded his goggles and glanced at the other three. He could tell they were waiting for him.

Light was now coming out of the mail car, flanking each side of the positioned truck. That meant the rail car doors were wide open to receive the transfer process. Henry moved and the other three followed. Across the open area and under the mail car the two teams moved. Henry looked for the legs of the guards beside the truck. He searched the lighted area and the darkness beyond, but no one was there. He looked at the others to see if they had any different information. He could see August make a big exaggerated shrug of his shoulders in response to the nonverbal question. No one could see the guards.

Henry could not wait. He slowly advanced from under the car and looked deeper into the area around the truck. No one. What was going on? Was it a trap? He moved to the edge of the mail car door and maneuvered one eye around the corner to view inside.

There they were. All four guards were in the corner of the mail car around a stove drinking coffee. He ducked down and gave a thumbs up to his three, indicating where the guards were. He took a deep breath…this was it. He found the loop step on the big truck and bounded from it into the car. He was the first one in. The disturbance brought the glance of all four guards. They did not have their guns. Only coffee cups could respond to his intrusion.

With both hands on his .45, Henry leveled the big gun in their direction. "Hands up!"

The sound came from him, but Henry did not recognize his own voice. With adrenalin flowing as swiftly as the day he faced the snake, his voice was reaching into another octave. The four guards had responded to his high-pitched order. The rush of his three companions around him made it quite impossible for the guards to resist in any way. Each of the three moved on a man to secure him and handcuff him to the wall of the car. Henry stood guard until the three had been subdued. Then he moved on the fourth man with his cuffs. He got to the man and was stunned by the sight of the man only having one arm. He stood there with a hand on each cuff and looked at the man's face. Everyone saw the predicament. The man just shrugged, as if to say, "Sorry, that's just the way it is."

Regaining his composure, Henry escorted the man to the mail desk and had him sit down on the floor next to the leg of the desk. The leg was bolted to the floor. He took the man's good hand, put one cuff on it, then wound the arm around the inside of the desk's leg. He then closed the remaining cuff on the man's ankle, which was on the outside of the desk's leg. Sammy came over to tie a gag around the man's mouth. As he did so, Henry pointed to the missing arm and asked the man, "The war?" The man nodded his head. Henry reached out and patted him lightly on the shoulder. "You take care of yourself." The man nodded again.

After surveying the four men and concluding they were no longer a threat, Henry took two of their fedora hats and motioned for his three to start loading the bags onto the truck. There were four white bags, two blue and two orange. These were the colors Appleby had told him to expect. Each color of bag identified the denomination of the contents. They loaded all the bags on the truck.

Henry grabbed the two shotguns leaning against the wall and ejected all the shells into the rain with quick pumping actions. He tossed each empty gun into the back of the truck. He jumped to the ground and trotted to the cab. The truck was still running. He moved it ahead three feet to give Sammy room to close the mail car doors and lock them. As Sammy bounded up into the passenger's side of the truck, Henry asked, "Are Josh and August in the back?"

"Yes!" Sammy yelled above the rain and the sound of the truck.

Henry treaded the truck through the crossover roads and swung around the south side of the yard to take the road back to the creamery. When he arrived opposite their exit door, Sammy got out and went about his job of opening and closing the doors of the creamery. Josh moved up into Sammy's place in the cab. They donned the 'borrowed' fedora hats to give the appearance of the original guards to the men manning the exit gate.

They exited the Yard at the same gate the truck had entered, just south of the main terminal. They saw two men at the gate, but neither bothered to challenge them in the rain. A simple wave passed them through. They proceeded on a normal course, which the truck would have taken back to the Federal Reserve Bank. Once out of sight of the two gatekeepers, they turned off and doubled back to the creamery. Henry let the momentum of the truck carry it up the ramp and passed Sammy's open door. Henry applied the brakes inside to bring the truck to its concluding part in the scheme. Sammy quickly closed the doors to prevent the red brake lights from sending out too much of a beacon into the rainy night.

The three men convened at the back of the truck, with August still up in the back. They swung their fists in the air, shook hands and celebrated in muted tones, their success. They took off their black outfits and used them to wipe the remaining charcoal from their faces. The gloves were left on, but the clothes were dumped in the trunk of the car. August threw down the colored bags and went to the white ones still on the truck. He cut them open to confirm that they contained only one-dollar bills. They did and were left where they were.

Henry cut through one of the orange bags on the floor and thrust his flashlight into it to determine the denomination of the bills inside. They were hundreds, just as Appleby had said they would be.

Henry reached in and drew out three bundles containing fifty bills each and raised them for the others to see. He took the $15,000 to the side of the drive where five, four inch pipes stuck out of the concrete about three feet high. They were there to prevent errant trucks from leaving the inside drive. All of the pipes had caps, but one had its cap off and on the floor. This was Appleby's invitation to deposit the funds here. Henry put the three bundles into the pipe and started screwing the cap back on. Josh was standing next to him and the math finally caught up with what he had seen Henry do. "That's too much money! Appleby only asked for $12,000!"

Henry finished screwing the cap on, then escorted Josh to the car with one arm around his shoulders in a 'fatherly' posture. "Remember the yellow envelope in Wichita? We're paying 'farmer' Appleby for the use of his 'barn' and his information. Everything he said was right on. Without him, we wouldn't have those four bags of money." He pointed to the bags being loaded into the back seat by Sammy and August. "Now I'm not going to sit around here and count money when we could be getting our asses out of here!" With that he gave Josh a friendly push toward the passenger's side of the car.

August was in the back seat with the money and Sammy was opening the door to the ramp. Henry backed out. The door was shut and locked then Sammy came bounding into the back of the car securing his presence just as Henry took off. They were on their way. Henry drove south up an incline and turned right onto a viaduct, which served vehicles traveling over the train yard. He reached under the dash and flicked the toggle switch back, so he again had break lights.

The four men broke into an uproar of celebration. Josh grabbed a bottle of whiskey from under his seat, cracked it open and took a big swig. While he was coughing on the effects of the whiskey, he handed the bottle back to August. The laughter and the bottle circled in the car, with the bottle by-passing only Sammy. No one could believe how well it had come off.

Josh imitated Henry's squeaky voice as he had given commands to the guards. Henry smacked Josh with his fedora and blushed in laughter as he realized they had all seen how nervous he had been. The months of planning and the stress of it all was now gone. Josh recounted how Henry had approached the one-armed man to handcuff him. Josh went through an exaggeration of the event to the laughter of Sammy and August. Josh laughed till he couldn't breath, then coughed his way back to teary-eyed laughing. Henry smiled and laughed with them, but wondered how his show of weakness would affect future dealings with the three. His thoughts drifted to the one-armed man and what he must have gone through in losing that arm. He knew in his heart the one-armed man was a better man than he.

Saturday, July 21, 1945

It was one o'clock in the morning when Henry drove the black sedan into the drive of The Riverview Motor Lodge. The other three men had been warned about this possibility and each had kept his thoughts on the subject. Henry offered them no options. He was going to bring this girl along.

Jean had been watching for a car. She had her California bus tickets in the event Henry did not show. Her suitcase packed for either event. She was relieved to see his car. That meant no one had been hurt. She believed Henry would not be here if it had happened otherwise. The rain had stopped and Henry bounded up on the steps to great her.

"Perfect!" He announced. "More than perfect, it couldn't have been planned to go that well!"

Jean accepted his kiss, then handed him her suitcase. Josh had his door open for her to enter, while Henry put her suitcase in the trunk. He grabbed two green army duffel bags from the trunk and tossed them in the back window as he went to the driver's door.

Henry made introductions as he was pulling back onto the highway. Sammy and August were busy transferring the bundles of bills from the original bags to the new green canvas ones. The green duffel bags were standard issue to all army personnel and were a common sight all over the States and the world for that matter. Nobody paid much attention to anyone carrying one of these.

When the transfer was completed, Henry picked a side road and turned off into the woods for a short distance. He, Sammy and August got out of the car with the colored bags in tow. Henry retrieved the black clothes and a shovel from the trunk. Together they went into the woods to bury the objects. Josh 'entertained' Jean in their absence. Soon they returned with only the shovel. Henry stowed it back in the trunk then they were off again. The revelry continued as each one of the men were eager to tell the attractive new passenger about the events of the evening. Their individual views on her presence had been affected by seeing her, although each man's thoughts were different. Josh was the most pleased. He felt lucky to be sitting up front with her. Her perfume multiplied his euphoria and stirred that special emotion that only a woman can reach in a man.

Next stop would be Omaha, Nebraska.

They arrived in Omaha, early that Saturday morning. Henry had laid out a plan for each of them to make their stay in Omaha as low profile as possible. They needed rest before going on the next stage, which would be a dedicated drive for the border. The three men dropped he and Jean at the railroad station, to give the appearance they had arrived by train. They parted with their luggage and one of the green GI bags. From the station, they took a taxi to the Butler-Stone Hotel. Jean and Henry got separate rooms using aliases, which had been provided for each of the party by Henry and his printing press pals. They had breakfast together and retired to their rooms to get some well, needed sleep.

The three men drove to the Blanchard Hotel. It was a block away from the Butler-Stone. They also used their aliases to register. Josh and August roomed together and kept the green GI bag with them. Sammy was pleased to have a room to himself. Without one of the GI bags, he was going to keep alert about the comings and goings of the other four. Sleep was a nagging nuisance to the three as they were still experiencing the euphoria of the night's enterprise. Aided by the alcohol they had consumed, sleep had its inevitable victory.

Jean and Henry got together at five-thirty in the afternoon to have dinner. Afterward, they walked to a nearby movie theater. The movie was a needed break from reality. They retreated to the hotel lounge and had a quiet evening enjoying each other's company. Henry felt all his waiting had been worth it. He was establishing his life in the fashion he had always dreamed. He slept well that night. He could not know this was to be his last good night's sleep for a long time to come.

Chapter 7

Sunday, July 22, 1945

Henry was awake early and decided not to disturb Jean. He went to the lobby by him-self to have breakfast. He bought a paper at the desk and went into the restaurant. Sipping coffee, he picked up the paper and was casually reading the headlines. Maybe he would see something about the work they had put in the night before. Most of the paper involved news about the war in the Pacific. American troops had "cleaning-up" operations on Okinawa and speculation about the impending invasion of the mainland of Japan had writers elbowing each other for the space available. Henry shook his head as he contemplated those poor bastards still over there slugging it out while the rest of the world had quit fighting.

He looked deeper into the paper. A photograph caught his eye. There were train cars in the background and two men standing in the foreground. One of the men was pointing to a rumpled bundle on the ground. “This must be it!” he said to himself as he read the caption under the picture.

“The body of Captain Loren Paully, of the Mid-Continent Railroad, lies where it was found early Saturday Morning. Pictured is Supervisor John Wakefield of the Railroad (Left) and Officer Eldon Appleby, who discovered the body.”

Henry couldn’t understand what this was. Why was Eldon Appleby in this picture? What had occurred in that train yard? He frantically searched the page, but didn’t pick up the headline, so he flipped back to the front page and examined it more closely. There it was, in unbelievable black and white.

“RAILROAD POLICEMAN KILLED IN DARING TRAIN ROBBERY!”

Sweat was beading on his brow as the hot flash of shock ran through his body. His mind was in panic and he couldn’t stay in the public another minute. He tossed a five onto the table and left. He went straight to his room so he could secure himself and find out what was happening.

After reading the entire article three times, he sat on the bed and restructured the events as related by the paper. Four men had held up a shipment of money destined for the Federal Reserve Bank. Federal Reserve employees notified railroad officials when the truck, used in the transfer of the money from the Railroad, never returned to the Bank. Investigation found three Bank employees and one Railroad employee handcuffed to the interior of the mail car carrying the shipment. Captain Paully had been shot to death during the night and his body had been found in another part of the Rail Yard. Officer Eldon Appleby was the one who discovered the body, but said there was no further evidence at the scene. A more intensive search was to start Saturday morning. Superintendent Wakefield had named Appleby as acting Captain of the Yard, in the deceased man's place and was now in control of the Railroad's investigation. An autopsy was scheduled for later that day on the body of Captain Paully.

There was a soft rap on the door. Jean's voice came just as softly, "Henry?"

Henry blinked as his mind moved from the paper to the door. Somebody…no Jean was at the door. He jumped to the door and opened it fast enough to startle Jean. He gently pulled her into the room so as not to alarm her further, gave a quick look up and down the hall then closed the door.

"What's…" she didn't get the rest out.

"Jean! Friday night, when we were in the railroad yard, someone killed a railroad policeman!" He shoved the paper forward to her.

"What?" This was from out of nowhere for her.

While she was reading the article he had pointed out, Henry nervously paced back and forth wiping the sweat from his head with his handkerchief. He spat out parts of the article as they came to mind and Jean tried to stay with her reading despite his broken narrative. Impatiently, he got to his point. "Jean, we didn't do that! Hell, we never even saw anyone but the men in that car and you know we didn't hurt them!"

Jean continued to read the horrifying account while Henry paced in his struggle to think. Jean finally said, "How can this be a coincidence?"

Henry stood with his hands running through his hair and felt she was trying to make an accusation. His anger rose and he demanded, "What in hell do you mean?"

She realized he mistook her so she back peddled as fast as she could. "No, no, no…you don't understand what I'm trying to say." She was calm and clear, the traits displayed by intelligent thinking. "To have a policeman killed on railroad property is a very rare thing. You almost never hear about it. Yet to have it happen on the same night you're robbing that train tells me there has to be a connection."

Henry protested again, "But we didn't do it!"

"I know you didn't Henry. If you had, you never would have stopped for me. Besides, with the amount of booze your partners were soaking-up on the drive up here, they would have said something." She followed her thinking further. "Henry, did anyone else know about the robbery?" She was pulling his thoughts together.

"Appleby!" Henry seemed to understand things. "It was Appleby! That son-of-a-bitch set us up. He killed his boss and now he's gun-a have us swing for it!"

"Who's Appleby?" she asked.

He moved to her side and pointed to the second page picture. "There! That's him. He gave us all the information on this job. He was the one who started this whole business. And we fell right into line. Man, I never saw it coming!" Henry was now angry with himself after this new view of the whole event. "Now he's in charge of finding us!"

There was another knock at the door. Jean and Henry looked at each other, picturing the police on the other side of the door. They remained frozen.

"Henry?" The voice from the other side of the door asked. "You in there?" It was Sammy. Henry let him in and again checked the hallway for anyone suspicious.

"We got trouble!" were Sammy's first words.

"I know, I know! I got the paper too." Henry gave in to the whole world knowing.

"Paper? What paper?" Was Sammy's perplexed question.

“This morning’s paper tells all about it!” Henry didn’t like to go through the repetition.

“They talkin’ about Josh and August in the paper?” Sammy was now confused.

“Josh and August? What about them?” Henry felt the confusion.

“That’s what I came up here to tell ya. They got liquored-up last night and decided it would be a good idea to break into a hardware store. So they did. I didn’t think it would make the papers already!” Sammy reported.

“What?” Henry was incredulous. “They get caught?”

“Naw, I found them sleepin’ it off in their room this mornin’. But they have shotguns, rifles and all kinds of camping gear around the room that wasn’t there yesterday.” Sammy was calm, because he knew he could take care of himself if this thing had fallen apart.Henry sank back on the bed and fell on his back with his hands covering his face. “OH SHIT!”

“What’s the paper say?” was Sammy’s question.

Henry just raised one arm and pointed to Jean. Jean took the paper to Sammy. She pointed out the highlights for him and showed him the picture. Sammy was calm as he took in the circumstances and announced, “Appleby done it.”

Henry’s head came up off the bed and he looked at Sammy as though someone in the room was totally nuts. “Am I the only one who didn’t see this Appleby crap coming?”

“Well, Henry, ya know ya can’t trust anyone in this sorted business. No sir, no one.”

Sammy seemed to now know more than Henry had given him credit for.

Henry stood up and dismissed all the bad news and started thinking and talking about where to go from here. “OK. We can’t split up now. One of us would be bound to make a mistake, like those two goofballs across the street, then they would pick us off one at a time.”

He thought some more. “We can’t go north anymore. Appleby knows that’s the way we are headed and there are bound to be roadblocks all over.

That leaves us west. We've got to go west and then up to Canada. No time to lose!"

"Sammy, where's the car?" Henry demanded.

"It's parked on a side street by my Hotel and I got the keys." Sammy replied.

"Alright. Look up a Federal Building address in the phone book, take the car over there and get a set of government plates off one of their pool cars. Ditch the Missouri plates and find some Nebraska plates to put on the car for now. When you get done, come back and check out of your room and help me get those two out of the Hotel." Sammy agreed and departed.

"Jean, if you need something to eat, you'd better get it now. No telling when we're gun-a get a square meal again." Henry said.

"Then what?" She asked.

"We've got to go west Jean. I don't want to split anyone away yet. Maybe we can find an opportunity to get you a bus ticket when the time is better." He looked at her realizing that this was more than she had agreed to. "Look Jean, if I had known about this killing, I never would have stopped to pick you up.

But now, I can't give the Feds anything to spoil our chances of getting clear. If they get a-hold of you, they have ways of threatening you and making offers that will look pretty good. When they have you alone, it can be nasty. You have got to go with us and have faith in me that I will do right by you."

"You really think that is what I would do to you?" She asked unbelieving his last statements.

"I only know what the Feds will do and how they can break anyone. Now is not the time to test your willingness to sit in jail. If we do this right, it won't come to that and you'll be in California with no more ties to us. Now please, get packed, eat something if you want and come back here to wait for me. OK?" He had said all he could in way of an explanation.

"I don't know if you're right or wrong Henry, but I'll do what you say until I know the difference." She was torn between friendship and lawful duty. She was also playing off safety for adventure. Despite the involvement of tragedy, this was the kind of challenge that was part of her nature.

Henry kissed her very quickly and left the room headed for the Blanchard Hotel.

Henry knocked on the door to Josh and August's room. He heard someone shuffle slowly to the door. The door opened with no questions. It was Josh, eyes half shut, a hang-over frown on his face. He looked indifferently at Henry, then turned and shuffled back to his bed. Henry followed him in and closed the door. He looked around the room; it was as Sammy had described it. The green GI bag was in the corner and looked to be intact. He walked between the two beds and with each arm, shook the two goofballs. "Alright you two!

Wake up and get up right now! We've got big trouble and we have to leave now!"

"Why?" was Josh's weak effort to protest.

"A cop was killed in the Yard the night we were there. Now they're gun-a come after us with a murder charge!" He got their attention.

Both started making noises about what was going on and how could this be, but both knew Henry was serious. He displayed how serious, "You two screwed up last night and it may bring this whole thing down on our heads. Right now I haven't got time to explain things! Either you move out and get on board or I'm gun-a have Sammy arrange for you to be left behind!"

They protested no more and started making motions to get out. Henry had used the threat of Sammy as a bluff, never intending for Sammy to hear about it. He felt this bluff would hold. He made sure Josh and August kept up a good pace while he waited for Sammy to return.

The wait for Sammy was long. But ended with his knock on the door. Henry let him in and checked the hallway then turned to Sammy, "How'd it go?"

"No problem, I got it all." Sammy was calm.

"Good man!" Henry was not calm. "Sammy, can you pick a lock on one of these doors down the hall?" Sammy nodded with confidence. "Take these rifles and shotguns and what ever else you can and hide them between the box springs and the cross boards under beds in these vacant rooms. Hide what ever else you can and what you can't get rid of safely, put in the car. Meet Jean and I behind the Butler-Stone and we'll get the hell out-a here!"

With little more explanation and only a quick answer or two, Henry rushed down the hall leaving Sammy and his bluff in charge. August and Josh were under the impression that Henry and Sammy had talked and neither wanted to give Sammy an excuse to carry out his "instructions". Sammy was amazed to see the two 'goofballs' snap-to at his every command.

Henry was down the stairs and headed for the front door. He took no notice of the lobby or any persons in it. His thoughts were on the current developments.

A man was walking slowly through the lobby reading a newspaper about a train robbery in his hometown. It was Skinny Ferguson. He had brought his wife to Omaha to visit her sick sister and they were staying at the Blanchard. The rush of a man across the lobby pulled his attention momentarily from the paper. He caught the last glimpse of the man before he was out the door. He thought it was Henry Lapointe, but didn't make a solid connection. He went back to his reading while he walked to the dining room. In the near future he would make the connection and relate his impressions to Tuffs Bellenger.

Monday, July 23, 1945

The five had gotten out of Omaha before noon on that Sunday. Henry drove straight west and avoided Lincoln, Nebraska to the southwest. Most of the time he drove dirt roads, which paralleled the hard top highways. He was in his element now. Driving the back roads and avoiding notice is what he had been raised doing.

For the first part of the journey from Omaha, he had to drive on the paved roads more than he wanted. He got the feel for the land and how the dirt road system worked. He could then make time on the dirt roads. While on the paved roads, he asked the three men to ride in the back seat and stay low to give the appearance of just a couple riding in the automobile. From the sounds of snoring coming from Josh and August, they apparently did not mind. But Sammy was a bit put out by having to share these conditions with the two 'goofballs'.

Jean had seen the intensity in Henry all day. She kept thinking back to his not offering her an option, in Omaha. She suspected he was clinging to her as the one sensible element in his life, which had now turned upside down. Maybe she wasn't ready to leave Henry now. Whatever the truth, they were still together.

Henry stopped behind a small gas station on the main highway. Being Sunday, it was closed. He called on Sammy's skills at illegal entry to search the inside for any five-gallon gas cans, which may contain gas. Sammy returned with two heavy cans and a funnel under one arm. They poured them into the car and Sammy retuned the cans and funnel to keep the disturbance by the intrusion down to a minimum. The fuel didn't fill the tank, but it was welcome, just the same.

At dusk, Henry was off the highway and on a dirt road headed west. They came upon a farmhouse that appeared deserted. Closer inspection proved that to be the case. It was still a working farm, but the original owners may have lost the land in the depression and now a neighbor was working the ground. The water pump at the windmill still pumped cool ground water and considered a welcome find for the five. They put the car in the barn and slept there for the night.

Early in the morning Henry was up first, getting the rest of them moving before the tenant farmer could come along. As they were leaving, he had Josh and August take elm branches and brush away tire marks and footprints in and around the barn.

They were driving west again. Sammy handed a map to Jean in the front seat. Henry saw this and asked. "Where the hell did you get that?"

"It was laying around that gas station. Figured it might come in handy." Sammy's reply was laid-back.

After studying the map, Henry set his sights on the intersection with Highway 30, which ran all the way across Nebraska. Once at Highway 30, he followed the pattern of driving dirt roads a mile or two north of the highway. The heat of July was always present. By midday they stopped at a cattle tank beside the road and refreshed themselves, again with the coolness of the ground water. Henry refilled his ever-present glass jug with its wet burlap jacket and Jean brought out three towels and soaked them in the water.

"Where did ya get those?" Henry asked.

"From the Hotel." Her frank reply.

"Shit, I'm surrounded by a pack of thieves that would make 'Fagan' proud!" He drew only faint smiles from two who understood his literary reference, Jean and Sammy.

Jean had each one of the wet towels closed in the top of three doors and posted the three men to hold the base of the towels against the wind of the open windows as they drove. The result was a very cool breeze whipping through the car for a slight break from the heat.

She sat between Henry and Josh in the front seat, kicked off her shoes, put her bare feet up on the dash and worked a crossword puzzle from a paper against her knees.

Josh watched Jean, glancing at her while she was deep in thought. He watched her hands move as she made the letters in the tiny boxes. He watched her lips move slowly and silently as she experimented with possible solutions. He watched her eyes move from the small boxes to the clues and back. He followed her legs to her bare feet on the dash. Everything he had surveyed was, to him, the most beautiful he had ever seen in one woman.

From her bare feet, his thoughts began to move up her legs, passed her knees. He brought his lustful journey to a halt by burying his face in the coolness of the wet towel he was assigned to hold. How could he sit beside her with their hips touching and not explode with desire? How could he carry this burden of being so near her and for how long?

Driving off the main road was consuming gas and time. But it was safer than the more visible concrete and asphalt. As Henry watched the gas gauge move toward empty, he started looking for another opportunity. They had passed Grand Island and Kearny and were running a stretch of small towns along the highway. Henry pushed it as far as he dared, then decided on a straightforward approach to the problem. First, he pulled to the side of the road and exchanged the Nebraska plates for the U.S.

government plates. He found a farm where it was obvious people were living. He could see a 500-gallon gas tank mounted on a stand holding it eight feet off the ground. Gravity was a useful tool on a farm. Henry felt sure there would be plenty of gas in that barrel.

Henry stopped in front of the farmhouse and got out of the car. An older man emerged from the barn and walked toward him. "Hello" Henry announced as he walked toward the man. "I'm Robert Hatch, of the Department of Immigration and Naturalization." As he said this, he reached into his coat pocket for the business card, which would support his claim.

"Yah, vot is it you vant?" The farmer replied in the same Americanized German Henry had heard from August.

"We're on our way to Colorado to process some German prisoners of war and get them ready to ship back to Germany." This was his prearranged story, but he wondered how it was going to play with this man of German heritage.

"Who's dat in da car mit you?" The farmer wanted all the pieces to the puzzle.

"That's my staff, from Washington. We were able to get to Chicago by train, but with all the military men on the move, we had to give up our seats for our servicemen." Looking back to the car, he thought he would try something impromptu. "August, come out here for a minute." Waiving his arm at his German-American.

August stepped out of the car and walked toward them. As he approached, Henry spoke again, "This here is August Kust, he's my interpreter." He said it loud enough for August to hear as he approached. "August, I was telling this gentleman about how we are on our way to Colorado to process German prisoners of war and get them ready to ship back to Germany."

August extended his hand to the farmer, not knowing what he was supposed to do.

The farmer took August's hand and said, "Hello, I'm Otto Pultz." Then the farmer started talking to August in German. August replied in the same tongue and he and the farmer struck up quite conversation. The farmer smiled as he talked, as if he was telling a dirty joke. The two of them laughed as the farmer slapped August on the back. August said something more and the two started laughing again.

Henry had no idea what was being said so he just stood by with a firm smile to support the situation.

The farmer tuned to the house and yelled for his wife. She appeared at the door and received some enthusiastic directions from her husband, then disappeared back into the house.

The farmer said to Henry, "You need some gas?" Without waiting for an answer he motioned for them to follow him down to the tank. Josh jumped into the drivers seat and followed the three walking men.

The farmer continued, "Sure, you can have all you vant. I vas telling August here, dat anything I can do to help you get dose German sons-a-bitches outa dis country, I'll do. I vas too old to go over dere and fight dem, but by Got, I can help get dem outa dis country." He laughed again.

They arrived at the tank and the farmer handled the hose, starting the flow of gas into the tank of the car. August walked over to the tank and felt its side as far as he could reach. The tank was cool to the touch, which meant there was gasoline at least to that level. The farmer saw him do that and said. "Oh, ve got plenty of gas, you don't vorry."

Then the farmer continued. "Ya know, ve been here a lonk time and ve earned mit our sweat und blood the right to be in America. But dose fellows you are going to see, day tried to take all of dis avay from us. Den day get captured and brought over here to vork in the fields, und enjoy da very life day want to destroy." He shook his head at the injustice. "No! It's better dat you get dem da hell outa here. Da sooner, da quicker!" He again smiled at Henry.

Henry responded as a typical bureaucrat, "We'll do our best to return them as fast as is possible." After all, he had been around immigration bureaucrats once in a while.

"Goot!" The farmer replied as he finished filling the tank. "My you got a pretty big gas tank on dat car. How many gallons does it hold?"

"I haven't the slightest idea Mr. Plutz, it's the government's car." He watched the farmer hang the hose up and put the gas cap back on.

"Now, Elsa vill have some food for you to take on your vay." He motioned them back to the house. Elsa was waiting with a bundle of biscuits, potato salad and cold chicken. She also had a box of cold beer setting on the ground.

The five accepted this unexpected bounty and expressed their delight and gratefulness. Henry stuck out his hand to Otto, "Thank you, you've been more than kind and we appreciate that so much. The government didn't have much to give us but train tickets and expense money. The tickets are no good now, but I'm sure the President would consider me a poor government employee if I didn't pay our way." He produced a twenty-dollar bill and extended it to Mr. Pultz.

"No, no, no, Mr. Hatch. Ve vant to do our share. The Mrs. and I are glad to help."

August stepped in front of Henry with a hand extended to Otto. He spoke to them again in German and all three laughed. August herded Henry back to the driver's seat as he spoke his good-byes to the couple. As the five drove out of the yard, Mr. And Mrs. Pultz waved from the front gate of their home.

Henry said. "Now there are some nice people! I wish they had taken the money."

From the back seat, August said, "No Henry, dese people have a lot of pride. It's a very dear thing to dem. You could have only insulted dem by insiting." Then he grabbed a chicken leg and took a bite.

"What were you talking to them about?" Henry asked.

"Just little talk. Day like it vhen day can talk in German." He said between bites.

"Well you did a good job with them." Henry said.

"Next time, it vould be better if you tell me vhat you are doing first, yah?" He smiled with a sigh of relief as he took a drink of beer.

That afternoon, they were nearing North Platte, Nebraska. Henry could see the toll the heat was taking on his group. He decided to find a place to rest for the night. His off road wandering brought him to a point of land in a bend of the River Platte. The point was fortified with big cottonwoods, isolated from view by the surrounding small bluffs. It was a good place for them. They got out of the car, stretching and working the stiffness out of their joints. North Platte was near so Henry announced he and August would go into the town. He had been so impressed by August's down-home endearment talents, that he wanted him along in the belief they might again run into local German-Americans. It was time to re-supply. He told Josh to keep an eye on things while they were gone.

Jean took her suitcase and announced she was going to the other side of the point to clean up. She was eager to get the dust, sweat and smell of the road off of her.

Sammy lay down in the grass under a cottonwood and quickly fell asleep.

Josh became idle. He couldn't sleep and didn't know what to do. Eventually his thoughts drifted to Jean. He gave her time to do what he guessed was take a bath, then he wandered in her direction.

Before he could find her, he called out, "Jean…Jean…"

He heard her reply. "Over here."

"Are you decent?" He inquired as he thought he ought to.

"My parents think so!" She answered. She was seated on a felled tree with her head bent down, drying her hair with a towel. She had her jeans and blouse on, but was barefoot.

Josh went to her and sat down beside her. "I just come to see that you was O.K."

"No problems here, Josh." She responded from under the towel.

Josh made small talk, speculating on what Henry and August were doing in North Platte and what they might bring back. Jean was polite to his chatter.

She lifted her head back quickly so all of her hair swung in an arch over her head and landed in place against her back. She leaned her head toward Josh and started working the towel through the hair hanging on that side. She had another dry towel neatly folded on her lap.

Josh watched her and his talk slowly dropped off to silence. He was captivated by her beauty. Good intentions placed so near such beauty cannot always be maintained by strength of will. Before he knew it, before she knew it, his arms were around her, holding her gently but firmly, her shoulder against his chest. She coolly stopped her grooming and looked at him without alarm.

"Look, I know you're Henry's girl, but I think you are the most beautiful woman I have ever seen. I want to…" His flight out of control was brought to a stop by the introduction of something to the cozy posture, which was completely out of place. It was a metal object pressing into his genitals. He froze as his mind concluded what it might be. He slowly lowered his eyes, searching for, but fearing confirmation. The blue steel barrel of a .45 pistol was placed firmly against his manhood. The gun was being held there by on of the hands he had so admired earlier.

Jean remained where he had pulled her, two inches away from his face. She spoke very softly and very calmly. “Now let me explain a couple of things to you Josh. Josh, are you listening?”

His eyes were riveted on the gun fearful of any sign that she might be squeezing the trigger. Only a portion of his attention was allowed to hear what she had to say. He weakly said “Yeah.” There was the slightest quiver in his voice.

Jean continued. “Number one. I’m not Henry’s girl. I belong to me and nobody owns me. Do you understand that?”

A slight nod was all Josh could muster, afraid of the results of any sudden movement.

“Number two. Never, I mean never grab me again! I am not an object and will not be treated as one! Number three. Friendship has nothing to do with how I look.”

She paused as she allowed him to take in her message. "The last thing I want you to remember is that my gun is bigger than yours. O.K.?"

He gave a final "O.K." from lack of options. She removed the gun from its formidable position, giving him his freedom. He took quick advantage of the release and jumped straight up and away. His anger flared now, as it could not earlier. "What the hell you doin', Jean? What if that thing would have gone off?"

She pulled back the ejection mechanism and it locked into place, displaying an empty chamber. "It's not this gun I was worried about going off."

Josh flushed with total indignity. He couldn't think of a single thing to say. He had crossed a social line and she had taken the best of him for it. He knew he deserved it, but did not want to accept her method of redrawing that line. He turned and stomped off. As his disgust carried him up the path, Henry was coming down. Josh passed without a look or a word. Henry tried to hail him, "Josh! Where ya goin?"

Josh said over his shoulder in very stern tones, "I'm gona take a leak!" Then as he continued on, he said to himself, "I'd like to see her do that with her gun!"

That night was one of those summer nights which old memories use to define all summer nights of youth. A super thunderstorm was to the south, in Kansas, slowly rolling its way east. The effects of the great mass of air and water to the south, was drawing cooler air from the north through the campsite of the five. Three of the men had taken advantage of the coolness to sleep, but Jean and Henry sat beside a small fire trying to stoke the illusion of being alone again as they had been so many times this summer before the robbery. They sat watching the great thunderheads to the south as the lightning illuminated the billowing clouds like great mushroom lamps. The display was magnificent as the yellow and, sometimes white, flashes were continuously in action. No sound reached them from that distance, so the surrealness of what they were watching could reach into their conciseness and loosen the imagination.

Henry spoke first. "My uncle used to tell me about being in the trenches of World War I. He said sometimes on quiet nights, like this, far away along the lines, the guns of one side or the other would start blasting away. He said this is similar to what that looked like." Henry pointed to the current show. "The flashing of light on the horizon and the soft unconnected booming as the sound eventually reached him. They would sit in their trenches and watch the guns and, to the man, give thanks they weren't the targets that night."

"Did your uncle talk about the war much?" Jean asked.

"No, only on rare occasions when he felt the need to talk. What he would say brought a very sobering sight to the hell he had found himself in." Henry looked at Jean in the fire's glow and wanted to talk on. "Ya know what ya see up there on the screen, news reels about this war?" Jean nodded. "Well according to Uncle George, that ain't the way it is. He said he saw a lot of men die, men who a few minutes before were his breathing, talking friends. The next thing he knew they were a mess of blood and gore. The mind has a terrible time with the quickness of that difference."

"You must have understood what he was talking about to be able to remember it again after so many years." Jean said.

"Yeah, I remember what he said alright. It was quite shocking to me to understand war was not just some great adventure where everyone covers himself in glory and is a hero forever. No sir, what goes on in war is a scary thing." Henry said.

"Is that why you wouldn't get into this war?" Jean asked.

"I think the grand illusions of war were wasted on me because of what I learned from my uncle. I just couldn't buy what they were sellin'. If they would have just handed me a gun and said lets get over-there right now and start shootin' these Nazis, then I might have jumped right up on the truck and said, 'Let's go!'" He took a stick and started poking at the fire. "But that's not the way it is either. So I knew I didn't belong in a uniform, pretending I agreed with the way they were goin' about things."

"Do you regret now, not going?" She asked.

"No. Don't get me wrong. I'm glad they beat the Nazis. Maybe I just regret there wasn't a way I could have been a part of it on my terms. That's a bit of nonsense isn't it?"

"I think so, but all wishful thinking and dreams have a bit of nonsense to them, or they wouldn't be." Jean spoke with the heart of a dreamer.

"What are you dreamin' about Jean? This business of California and so on?" He was glad to get off the subject of war.

"Oh, I don't know. California just seems like a good place to start. I have this urge to go places and see things. To be a part of the things I've read about and experience what this world has to offer. I don't know where exactly, or how, but I do want to go!" Her eyes were fixed on the flashing clouds.

"Where do you think you will end up?" He asked, trying to gauge the completeness of her plans.

"It's something I'll find out when I'm there. But I hope it's all so wonderful and exciting! I hope I'll have someone to tell it all to in the end." She couldn't help the smile brought on by her hopes. "What are you going to do once you get to Canada?"

"That will be the easy part. If I can get these three up there, I know exactly what I can do. I know a lot of people from my bootleggin' days and I know they can help me. We can get new I.D.'s and, as big as Western Canada is, there are places we can hide in plain sight. The R.C.M.P.'s are a sharp bunch up there. I worry about those fellows."

"The R.M…who?" Jean interrupted.

"Oh, the Royal Canadian Mounted Police. Canada's Finest! They are a smart, dedicated bunch of Son's of Canada. I worry about them because of these three Americans here. I'm afraid these guys just won't understand how important it is to walk the straight and narrow while we're up there, avoiding any and all attention. I know how to do it, I just don't know if I can make these three do what I know."

Jean glanced around at the three sleeping figures on the ground. "I don't know Henry. These aren't the Three Wise Men you're dragging along!"

With that Henry broke with a stifled laugh, trying very hard not to be too loud. Jean joined in as she enjoyed his getting tickled at what she had said. They worked together to control their laughter. The more they tried the worse it got. Henry would always remember this evening with Jean. The two had shared wonderful moments together, but this might have been the most endearing.

Tuesday, July 24, 1945

Among the supplies August and Henry had brought back from North Platte, were blankets. Each one in the party was grateful for the addition to their comfort during the cooler night. They all slept-in that morning. Once up and stirring, all were reluctant to get back in that cramped car and start the monotony again. Time floated into afternoon and Henry's voice started asking for action to get moving. He was feeling a loss of opportunity from the delay.

Josh felt different about Jean on this day. Her beauty ceased to be an issue within him.

Not because of her request, but rather because of the incident. Jean turning on him now made him indifferent to her. As far as her statement of friendship, he had no idea of what she meant. He had never examined what was inside of him and it had never occurred to him to even think about what someone else might be made of. The issue of friendship was no longer practical between the two. Josh kept his distance from Jean.

Henry finally got everyone and everything in the car and started moving again, back on the highway headed west. They passed through Ogallala, Nebraska and the routine of the trip set back in. Josh was in the back seat with Sammy and August. The later two were not pleased to have to give up room for Josh, but the moody young man ignored their protests. For the moment, the three were reclining low in the seat trying to fight boredom with closed eyes.

Henry topped a hill and took the long gradual slope toward the bottom. It was at least a mile to the bottom, before the grade started climbing an equally long slope up the side of another endless string of hills. There was a car coming from the opposite direction and Henry felt a chill as he recognized the black and white design of the vehicle closing on him. He set out the warning, "Stay down in the back seat! We have a cop coming at us!" He made a quick glance to the back seat to make sure the three were out of sight then settled in to await the close encounter.

As the cars passed each other, Henry gave a small friendly wave as any two drivers in this desolation would do to great each other, but maintained his attention forward. As soon as the car was by he looked in each of his rear view mirrors for signs of the policeman slowing to turn around. The police car continued to the top of the hill and, just before it disappeared over the hill, Henry saw the brake lights come on. "Shit!" That did it. Henry pressed his foot against the floor to bring the big V-8 into action. Everyone in the car was aware of the spot they were now in. As he neared the bottom of the hill, Henry spotted the short bridge guards on either side of the road that indicated a drainage tunnel running under the highway. He reached under the dash and flipped the toggle switch, which disabled his brake lights, then came to a screeching halt.

"You three get out and under the highway!" pointing to the side of the road. While they jumped out, he explained further, "Jean and I are gun-a get this cop off us, then we'll be back to pick you up!" His car was moving again at his last words. Henry was not interested in speed now, but knew he was going to have to face this cop's curiosity. He flipped the toggle switch back on to give the cop something less to be curious about.

In the rear view mirror his worst thoughts were coming true. The police car was coming after him with its red light flashing. "Damn! Here he comes Jean! Just play it cool and follow my lead. We'll be ok if we don't panic!"

Jean turned in her seat to watch the on-coming red light. She had never been stopped by a police car before this.

At the proper distance, Henry pulled to the side of the road. He had not progressed too far beyond the bridge. The policeman pulled up behind him, but didn't get out of his car. They sat waiting for him. When the officer did get out of the patrol car, Henry could see he was a Nebraska Highway Patrolman. The officer stopped at the back of the car and made a note of the government plates, then proceed to the back door window and examined the interior before nearing Henry's window.

"Is something wrong officer?" Henry asked with a tone of genuine innocence.

"Could I see your driver's license?" was all the officer responded with.

"Sure." Henry replied as he dug for his wallet.

"Do you have identification too, ma'am?" The Officer addressed Jean.

Jean started into her purse to get her recently printed I.D.

After they handed him the requested items, the officer instructed them to step out of the car, specifically asking Jean to slide across the seat and exit on the driver's side.

The officer examined the license of Robert Hatch and Jean Miller, the first of Washington, D.C. and the second of Alexandria, Virginia. Henry's time and money spent at the Kansas City printing presses was about to show dividends. "You're Robert Hatch?"

"Yes, with the Department of Immigration and Naturalization. And this is my assistant, Jean Miller." Henry handed him a business card to back up the story.

In a slow drawl, the officer began his reasoning. "There have been some problems goin' on back east of here. Missouri authorities have asked that we check out all unknown persons in our area."

"We're headed for Fort Collins, Colorado, to help process the German P.O.W.'s from that area." Henry volunteered with his pat story.

Un-interested, the office asked officially, "Would you lock up your car and come with me?" The question was not a question.

"But I work for the government, Officer! We've got to get to Fort Collins." Henry felt the control settling with this veteran Trooper.

"I work for the government too, sir. If you do as I ask, we can have you on your way a lot quicker." Further protest was not welcome.

After the car was locked, the officer took the keys from Henry and escorted the two back to his patrol car. Before he allowed them to enter his car, he had them "spread-eagle" against the fender. He frisked Henry thoroughly, finding nothing. He was careful with Jean, only touching her on the parameters and concentrating on her purse. Satisfied, he asked them to get in the back seat.

"I protest at being treated this way! I can't believe this is happening!" Henry's amazed expressions were designed to flow with the character of an innocent government employee, but he knew it was only a matter of time as long as this Officer continued on his determined course. Once in town, the Officer would keep them under custody until he verified their identity and plates. That verification was impossible. He also knew that his car would soon be gone along with the two green duffel bags in the trunk. Lack of a key would be no obstacle to Sammy.

The big cruiser swung around in the road and headed east. To himself, Henry uttered "Shit!" That seemed to cover the entire situation.

As they approached the small bridge from the west, the Officer let off the gas pedal and asked, "What the hell is this?"

To the left of the road were two men struggling up from the ditch. One appeared to be injured and the other man was working hard to lift the mostly dead weight of his companion. The able man waved anxiously at the officer. The police car came to a stop and the Officer got out very cautiously. "What's goin' on here?"

"We've been robbed!" the man called out. "It was two hitchhikers what done it!"

The Officer didn't like what was happening, but didn't understand it yet. He moved to the front of his vehicle to give himself more options and reached to unhook the leather strap on the hammer of his revolver. He commanded, "Stay right there!"

Another voice responded from the Officer's back. "Freeze deputy! I don't want to see you move an inch!"

The Officer froze, but slowly turned his head to take in the threat. Fifteen feet away was a man with a big .45 aimed at his head. A glance back to the original two showed each of them had a .45 also. He slowly raised his hands. They disarmed him and used his own cuffs to secure his hands behind his back. Jean and Henry were out of the car, Henry looking east and west to see if anyone was coming upon this nasty little scene. Henry had to take quick control of the situation to prevent the three gunmen from pursuing their present course of action. He stepped between the guns and the Officer and retrieved his belongings plus the officer's note pad. He searched the Officer for any other items of importance then pulled out his revolver, emptied the cylinder into the ditch and heaved the gun as far as he could into the pasture.

He pointed to August and Josh, the two "victims" and without using their names gave them orders. "Take him down under the bridge and see if you can find some wire to tie his feet"

He tossed the keys to Sammy and told him and Jean to take the cruiser and retrieve their car. Then he trotted after the trio down the embankment. August had scooped up a piece of loose barbed wire per instructions.

Under the bridge, the Trooper was seated in the silt and sand as August wrapped the wire around his boots. Henry motioned the two out as he knelt down beside the Trooper. “I don’t suppose there are many cars that come along these days, but when you make it back up to the highway, I think you’ll be rescued soon. Just don’t start outa here too soon. Them boys with the guns don’t really like cops. You’re a damned good cop. We just had too many people for you to handle.”

The Trooper was burning with anger at falling into the trap. He felt like one of the worst cops for not approaching this whole event differently. He hadn’t even had time to radio the fact that he was bringing the couple in. Things had just happened too fast.

Henry was back out of the ditch and up to the cars. He had the Trooper’s hat in his hand and tossed it to Josh. “You drive the police car and follow me.” He started around his car to the driver’s side and assumed everyone was getting in to leave. Before he sat down he caught a glimpse of Sammy headed back toward the bridge, gun in hand.

"Whoa! Whoa!" Henry cried out as he sprinted around the car to cut Sammy off. He crossed Sammy's path a few yards ahead so as not to confront him directly. Henry held up both hands in a motion for Sammy to stop. He eased into the volatile problem. "Sammy, where ya goin'?"

"I can't leave that cop here alive!" Sammy had the blank expression of a man without a soul on his face. His eyes were cold and frightening. This was the side of Sammy he had heard about, but thought he could control. Unarmed, Henry only had words and a short amount of precious seconds to use.

"Sammy, we can't do that!" He said calmly.

"The hell we can't! That cop is gona tell everything about us. I can't let that happen!"

Sammy set his jaw and started to flank Henry's position. Henry retreated and again blocked his path.

"That's what WE want him to do, Sammy!" This illogical statement stopped Sammy.

He looked at Henry like he was nuts.

"What the hell you talkin' about, boy?" A little bit of soul could be seen entering his expression. Henry knew he had achieved a step in the right direction.

Henry repeated the statement in a more earnest tone, "That's what WE want him to do." Henry's use of the term "WE" was a deliberate attempt to psychologically embrace Sammy as already being part of a different plan of action. "We want him to tell-all about us, everything he knows and anything he can make up!" Sammy just looked at him.

"Look," his tone stepped down to lower the tension, "if we kill this cop, the story he'll tell as a dead man is gun-a be the worst thing that could happen to us."

"Henry, dead men don't talk!" Sammy was trying to talk about reality. Henry heard Sammy use his name and he viewed that as further progress, so he got bolder.

"Yes they do, Sammy, yes they do! They talk louder and longer than any live man ever could. If they find this fellow dead, every law officer in the west is gun-a bust their ass day and night to get us. If they find him alive, they're gun-a ask him hundreds of questions and all that information is gun-a take time to sort through and figure out. That's time we can use! Don't ya see Sammy, we've got a better chance with him alive?"

It sounded convincing and Sammy's state of mind was not positioned to sort through this story for any verification of truth within it. He could only understand the surface elements for which he didn't have the thought process in gear to counter. He turned and walked back to the car. The look on his face was unsettled anger, but the cold, soulless face was gone. Henry's insides turned over, as he realized how close they had come to a great tragedy. The other three breathed the same sigh of relief.

Josh was wearing the Trooper's hat as he drove the cruiser and followed Henry. They reached a fork in the Highway and Henry took the left fork with a sign reading, "Fort Morgan, Colorado". Josh followed. Henry was just hoping Josh wouldn't turn on the red light or the siren. If he could get by without that happening, he could keep a steady course on his intentions.

In the distance he saw another small bridge crossing, just like the one they had left the Trooper in. There was an entrance road to the pasture just this side of that bridge. Henry braked to a stop just beyond the entrance to set Josh in a position to make the turn.

Henry jumped out of the car and ran back to Josh. "Take the car in here and drive it down under that bridge. O.K.?"

Josh followed the directions after Henry had opened the gate for him. He drove the black and white cruiser through the pasture, off a short embankment and down into the dry wash. He picked up speed and drove under the bridge. The engine's rpm's sang louder and louder as he tried to make headway through the mud and sand, but the car bogged down and died. He was far enough in so no one could see the car from the highway. Henry yelled for him to come on and leave the hat! August and Sammy had removed the U.S. Government plates and put back the Nebraska plates while they waited for Josh.

Once back in the sedan, Josh displayed his thrill of driving a police car. His joy seemed out of place under the circumstances. Henry doubled back to the fork in the highways and turned west. The sign in this direction read "Cheyenne, Wyoming".

Wednesday, July 25, 1945

They drove through the night and ended up southwest of Cheyenne in the early morning. Henry pulled off on a dirt road and worked his way up a draw and around a bend.

They were safe for the time being and used the time to take care of their personal needs.

They finished the last of their food and broke out their equipment to rest. Everyone was on edge. The long drive and the pressure of being on the run were getting to be too much. Sammy broke his silence in the presence of the others. "We should never have let that cop go." His darker personality was returning.

Before Henry could gather his thoughts to fight this battle again, August spoke.

“Ya know Sammy, Henry vas right.” His voice was calm and had the air of authority to it. “Ven I lived on da farm, every once in a vile, ve would have some coyote trouble. They would start takin’ calves for their meals instead of the rabbits and other varmints. Da farmers would leave the coyotes alone, until they would start dat business. Den something had to be done. They would call in dees coyote hunters dat had special built trucks with dog boxes on da back of dem. They had greyhound dogs.”

He looked up to the others and saw he had everyone’s attention.

“I seen dem work one time. Day would get a coyote up an’ going and day would chase him mit deir trucks. When they got right up on him, day would slam on da brakes and let da dogs out. Dose dogs ver smart. They lived for dis moment. Most of da time, da chase didn’t last long. Da lead dog would bite da coyote’s back legs und trip him. Then da rest of da dogs would pile on. I tell you what, I never seen something so vicious in my life. They would stay on dat coyote until they killed him. Even den, they vas hard to pull off."

"Ven you see something like dat, you don't forget it. Vhat Henry, here, is trying to tell you is dats vot would happen to us if day would have found dat policeman dead. Now dats da truth Sammy and you had better know it!"

Henry was grateful for what August had done, a totally unexpected rescue from a surprise source. This crisis was maybe over. But the group was an uneasy bunch as direction was being lost.

Through the day, the men talked about what to do next. The three Americans wanted to go to Mexico, but Henry held out for Canada. He pointed out all the negatives of going to Mexico, including the lawless bandits roaming the border areas and the fact that Mexico was too obvious for the authorities. They would be concentrating on the Mexican border.

Finally, Sammy brought the arguing to a close. "Henry, you've done a lot of talkin', but I don't see us gettin' anywhere. Now if you don't know what to do, we're goin' south!"

The ultimatum was not commented on by Josh or August. They didn't have any ideas either, so if south was the only option, they were with Sammy. No one asked Jean about her intent or ideas. She listened, but knew none of these people were going to decide for her in any case.

Josh and August drug out the two GI bags and started counting the money. Sammy gathered up the guns, except Henry's and then spread them on a towel to clean them.

Henry spent his time thinking and sitting with Jean in the shade of the car. No ideas were forthcoming. It was getting late in the day. Finally, he walked up to the top of the ridge where he could see the tree enveloped town of Cheyenne to the northeast. He knelt down and looked at the town for a long time. Still nothing. The sun was going down to his left.

He looked toward the sun and asked, "You're not going to hide me sundown, are you?" He received no reply. "I didn't think so."

Chapter 8

Wednesday, July 25, 1945

Henry was looking at the town when he heard someone coming up the hill. It was Jean. She was welcome. When she knelt beside him, she handed him a pair of binoculars. "Josh and August went to so much trouble to get these from that hardware store, you might as well use them."

"Thanks. Ya know, that day in Omaha seems like a century ago." Henry accepted the aid, which he knew would do no more for him in finding an answer, but he was grateful for Jean's thoughtfulness and put the binoculars to his eyes. The light was dimming, but he scanned the top of the trees anyway. He saw the water tower, two grain elevators, a church steeple and lots of trees. He completed his sweep across the city and started back for one final look. As the binoculars made the slow sweep, they were suddenly filled with a burst of lights from the tops of the trees. What was that? He fixed on the lights and focused the binoculars to try and make an identity. Then he had it!

Still looking through the glasses, he asked, "Jean, do you like baseball?"

Puzzled, she answered honestly, "No, not particularly. Why?"

"Let me ask you this, then. Do you like hot dogs?"

Now she could relate to this question. "Right now I'd like nothing better!"

"If I'm right, we're gun-a have a hot dog and see a baseball game!"

The announcement of a meal waiting put everyone in motion. The car was packed and they were off. Henry explained the need to hurry, because if there was a baseball game going on, it was probably close to being over.

Henry drove into Cheyenne, selecting streets that would lead to the bright lights of the ballpark. They found the park and entered the dirt parking lot. The headlights of the car caught a gleaming new bus parked on the tree-lined edge. Henry read to himself the painted words on the bus's side, "Rocky Mountain

Victory Tour". The lot was only half full, but that was common during the war. People walked instead of wasting gasoline to drive. Walking was a patriotic duty.

The five walked to the main entrance to the field and Henry was mildly surprised to see they were still selling tickets. He purchased the five tickets and felt they had a good chance to catch the concession stand still open.

In Cheyenne, rodeo was king, but baseball had a place in the hearts of the citizens. This was reflected in the grandstand structure built for the field. Entirely of wood, it resembled a big league park in miniature. The concessions were on either side of the tunnel leading up into the stands. Each of the men got two or three hot dogs, but no beer was being served. Soft drinks were a reluctant substitute. The five carried their high spirits and hot dogs up the stairs. They were each grateful for the chance to eat and relax for a short time.

Jean and Henry enter after the three men, giving the appearance of the five not being together. The grandstands were almost full, with the exception of areas behind the visitor's dugout on the third base side of the field. Jean and Henry sat in this area and settled in to eat. It was the third inning according to the manual scoreboard in left field. There was no score for either team and the home team was at bat. Jean paid little attention to anything on the field, instead she discovered a thick newspaper tucked under the wooden bench behind her. It was yesterday's copy of a Denver paper. She was quickly absorbed in the news while she balanced her hot dog and the paper in such a way that she could quench her physical and intellectual hunger at the same time.

The paper headlined the Potsdam Conference going on in Europe with the leaders of the victorious Allied powers meeting to put the conclusions on the war, recently ended in Europe. They also had an agenda to pressure Japan for an equal conclusion in the Pacific. Okinawa had been secured the previous month and no major land battles were taking place. The air attacks on Japan were the major active effort of the American air command, while other articles told of the preparations for the land invasion of the Japanese home islands.

Henry watched the ball game with casual interest. He looked for the other three men and saw Josh and August sitting together, higher up behind him. Sammy was off to their left. All three were into their hot dogs. It was a moment of satisfying relief from the pressure of trying to keep this group involved with staying together. He was committed to his idea of getting all to the sanctity of Canada. His belief in this being the best choice was under assault by frustration and the immense expenditure of effort it was taking to accomplish. Maybe it would be better to split-up now and everybody take their chances.

He finished his hot dogs as the inning came to a close and the two teams changed positions on the field. He watched the visitors trotting toward the dugout in front of him, in their new gray uniforms with the letters "R.M.V." in a slight arc across their chests. Henry had been around baseball in Canada during the summers, but his sport was Canada's own, ice hockey. He had not the skill, nor the time to play either sport for long in his youth, but the attachment remained.

As team members emerged from the dugout to take their place in the batting circle, Henry heard a single voice calling each by name. It belonged to an older man, sitting by himself, behind the dugout. Henry figured he must be with the team in some capacity. He watched through the half inning as this man sang out encouragement to each batter. No runs were scored, although the visitors managed a hit and a walk before a double play ended their chances for a run. Henry was brought away from his involvement in the game by a stern tug on his sleeve. It was Jean.

In a harsh whisper, she was talking to him at an excited level, "Henry! Henry! Look at this!" She thrust the paper into his hands. Her index finger pointed to a small article on an inside page.

The bold type leading the article declared: "KANSAS CITY HEIST PERPETTRATORS STILL ON THE LOOSE!" Jean's finger directed Henry's eyes deeper into the article, towards the words "Autopsy results…". Henry leaned into the paper to get the best view of the words. His excitement level now matched hers. It related that Captain Paully had died as a result of three gunshot wounds to the upper chest, from a .38 caliber weapon.

"Jean!" He responded in the same harsh whisper, "Do you know what this means?"

"Yes!" She had known from the moment she had read the words.

"None of us had a .38!" Henry had to vocalize it as if that were necessary for it to become true. "It ***was*** Appleby! Lawmen still carry .38's!" He turned to look for the three men behind him, but this wasn't the place to be sharing the news with them. He then realized the major significance of the news was currently between he and Jean. This verified he had not brought her into this, knowing a man had been killed. Although logic had told her so at the beginning, she too was happy for the veiled vindication of the four men. They both knew this did not change the fact that the law of the land still was looking for them as the responsible parties. They were again thankful for being able to keep the Nebraska Trooper alive.

"Look, keep this paper and any other paper you find. We need to know what's goin' on out there." Henry's energy was renewed and his mind was again working on finding a solution to their problem. He became unsettled and restless sitting there on the bench. He wanted to get up and do something, but there was nowhere to go and nothing to do.

Then he heard that single voice again, calling to the team in gray. A strange curiosity aroused in him the means to quell his restlessness. He was up and moving toward the older man. Before he had thought it completely through, he found himself sitting down beside the man.

"Hello there." He said with a disarming smile. "Are you with the team, out there?"

There was a slight pause as the older man looked at his surprise visitor and then behind him to see if any other persons were also 'visiting'. The man was leery of opposing fans from experience. "Yes, I'm with the tour."

Henry remembered the writing on the bus. “The…Victory Tour?” He openly sought the man’s participation in helping him recall the exact text.

“Yeah…The Rocky Mountain Victory Tour.” The man extended his hand, “I’m Walt Chambers, from Denver.”

Henry took the man’s hand and responded, “I’m Henry Lapointe…” he kept the smile on his face despite his realization that he had given his real name. Then he tried to pick up the pieces by continuing, “From Washington.”

“Is that the state or D.C.?” Walt’s question was quick, catching Henry off guard about the possible confusion of the two Washington’s.

“Ah…D.C. The Department of Immigration and Naturalization.” He was still fumbling with too much information, feeling he was on Walt’s home turf. He moved to get to his interest. “What is this Rocky Mountain Victory Tour?”

“Oh, the Governor of Colorado and some of those Congressmen, down where you come from, got together and decided it was time to bring baseball back to the people." Walt was talking now, something he enjoyed when it was his subject. "Everyone, including Harry Truman got into the act and hailed it as the thing to do. With the war, the American people haven't had too many chances to see baseball. If ya look around at the stands here, ya can see it might be just the thing they need." He directed Henry with a quick flick of his index finger to the nearly full stands.

Henry looked over his right shoulder to the crowd in general and noted all faces were directed at the playing filed. Before he turned back to Walt, he started his next question, "So you're takin' this team around the area on a road trip?"

"Yeah. We're going up the front range of the Rockies into Montana and then back down the Western Slope, through Idaho, Utah, then back across Colorado from Grand Junction. We'll be at it for about four weeks." Walt was on a roll.

Henry had heard Montana. "How far north do you go?"

"I think Great Falls will be the last stop before we go over the Continental Divide and head for Idaho. I think that's the schedule." Walt was trying to remember the written schedule, which he had looked at several times, but had not conquered in detail yet.

"You head up this tour?" Henry was feeling his way around.

"Nah, not me. I'm takin' care of this crew." Again flashing his index finger in the direction of the players. "I drive the bus, take care of the equipment and do what I can to help Father Sullivan keep these boys in line."

"Who's Father Sullivan?" Henry asked.

"He's the one who heads up this tour." Walt added, "Yes, he is a priest and a darn good one too. He was also a good ball player, in his day. He spent four years in the minor leagues before he found out he wasn't gona make it to the big leagues. So he became a priest. He's been using baseball to keep kids on the straight and narrow. He claims if a kid is playin' ball, then there ain't too much else that's gona be on his mind."

"Are these players professionals?" Every time Henry asked a question, the talkative Walt Chambers gave him more information than asked for.

"No, not a single one of them. But they're all damn good ball players, even the kids; those two tall kids, the one pitchin' and the other in center. They're both just outta high school and the major leagues have already been calling."

"What's your next stop?" Henry was feeling something in the way of an idea.

"We leave tonight after this game and drive up to Casper. Then it's on to Sheridan and into Montana. I think we play two or three ball games at each stop."

"Well, good luck with your trip." Henry extended his hand. Walt shook it, but seemed a little surprised at Henry's sudden intent to depart. But he expressed his thanks dismissing the brief encounter as Henry left. Walt's attention was immediately again on the field. Henry was back sitting with Jean, his mind building a solution.

Thursday, July 26, 1945

The game had ended and it was now after midnight as the team from Colorado prepared for the night drive ahead of them. Most of the players were dressed and moving toward the bus. Walt was with Father Sullivan in the locker room, both busy packing the gear and making sure the locker room was left in an order as was consistent with a good guest.

Father Mike was the first to notice a presence in the room, beyond Walt and himself. Sometimes players straggle back in to retrieve a forgotten item, but this was different. Father stopped gathering towels and turned toward the entrance. Three strangers were standing there. They could not have been more out of place.

Unsure of the unusual event, Father Mike asked, "Is thur somethon I cun help you with?" A touch of Irish garnished his question.

"Hello Walt." The man in the middle addressed Walt very politely with a nod toward the man on Father's left.

Father Mike looked at Walt expecting to understand based on the friendly greeting. Walt looked back with a blank expression and shrugged his shoulders.

"Are you Father Sullivan?" The man spoke again and Father retuned his attention from Walt.

"That I am. And who might you be?"

The man took two steps forward as he spoke, "Father, my name is Henry. Now Walt here, wasn't expecting me…us." As he turned to motion to the two men still standing at the door. "Walt and I chatted a bit up in the stands and I understand your ball team is on a tour goin' north."

Father nodded but would not participate in this until he understood what was meant. There was something familiar to him about being in the company of these men, something from his childhood growing up on the north side of Chicago. He had known this feeling from the thugs and hoods in his neighborhood twenty years ago and he didn't like the intrusion again in his life.

"My friends and I have an urgent need to get up north and we find it necessary to impose upon you and your team in order to do what we have to do." Henry was calm and in control. He knew exactly what had to happen in order for his long-standing plan to have a chance. Without being hidden among the ball team on the way north, the five of them in one car would be easy pickings for radio and telephone informed lawmen throughout the west.

"I'm sorry, but that's impossible. We are not takin' riders on the bus." Father was emphatic and wanted to make this the end of their conversation.

Henry walked up to Father Mike. His voice did not carry the high-pitched nervousness that was present on that rain-drenched night in Kansas City. "Sit down Father." He said motioning to the players' bench. Father started to balk, but Henry said again, "Please, just sit down for a moment and let me explain this to you."

Father looked at the two men at the door and then to Henry. Henry again motioned with his hand for the Father to take a seat. Reluctantly, Father Mike sat down. It was the first time in years he had not been in control of one of life's situations.

Henry reached for a chair and pulled it up in front of Father Mike, sat down and calmly started talking. "I'll let ya know right out, we're on the run. There are some things that we've done and the law has a right to be comin' after us. One of the things they have all the dogs out for, is the murder of a cop. So as you can see, we are not really asking you for your permission. It's something we gotta do."

Father looked again at the two men at the door believing fully from their appearance that murder could be apart of their lives.

Henry continued. "We are out of options, except for the one you are going to provide. Now, here's how it lays. We could hold a gun to your head and it wouldn't make you budge an inch. We could hold a gun to old Walt's head and he'd just spit in our eye. Or we could go out to the bus and hold a gun to your ball players' heads. Now, I think that would convince you to do what we tell ya ta do. So lets just say, as of right now, we have a gun on your players. You and

Walt are the only ones who need to know who we are and what we are doin'. I want you to tell the team we are administrative personnel from Washington, here to analyze the benefits of this tour and that it would be best if there was as little contact between our groups in order that we can do our job."

"Now Father, being hunted the way we are, if the police or FBI or any local law get wind of who we are, then that will place your people in a very bad position. We are serious about you and Walt staying quiet and keeping your players from getting any ideas. The last thing we want is to get someone hurt. Just do what we say and once we get up north far enough, we are gun-a cut away and make our way outta the country. Until then, you do as I say."

Henry looked at Father Mike, waiting for a response. Father Mike said, "Son, you know this isn't right?"

"Oh yes, Father, I know it isn't right at all. But ya see, we've been doin' wrong for so long that right or wrong is no longer the issue. Now the way I figure it, when we get to Canada, maybe then we can start makin' better choices about right and wrong. Until then, do what I ask. Play your schedule as it is and in a short while, we'll be gone. Keep control of your team and keep quiet and I can guarantee that nobody gets hurt."

"I don't put much stock in any guarantee from you or your friends. I've seen too many of your kind, thugs who want to combine moral values with criminal acts. I'm tellin' ya, the two don't exist together and never will."

"O.K. then, just do as I ask." Henry's tone had an end-to-the-conversation quality about it.

Father looked up at Walt. "Walt?"

Walt's reply was a dry matter-of-fact, "Father, they're the ones with the guns."

Father sat on the bench in thought, his lips pressed together with the strain of the unacceptable answer he was left with. "If one person so much as gets a scratch because of you and your goons, I'll personally haul your carcass up the court house steps and put you behind bars without the benefit of opening the doors. Do I make ***myself*** clear?"

“I’ll take that as a ‘yes’ Father.” Henry stood up and moved the chair back. “Oh, one other thing. Another of us is waiting out by the bus with our things. With him is someone who is not one of us. She has had the unfortunate experience of accepting a travel invitation without knowing what this was all about. Her co-operation is on the same basis as yours and let it be further understood, she has in no way been harmed by anyone of us.”

“Good God man, in addition to all else, you’ve kidnapped a woman?” Father was incredulous.

Henry turned and cocked his head a little to the right as he replied. “Again Father, you put it in terms we haven’t givin’ much thought to. So don’t waste time makin’ lists of things we’ve done wrong. There are plenty of other people doin’ that. Now, can we help you carry some things to the bus?”

Father Mike couldn’t believe this was happening. “God give me strength!” was the short prayer he offered as he arose to take on this new challenge against the peace and sanctity of man and the Church.

As they walked to the bus, it was as Henry had said. A woman and another man were standing at the side of the bus surrounded by suitcases and two large green GI bags. Henry had been busy since his original chat with Walt. First he had let the three men know about the evidence described in the paper, which could potentially clear them of the murder. He used this information as a springboard to enlist them into his next plan. He explained the bus and how once it got close enough to Canada, they could hop across the border and continue with his original plan.

He had ordered Josh and Sammy to take Jean and the car a few blocks away and park the car where it would not be conspicuous. He wanted them to wipe down the interior for fingerprints, remove the plates and carry all the belongings back to the bus. He and August would stay in the stadium, watch and count the players so they would know how many people needed to be on the bus and out of the locker room before they made their move. They also scouted the area and managed to get a couple of more hot dogs from the concession as it was finishing cleaning up.

Sammy returned inside the ballpark when his tasks were completed and the three men waited for their opportunity to confront Father Mike and Walt. Henry had found the solution to their problem. There would be no more talk of Mexico.

At the bus, Josh and August helped Walt load the equipment and the newly arrived baggage into the luggage bins under the bus. The exceptions were what Jean would carry onto the bus and the two green bags. Henry and Sammy followed Father Mike onto the bus.

The bus was noisy with the excitement of a fresh victory, as the Colorado team had won six to nothing. The victory was going to take the edge off the night bus ride to Casper.

Father stood at the head of the isle, asked for and received the attention of the players. "I have an announcement to make." The respect he commanded was evident. "We have a party of five joining us for the trip up the front-range. These people are from Washington and are here to observe the tour and report on its success to a Congressional Committee. Please give them every courtesy, but they want to remain independent of the team. There will be no interruption of our schedule and you will be asked not to interrupt them in their duties. I would ask that you just play ball and leave all else to me."

At this, Jean came aboard followed by Josh and August. Henry signaled them to the back of the bus where a bench seat stretched across the entire width. Henry and Sammy took seats up front on either side of the isle, behind Walt.

The dim interior lights identified Jean as a woman to each of the seated players. Silence and stares greeted her as she made her way, followed by the two men lugging the big bags. Then a very well practiced wolf whistle sounded from among the players. The tone of the whistle was pure and perfectly timed to express the single thought possessed by each of the young men.

Chapter 9

Thursday, July 26, 1945

The three-hour trip to Casper was uneventful. Everyone was too tired to exchange the usual light banter of a ball team. A few questioning glances were directed at the newcomers, but Father Mike's instructions were clear and that was that. Father Mike also viewed the quietness as a reflection of the intrusion of the five. It would not have a good effect on the team, even explained as it was. Had the players known the truth, he knew they would not have stood for it and some kind of reaction would be inevitable. He could not allow that. Father Sullivan had to walk the middle ground for the protection of all. This would be his first priority. His second priority would be to look for opportunities to get the intrusive party to give up this insane measure.

They arrived in Casper at twenty minutes before five in the morning. The local representative for the city of Casper was there to meet them at the high school, along with two of the high school's custodians. The gymnasium had been opened and army cots had been placed in rows on the gym floor. The gym was a multipurpose facility, like hundreds of high school gyms in the mid-west. Its smallness accommodated the community, but not a full sized basketball court. The half court lines overlapped almost to the top of the free throw circles. Concrete stands occupied one side of the court, with a balcony structure above and down each end of the building. A stage occupied the remaining wall, with locker room doors on either side of the stage leading down to the dressing and shower rooms, below the stage. One was marked "Boys' and the other "Girls".

When the local man found five more people than he had been told, his apologies were followed by requests of the janitors to get more cots, blankets and pillows. The war had brought these kinds of surpluses to even the remote parts of the States. For Jean, they placed a cot up on the stage and drew the curtains. A hand written sign was taped across the "Girls" locker door and now read, "Women Only". The men from

Casper were very accommodating and announced a breakfast was to be brought to the gym at 8:00 am. Father thanked them sincerely for their hospitality and then went about getting his players settled in.

All were free to do as they wished for the next three hours. Most took advantage of the cots. A few, plus the four strangers, took turns in the locker room showers until the hot water gave out. Three of the strangers remained on the gym floor at all times. They were very careful to distance themselves from the players and keep their .45's out of sight.

Jean slept for two hours and then took full advantage of having the women's locker room to herself. The hot water was back, so she enjoyed the great pleasure of a hot shower again.

The eight o'clock hour was approaching as Father Sullivan, roused his troops for the breakfast, promising they could go back to bed after the meal. He made his way to the stage. Standing in the middle where the curtains would part, he reached out and rapped his knuckles on the stage floor, politely substituting for the privacy of a door. "Pardon me Miss, but are you awake?" There was no response. "Miss, are you there?" He requested louder.

This time movement occurred at the break in the curtains. A beautiful face appeared topped with a full head of dark, curly, wet hair.

"Pardon me, lass, I'm Father Sullivan and I wanted to let you know breakfast is going to be served here within the half hour."

She looked across the floor at the men slowly milling from their cots and then back at Father Sullivan. "Thanks, that sounds good."

"By the way lass, what is your name?" He inquired.

She came out from behind the curtains in here jeans and a bloused shirt, tied in a knot at her waist. She was barefoot and carried her towel. She walked to the edge of the stage and sat down at Father's level. "I'm Jean." She offered her hand for the greeting.

"As I said, I'm Father Sullivan, but most call me Father Mike." He took her hand but did not give it a shake, as he would have a man. Then his tone softened and turned to concern. "Jean, are you alright? No one has abused you in any way have they?"

Jean was surprised by this question, but started rubbing the towel against her hair and said, "No, I'm fine."

Father leaned in for privacy and spoke again. "This is a very serious situation we find ourselves in, so if anyone bothers you, in any way, I want you ta tell me straight away!"

Jean was even more puzzled, as she had not been privy to Henry's explanation of her circumstances. She leaned toward Father Mike and spoke with his same softness, "Father, if anyone bothers me, you will be the first one I come get, cause ***they*** are the ones who are going to need your services, not me." She gave him a big smile.

Surprise was now on Father's side of the court. He said, "Ah, this rose has a very formidable complement of thorns!" He leaned toward her and spoke again, "In that case, be quick about tellin' me, I wouldn't want their poor souls to linger in anguish too long!" He reached up and gave her cheek a light squeeze and winked as he left.

She smiled at their light moment as she watched him walk away. She looked up and her eyes took in the scene on the gym floor. Every ball player had stopped in his place, each with the same look of wonderment on his face, each staring directly at her. She was center stage all right and had everyone's undivided attention. She gave a quick smile, which was not missed by a single player and just as quickly retreated behind the curtain. Once to safety, she felt the flush of self-consciousness fill her cheeks. Then a voice near the stage broke the silence from the all male side of the curtain. "Carl, you can shoot me now 'cause I know what Heaven's like!" The down home drawl of the voice broke everybody's ability to control his laughter. Jean covered her mouth and laughed with them.

After breakfast and organizing his three partners to keep control, or at least, give the appearance of having control, Henry took Jean on a walk down town. They did some shopping, although the main clothing lines consisted of western wear, Henry and Jean both found new clothes to completely shake the dust of the Nebraska road trip. Henry also stopped at a hardware store and bought some odds and ends, including a pair of scissors and a white canvas utility bag, similar to the bags used by the team to carry their equipment. They walked the town window shopping and had lunch at a diner.

During lunch, Henry explained to Jean his need for her to be by his side during the last leg of the trip. He asked her to do something for him. Included in his instructions was for her to purchase any paper she could get her hands on and thoroughly search them for information about the five of them. She was to cut the articles out and keep them for him to possibly use to support his position and directions to the other three. He detailed other assignments for her and explained she was the only one he could trust.

They walked back to the school and each of the other three men took their turn, during the afternoon, to go into town. Individuals from the team also made the walk, but Henry always had a good part of the team under watch.

Jean was on stage with the curtains partly drawn, going through several newspapers purchased on their walk. She found one of the articles Henry had asked her to look for and soon got Henry's attention to come up on the stage.

"I found an article on that Nebraska Patrolman!" She announced as Henry arrived.

She pointed to a second page article from a Cheyenne newspaper:

"NEBRASKA TROOPER HAS CLOSE CALL WITH FUGITIVES!"

Henry read. "Nebraska State Trooper, Bob Hansen of Ogallala, Neb., was found Tuesday evening handcuffed beside Highway 30, about twelve miles west of that Nebraska town. He said he had made a routine stop of a man and a woman, who were driving a black sedan with U.S. Government plates. As he was taking them in to confirm their identities, he stopped to assist two men who appeared to be injured beside the road. A third man emerged from behind his car and held him at gunpoint while the man and the woman were freed. He was left bound, but unharmed, under a bridge and managed to crawl to the road where a passing motorist came to his aid."

The article continued. "Federal authorities say four of the five persons involved are quite possibly the ones responsible for the robbery of a Federal Reserve Shipment and the killing of a railroad policeman in Kansas City on July 20th. All available personnel from three federal agencies, along with law enforcement jurisdictions from five area states have been mobilized to find the fugitives. The FBI is leading the investigation. The fugitives are considered armed and dangerous. No other information was available at this time."

He let the paper wilt in his hands and looked at Jean. "Well, just like I thought, we've got everyone with a badge this side of the Mississippi lookin' for us."

"I know." Jean answered. "Thank God you stopped Sammy. I only hope you can keep anything from happening to these boys."

"Yeah, I think I can. I've just got to keep an eye on Sammy most of all. I don't think Josh or August would initiate anything on their own." He stared straight ahead. "Jean, why are you still here?"

She stared with him as she struggled for the answer. "Sometimes I think I know why, then other times I ask myself what the hell I am doing. I feel like I'm doing something wrong, yet at the same time, I don't feel I'm a part of this. Right now, I think I can help keep anyone from getting hurt. That's what concerns me most."

"Well, the only hold I have on this team is a bluff. I'd give myself up before I'd go through with shootin' someone. Trouble is, I have to play the same bluff on Sammy, Josh and August. I believe traveling with this team is the one shot we have at getting out of the country. If this falls apart, I'm ready to take my medicine. Until I believe it isn't gun-a work, I've got to keep goin' and see if I can get a better life."

He looked at Jean. "Now I've told you how important you are to me in this and I don't think I could do it without you. But anytime you want out, you just tell me and you get a bus ticket. OK?"

"Thanks. I'll keep that as an option." She needed options, although they might be too late to benefit her guilt or innocence and future freedom.

That evening all climbed aboard the bus and drove to a modest ballpark to watch the opening game of the round-robin tournament. Casper was hosting Rawlins. The nightcap would feature the Colorado team versus the team from the Douglas, Wyoming area. The two green bags were aboard the locked bus with Jean. Jean didn't mind the time on the bus. Her lack of interest in baseball would make sitting in the stands tedious at best. Here she could read books and take care of the newspapers as Henry had asked her to do.

Sammy was near the bus, keeping guard on Jean and the two bags, or more to the point, the two bags. Josh and August would rotate with Sammy during the evening. One would be in the dugout with Henry, the other in the stands.

Henry would relieve Jean on the bus, so she could eat and stretch her legs. None of the other three wanted to spend time sitting on the bus, so they were well entrenched in being the visual threats to Father Mike and Walt. Henry had explained to the three, their options for a clean get-a-way were now down to a narrow corridor through which the team bus was going to take them. If anyone didn't do exactly as Henry said, then there was a murder charge waiting for all of them to face in court. For right now, he felt he had control. It was going to be two weeks of this before they were close enough to break for the border. He doubted it would all hold together that long.

Sunday, July 29, 1945

And so it went for the next two days in Casper. Sunday was departure day and Henry was glad to start putting more distance between them and Cheyenne. Jean's news reports had turned up an article on the discovery of the Trooper's cruiser. Maybe the feint toward Fort Morgan, Colorado would send some of the heat south. Not much news reached them from Kansas

City. All Henry could hope for was that he had left so small a trail to pickup; the Feds would go around in circles while he made this time-consuming journey on the bus.

Next stop was Sheridan for the team. They were undefeated to this point and spirits were high among the players. Their success took their minds off the constant presence of the four men. Jean's presence, however, was tolerated quite nicely.

Sheridan was another four team round robin with a team from Cody and one from Gillette, filling the bill. People from all around the area were coming to the games. A packed house testified to the success of the tour.

The Potsdam Conference was the major news coming from the war. The Allied powers had issued the Potsdam Proclamation to Japan, formally restating their insistence on an immediate and unconditional surrender by Japan. Fearing their Emperor-god would fall into the hands of the barbarian Allies, Japan rejected the proclamation.

In the low levels of news coming from the Potsdam Conference, were a few paragraphs Jean was now reading out of a newfound interest in world affairs. The article stated a young patriot from Indo-China had attended the Conference, in the hope of convincing the Allies not to return his country to colonial rule under the French. The Allies took no action on the nationalistic requests by the young Asian. As conquerors do, dividing the "victory pie" was reserved for only the top, powerful countries. One was France, so the request received no action as the "victorious four" awarded France back its pre-war "possession". The article related the young man's name as Ho Chi Minh. Jean's immediate reaction to this was that millions of people had just died to free countries from ownership by bigger countries. Why would they go right back to the same policy that started this war in the first place? France and the United States would later know this country as Viet Nam. This would visit Jean again, in another generation, when her son would be sent to this place.

Bombing of the major Japanese cities had continued, although the Army Air Corps was running out of targets. American war planers were developing the final invasion plans of the war. It would be the invasion of the home islands of Japan. It was believed this invasion would cost the United States at least one million casualties. It was also believed that Japanese casualties would be many times that number. Extreme measures were being suggested to lessen the impact of death and injury to the American soldiers. One of these suggestions proposed the use of poison gas for the first time in this war, by the Allies. Washington steered clear of even considering the widespread duplication of the horrors of World War I. There were only a few men in Washington who knew of another option.

Another high school, another little ballpark and a large festive crowd for three days brought three more victories to the Colorado team. They would travel on Tuesday night, July 31st, to Billings, Montana. Two games were to be played there, then both teams would travel to Helena on Friday, August 3rd, for a full weekend of baseball. The caliber of competition would increase, as teams from Butte and Bozeman would be supplied with good ball players from large military bases in the surrounding area.

Tuesday, July 31, 1945

Not much conversation had passed between the players and the "administrators" in the first week of traveling together. But time and human nature work in concert on people kept in close proximity. Soon cheers of encouragement could be heard from Josh and August when they had their post in the stands. They had begun to look forward to that duty.

During the last game in Sheridan, the third baseman for the Colorado team was stretching a single into a double and went in hard at second base. He was tagged out on the play, but of more serious consequence to the team, he sprained his right ankle. He spent the remainder of the game with an ice bag on the bench. His name is John Houser and, aside from Father Mike and Walt, he is the oldest man on the team, at the ripe old age of twenty-five. He looked older than his years because of something else about him. He was a Marine. Father Mike had recruited players from all corners of Denver. If they were good ball players, he knew about them and had the strings to pull to get them on this tour. John was a Marine Recruiter assigned to Denver and played third base like a Marine in a bayonet fight. He was a hard throwing, hard hitting, no-nonsense player. That was his nature off the field as well.

Father Mike had taken opportunities to talk to Henry and Jean, both together and individually about his players. He felt the more they knew these men as people, the less likely it would be to summon the meanness to harm them. Father Sullivan also tried the same tactic on the other three men, but August and Sammy kept their distance and Josh seemed more entertained than informed by the talks. So his most viable entry into the group's conscience had to be through the two who had consciences.

As they were departing Sheridan that evening, John was helped aboard the bus by the second baseman; who doubled as trainer for the team. This is Larry

'Doc' Goodman, a twenty-three year old Navy Medical Corpsman. Father Mike had found him at the Fitzsimmons Army Hospital in Denver, where he had been loaned by the Navy to train Army personnel in treating battlefield wounds. Father Sullivan, as one of his tactical disclosures, had told John and Doc's stories to Henry and Jean. He looked at the unfortunate injury to John as an opportunity to work on Jean's mind and through her, he might reach Henry.

Jean always road the bench seat at the back of the bus and Father felt John 'needed' to have his ankle elevated and on ice, during the trip. The best seat for that was the middle of the bench, where his leg could be supported straight out into the isle. He instructed Doc to put John there; and to his delight, Jean kept her place.

It was getting dark when the bus pulled out of the parking lot. Henry was in the front seat opposite the driver's side with Father Sullivan directly behind him. Now, Father issued a small prayer to have the human nature of man and of woman, work for his purpose.

Jean watched the man beside her as he dealt with the uncomfortable sprained ankle. He shifted to keep himself and the ankle in place as the bus made a few corners on the way out of town. Once on the highway, he could spend less energy staying upright and relaxed as much as he could. Twenty minutes passed and neither he nor she said a word to each other. The hum of the diesel engine below and back of them, soon provided a mask, like a physical separation from the ears of other people on the bus.

Jean spoke first. “Does that still hurt?”

John looked at her rather indifferently, but was polite. “I’ve had worse.”

“Are you going to be able to sleep with it?” She ventured small talk.

“Not likely.” He replied. “I don’t sleep well on buses anyway.”

“I’m Jean.” She offered her hand.

He looked at her hand and gave in, “I’m John, John Houser.” He gave her hand one quick shake.

“Father said you are in the Army.” Conversation now would be more enjoyable than trying to sleep.

"No, no..." He was low key about the mistake, but was going through the same explanation for the thousandth time. "I'm a Marine."

Taking a clue from his reaction she said, "Obviously there's a difference."

"Oh yes ma'am, there is a difference." He looked at her and she had a slight smile inviting him to explain further. "The Army is the Army and I don't want to say nothin' bad about those fellas, cause there's room enough in this fight for everyone. But the Marine Corps is special. We are under the Department of the Navy and are deployed by the Navy as their ground assault forces. While the Navy personnel do their fightin' from ships, it's the Marines who go ashore and fight on the beaches, in the jungles or any other stinkin' place the enemy needs to be kicked out of!" His last words gave way to a bitter tone.

"Father Sullivan said you were fighting the Japanese on an island." Jean said casually, to keep the conversation going.

"He did, did he?" John strained his neck to look for Father Mike in the front of the bus.

"Maybe you ought to get him back here to talk to you some more."

"Relax." She looked with him to spot Father Mike. "He can't tell a story very well anyway. I got lost in what he was trying to say."

"Well, it's not something I like to talk about." John said with dismay.

"That's O.K. If you don't want to talk you don't have to." She changed her position to direct her attention straight ahead.

He noticed this and looked at her. "What do you wanna know for?"

Her head tilted toward him and a passing car's lights momentarily lit the beauty in her face. "I don't know what happened out there. It's been four years and I still don't know what happens when men go to war. I think it's time I understand what you guys went through."

John resisted the temptation to flay into her for not noticing a world war that had been going on for six years. Maybe it was that small glint of beauty that had caught his eye. Maybe he didn't have the mean spirit in him tonight. Instead, he adjusted his seating posture to get more comfortable and looked at her. He began his private journey, again.

"I joined the Marines before the war started. I had a year in before Pearl Harbor, so we were one of the first organized divisions sent to fight. Did you ever hear of Guadalcanal?"

"No. What is it?" Jean asked.

"It's an island in the Solomon chain, northeast of Australia. In the summer of '42, our intelligence found out the Japanese were building an airfield on that island. From there, they could launch a strike at Australia; maybe even use it as a springboard to take the continent. I was in the First Marines of the First Marine Division. We were sent in there to take and keep that airfield. We landed on August 7th. There weren't too many military personnel on the island, mostly construction troops. They headed for the hills when they saw us. But the Japanese got very serious, very fast about losing that airfield and started landing troops to take it back. Their ships came in almost every night and shot up the place. They sank a lot of our ships who were trying to defend us."

"My battalion was put on the eastern side of the air field with a river called the Tenaru to our front. I was part of a .30 caliber machine gun crew, so they put us at the very point. We were less than twenty yards from the river. No other Marines were in front of us. We dug in and stayed there for days.

He chuckled as a thought came to mind. "Once in a while, at night, someone would think they saw something in the Tenaru and would open fire on it. All hell would break loose up and down the line. It would take the officers twenty minutes to get the firing stopped. We later found out from natives that what we were seeing in the river were crocodiles. After that, we left them alone. Figured they were our first line of defense." He chuckled again.

"On August 20th, the Japanese finally hit us." His eyes fixed into a stare as his face lost the creases from the chuckle. He recounted the terrible events from his mind, so far away now. "They hit us at night, with over a thousand men. They came right at my gun. I started firing even though I couldn't pick out individuals. Green flares went up from our side to help us see. They turned the whole area into a ghostly scene. We just poured fire into them and kept it up. Most of them never got across the river, but isolated pockets did. One group came at us from the side so we didn't know they were there until grenades started going off around us. Ned Fisher and Roland Tomack were on my gun crew. They started shooting with .45's and tossing what grenades we had. I never saw Roland go down. He was on my left, feeding ammo into the gun. He caught a bullet in the forehead and died before he hit the bottom of the trench. Ned was on my right, shootin' and yellin' for me to fire here, then there! It really got bad. He must have known a grenade had come into our position, cause he yelled it out and I stopped to look at him. That's when it went off. He took most of the blast and died right then. Part of the blast took my right side, from my knee to the shoulder."

"They got me out of there the next day, but I don't remember anything for the next four days. The crossfire from the guns behind us cut down all the enemy, but not in time to help Ned and Roland. In the deal I lost my right kidney and got a ticket home."

There was silence for a long period of time as both of them absorbed what he had said. The hum of the diesel engine was the only sound that accompanied each on their journey through their souls.

"I found out later that our battalion killed some 800 Japanese on the river that night. We suffered only ***light*** casualties. For Ned, Roland and me, I think the casualties were pretty heavy. You want to know about war? That's what war does. It takes the death of a man and turns it into a number. After those numbers get big enough, somebody has to quit fighting for a while until they can get more men. You kill enough of them and they might quit fightin' altogether. Who knows what that number is?"

"Father said you earned a medal." Jean's voice was soft as the story settled on her heart.

"Yeah, they gave me the Silver Star and the Navy Cross. Ned and Roland got both medals too." There was another pause. "They gave me medals, but I didn't find much glory in watching my buddies die."

Jean was silent. She didn't know what to say.

John came back to the present and spoke with a much more enthusiastic tone. "Hey, ya know Doc?"

Jean was not with him. "Who?"

"Doc, the guy who was workin' on my leg when we got on the bus. He's our second baseman and his name is Larry Goodman."

"Oh yes, father talked some about him too."

John started talking right on the heels of her statement, as he was primed to talk about Doc. "Doc was on Guadalcanal at the same time as me, only we didn't know each other. He was with the 5th Marines. He's Navy ya know. He's a Navy Corpsman." He looked at Jean and saw that more information was required. "You know, a medic, guys that give first aid on the battlefield. Only the Navy calls them Corpsmen. The Navy furnishes all the Corpsmen for the Marines. They are really special people. Each one of them is a jewel. They'd do anything to help a wounded Marine. Doc's one of the best of the best!"

"Doc lasted longer than I did on that island. He got his up on what they call 'Bloody Ridge' in one of the biggest attacks the Japs had. Some Marines were out on point with a machine gun, just like I was. There were two foxholes of them and they took the brunt of the first few attacks. In between attacks, ole' Doc crawled out there and found all of them wounded. He made three trips dragging a man back each time. On the fourth trip, the Japanese came again and that's when his luck ran out. He got hit five times, all in the same volley, once in the thigh, once in the hip, once in the upper chest and once in the shoulder. They say the one that was headed for his heart hit his left hand instead, as he held onto that Marine's uniform. You can see his left pointing finger and part of his middle finger are gone. It took him a long time to get over that hip wound. It's a wonder he can walk, let alone play baseball. But he does real good out there."

"You mean he's O.K. now?" Jean hadn't noticed the second baseman at all.

"Not bad for a guy who's been shot up like he was. Father Sullivan found him at the Fitzsimmons Army

Hospital, not as a patient, but on loan to the Army to teach medics about battlefield wounds. He was playing softball for the Hospital team and Father knows how to find ballplayers. And good men for that matter."

Jean was deeply affected by what she had heard in John's first hand account of what happened in war. It made her sick to her stomach to think about it. It was so brutal and these men had no choice but to walk into it. She shuddered at the thought of having to do that. "Doc got a medal too, didn't he?"

"Oh yeah, he got the Navy Cross. Our division commander recommended him for the Medal of Honor, but to my knowledge, nothin' ever came of it. If anyone deserves that medal, it's Doc."

She and John talked all the way to Billings. The trip went by fast for them. They had a new appreciation for each other after that night. Jean also learned something about the other man, Doc. These two had gone through so much, had lost so much and still were giving more of themselves. She tried to put that into perspective with her own life.

Just as the bus trip had started for Jean and John in the back of the bus, the front of the bus also held two people bound in conversation. Father Mike had gotten Henry to start talking and Father was using all his skill to maneuver the younger man away from his present course.

Father started by asking where Henry was from. Although Henry did not give information freely, he soon was talking about his life in a limited fashion.

"How long have you been involved outside the law?" Father asked keeping his voice just between the two of them.

"Since I was thirteen, I guess. Haven't known much of a life other than that." Henry was going over old ground.

"I'll tell you something Henry, I grew up on the north side of Chicago where there were plenty of boys and men choos'n a life of crime. I knew everyone of them. They were kids I grew up with or men my father grew up with. You would see them every day goin' about their business of steeling money from the hard workin' people in the community. They looked like they were successful; big cars, fancy suits an' new shoes. Kids would see that and the lure of easy money would be passed on to the next generation. Ya know, nearly every one of those men ended up dead or in prison. None of them lived long on the outside."

"I know Father, I seen plenty of that myself." Henry added.

"What does that tell ya son?" Father was extending his point.

"It tells me that I'm takin' my last chance ta turn my life into something before it's too late. When I reach Canada, I'll be able ta get out of this life and have enough money to leave it far behind." Henry was resolute in repeating his plan.

"But look what you have ta do to other people. Look at what you're doin' to these people on the bus. Don't ya think that's a wee bit selfish?" Father kept throwing points.

"Yes…I guess you're right about that. But it's done now. Besides, I never looked at it like I had a choice." Henry said.

"Ya do have a choice man! That's what I'm tellin' ya. You don't have to go on with this. End it now; turn yourself in. I'll do what I can for ya, if ya do that."

"You know what they would do to me! No, I've got ta go to Canada."

"My God son, do ya know what you're sayin'? You could get people hurt or killed here…for what? A sack of money you think is goin' ta buy your dream? Money doesn't change your life. It only changes the way people think about you. To change your life, you've gotta do it from the inside using your God given tools of humanity. Now is the time ta start changin' your life by bringin' this thing to an end!"

"Right now, Father, I don't know how to do what you're sayin'. I've got to get to Canada. I know what I can do then." Even if it was just a plan, it was all he knew.

"These men that are after ya, they could kill ya. Doesn't that mean anything to ya?"

"Well, if that happens, I'd be requirin' your services for the last rights." Henry wanted to end this pointless circle he and Father were on. “What about you Father, why didn’t you choose to join one of those gangs in Chicago and go for the easy money?”

Thinking this would be a good entry into a new tact, Father answered Henry’s question. “Not everyone in North Chicago is a criminal. I came from a very lovin’, hard workin’ family. We put our faith in God first, then each other. My father was an expert carpenter…always considered that a bit of an irony…always had a job due to his skill with tools. Mind you, we weren’t wealthy by any means; we had a lot of bad times to go through. I had two older brothers, an older sister and a younger sister. My oldest brother, Tom, was the person I looked up to the most. He’s a fine man. He entered the priesthood and that started me thinkin’ about a vocation in the Church. My love of baseball kept me away from the influences of the street and, for awhile, away from my true callin’.”

He broke from his story to include Henry, “You ever play baseball?”

"A little. Some hockey too, but I guess you could say my vocation kept me away from the influences of the ball field." Henry played on Father's words.

"You would have been better off to pick up a bat at thirteen, I'm tellin' the truth. I found I had a talent for the game around that age myself. Being left-handed limited what positions I could play. I wanted to be a shortstop, but no one ever has a shortstop that throws from the left side. It goes against the nature of the game. Now if they ran the bases clockwise instead of counter-clockwise, I could-a got my wish. But the world doesn't change for ya. I didn't have the arm to pitch or play the outfield, but I could shag balls. I found they valued me at first base because of my glove and I could hit too. Played high school ball and as much ball as I could during the summers. The Cubs found me and signed me to a minor league contract. I thought, 'this is it'. I'm goin' to the top. But the further I went, the better the pitchin' was. I soon found out that beside a left-handed shortstop, another thing baseball didn't need was one more .200 hitter. So I followed my brother into the priesthood and we use baseball to help young kids find a place in this life."

"North Chicago must have been rough during those days!" Henry had heard all the stories.

"I'll say." Father enthused. "Some days you could hear guns goin' off in the next block. Ya had to stay down until all the ruckus was done, then we'd sneak around to find out what it was all about. Did that on Saint Valentine's Day once."

"No lyin'? You were around for that?" Henry was amazed.

"Sure was. I was home for the winter after playin' minor league ball, when me and a buddy heard about a big shootin'. We went over to that garage, but we weren't satisfied to just stand in the crowd and see nothin'. So I followed him into an adjoining building and up ta the roof we went. We crossed over the roofs and crawled up to the top of the garage were this windowed structure was, you know, to let sunlight into the garage. We looked down into that place as the flash bulbs were goin' off from cameras. Every time one of them went off, all I could see was red blood all over the floor. With seven men shot to pieces, you can imagine how much blood there was. The sight made me sick, so I started back down. I met the police comin' up. They escorted us back behind the barricades and warned us not to do it again. We were besieged by people askin' what we saw. My friend started tellin' them all about it, almost like he was enjoyin' it. I just walked away and went home. Anyone wanting to know about the reality of a life of crime should have been on that roof with me."

Henry thought for a moment remembering the hobo in the train yard. He agreed with Father's reaction to the sight, but said nothing.

"Tell me again, how does Jean fit into all of this?" Father asked, seeking to work Henry from another angle.

"Jean?" Henry was aroused from his thoughts about Father's story. More alert, he responded, "She's not part of this. She's just a girl tryin' to get to California and we were a ticket outta town."

"Nobody's bothered her have they?" Father wanted to express where he drew lines.

"No, no. Jean's not the type of girl to take advantage of. I believe if any guy was dumb enough to try, he'd find out she would consider it a matter of kill or be killed. And I'm bettin' on her to win." He smiled as the picture of her defiance stood in his mind.

"Are you in love with her?" Father had seen Henry soften as he spoke about Jean.

"In love with her? Hell, Father, everyone's in love with Jean!" Henry leaned forward to get a look at Jean in the dimness of the back of the bus. "Even your injured player, there." He gestured toward the two in conversation. "He's probably head over heels right now."

Father glanced over his shoulder at the two. "John? Not John. He's as tough a Marine as they come."

"Well no doubt Father, but Marines have hearts too." Henry had seen Jean's charm enlist many an admirer.

Father looked again. Henry had a point. "That doesn't upset you does it?" Father was trying to determine if there was trouble coming.

"In another time, in another place, I might take exception; but not now. Not with who I am and who she is. A guy like me doesn't end up with a girl like that. Any fool can see that. I just wanna see that she don't get hurt!"

"Why don't you let her go?" Father asked.

"Good question Father. Why don't I let her go?" Henry was thinking in different terms than Father Mike. The question, on each base of thought, went unanswered.

Two days earlier: Sunday, July 29, 1945

The Cheyenne neighborhood was a-buzz with activity on a normally calm Sunday.

Police and FBI agents were all over the place. Their center of attention was on an abandoned car with no license plates. A resident had reported it to the local police the day before. The police immediately recognized the possibilities. The report brought a quick response from all agents near the area.

Leading the investigation was special agent Jack Frazier, of the FBI. One of the agents working with him was Raymond Castle. Jack's theory held that this is where the five people split up. The car would be the starting point to pick up the different trails. Everyone was in agreement, with the exception of Raymond. He couldn't get a clear understanding why, if the five had split up, no one had reported any crimes, such as a stolen car, prowlers, or break-ins, which at least some of the five should have committed in their separate flights. It was possible they could have gotten away without committing another crime, but Raymond felt the odds were against it. His boss felt differently.

Because he had no leads, just like everyone else, he got his assignments based on the prevailing theory. He was told to go through the neighborhood and ask questions.

He walked through a crowd of on-lookers and stood in the intersection of the streets just north of where all the activity surrounded the abandoned car. He looked west and east seeing only residences. To the north were more residences, but at the end of the next block was a parking lot. Open dirt, lined by trees. It was the only unusual thing about this residential area. He approached a man standing nearby who was taking in all the big time police work. Displaying his badge, "I'm agent Castle of the FBI. Do you live in this neighborhood?"

"Shore do," the man responded with delight. He turned and pointed to the house on the northwest corner of the intersection. "I live right there."

"Did you see anything unusual concerning this car we found…any people around it or walking or running away from it?" The agent asked.

"No. I didn't even know about something goin' on 'til I seen all the people around this mornin'." The man replied.

"Thank you." The agent started to walk, but his eyes saw the parking lot again. He turned his voice back to the man. "Can you tell me what that parking lot is for up at the end of the block?"

"Parkin' lot? Why that's the ballpark." The man answered as if everyone knew that.

"Thank you." The agent turned to walk again.

The man continued talking. "Yeah, we had a big crowd up there last week. The most people in that ballpark since the war started. Wasn't as excitin' as today, but the place was packed."

"A ball game?" Raymond stepped back toward him.

"Sure. There was a team on tour that came up from Denver and they had a couple of games here with our boys and some boys from Laramie." The man was an expert by now.

"They were on tour?" Raymond's experience was leading him.

"Yeah, a tour. Ya know, like with a bus and all, travelin' around from town to town." The man thought the agent was asking dumb questions. "They had a brand new bus all painted up with signs and stuff. They was makin' a big show of their baseball tour."

"Did you go to the games?"

"Au-huh, but we got beat. Our boys could-a beat them if they would-a had some time ta practice…" He was off and going on his own.

Raymond interrupted him with a more immediate request. "Do you have a program from the games?"

"Sure do. I could get it for ya if ya like." The man now felt he was a part of this investigation.

"Could you please?" Raymond said.

The man turned and yelled at a woman standing on his front porch. "Martha, go in the house and get me that baseball program from the other night! This here FBI man wants ta see it!" The man turned back to Raymond and said, "It'll be right along."

Raymond started walking toward the house to shorten the distance the woman would have to travel. The man was in his wake; excited by the attention he was receiving from a real FBI agent. Martha met them on the porch with the program and handed it to the agent. "Thank you ma'am. I appreciate your getting this for me." She smiled and nodded approvingly.

"You can have that if ya like." The man jumped back in.

"Thank you sir, I think I can use this." Raymond turned and started down the steps.

The man called after him, "Don't ya wanta know my name or somethin'?"

Raymond answered back over his shoulder. "One of the other agents will be by to get your name!" This seemed to satisfy the man and he turned his attention in the other direction to await confirmation of his importance. Of course, his wait would be in vain.

As Raymond walked toward the park, he examined the program. In the crowd of people, agent Castle's lone walk to the north went unnoticed, with the exception of one set of eyes. They belonged to a big man whose size was his only distinguishing feature in the crowd of on-lookers. He wore a brown fedora hat and a white dress shirt with the tie and collar undone at the neck. He carried his jacket over one arm and had a soft drink bottle in the other hand. He would take a sip now and again as he watched the lone agent in his progress north.

The large man walked north too, remaining on the sidewalk and to the rear of the agent. Trees lining the street helped to veil his presence, but his main asset against notice was his completely calm demeanor. He watched the agent walk into the parking lot and approach the billboard sign, which stood mounted on wooden and concrete legs, next to the street. It still proudly announced the "Rocky Mountain Victory Tour Baseball Game, TONIGHT."

He saw the agent whirl in his tracks briskly walking back the way he had come. The big man crossed the street and stood under the sign. He took his last drink of the soda and sat the empty bottle down on the concrete base, which secured one of the sign's legs. Satisfied, he turned away, to continue his assignment.

Chapter 10

Wednesday, August 1, 1945

The Billings High School gym was the team's current residence. Sleep was the primary need for the bus riders. The morning and part of the afternoon passed in this pursuit. Two games were to be played here, both at night in the form of a twilight double header. A late lunch was provided by the women of the local Methodist Church. Among the sandwiches and potato salad several copies of newspapers were available. This was a welcome gesture to Jean who didn't think she would have the opportunity to leave to gather the news.

Early in her search through the papers, she found the important news from Cheyenne. She got Henry's attention and together they reviewed the article. The FBI announced they had possession of the car believed to be the one used by the four fugitives in their flight from Kansas City. It has been identified by Nebraska Highway Patrolman Hansen as the one used by the five persons who accosted him outside the town of Ogallala, Nebraska. The article went on to say the FBI had taken possession of the car and were examining it for evidence. Lead FBI agent, Jack Frazier, was quoted as saying they were following all leads in the case and were studying the possibility the five people had separated in Cheyenne and were now, possibly spread over a wide area.

The article recounted the known events of the July 20th robbery and a description of each of the persons sought. Henry leaned back against the bench row behind him. "They're lookin' for us all over now. One good thing is they are thinkin' we split up. That ought to keep them busy for a while. When did they find the car?"

"On Sunday." Jean retrieved the information from the article.

"I wish this tour would move faster. The slowness is beginning to eat on everyone." Henry again went over all the circumstances in his mind to evaluate what could be done to help the situation. Jean went on looking for more in the papers.

That night's ball games were played as scheduled, but Father Sullivan knew the quick pace of the tour was starting to catch up with his team. John Houser did not play in either game and remained in the dugout. Henry, Father and Walt were also constant occupants of the dugout. Jean spent most of the evening on the bus, with Sammy as the primary lookout. Josh and August were in the stands sharing their duty as 'imposing' figures for the benefit of Father Mike and Walt.

Sammy had received a rotation of duties from the two 'fans' and was now back at his station watching the bus. Darkness was coming fast as he listened to the crescendo of the voices in the ballpark rise and fall with the fortunes of their team.

The monotony of his job was getting to him. He was starting to question what in the hell Henry was doing. Tagging along with this team was the dumbest thing he could think of.

Movement! Out of the corner of his eye, he thought he saw movement among the cars in the parking lot. He focused on the spot where the light and dark forms were breaking as a figure moved through his line of sight. His brain was sorting the information, putting together the puzzle, which would give definition to what was taking place out there. It was a lone man; a big man. He was moving slowly in the direction of the bus. He would stop every few steps to give the bus and the parking lot a visual inspection.

Sammy had been leaning back in a chair against one of the supporting pillars under the grand stands. He brought the chair down on its four legs and pulled the .45 from his pocket. He chocked it. The metal action seemed to reverberate through the back of the stands, but the crowd noise kept the sound from traveling. Sammy started moving in a flanking manner toward the man. He intended to cut him off before he got to the bus. He kept the .45 low to his side, until he could determine who this was.

The big man was nearing the bus when his latest glance brought Sammy into view. He stopped. Sammy kept advancing. Sammy's blood was pumping and the anger was building with each of his steps. He would use this anger as a tool against the big man, if the following seconds brought the need. The big man stood in his place and made no effort to retreat. Sammy stopped about fifteen feet from the stranger. He knew the man could see the .45 at his side, so he didn't raise it. It would be very effective where it was. Sammy had never seen the man before, but he was now ready to kill him. Through his anger Sammy asked, "What the hell you doin'?"

The big man remained calm and offered: "I drive a bus for a livin' and I taught I would look at dis new bus to see what it's like." There was no warmth in his explanation.

Sammy knew he was facing a man who was not a bus driver. He felt the calmness in the man, a calmness that only a professional killer would have under these conditions. A shudder went through him as he realized his danger. "This bus is off limits! Now you move on and keep the hell outta here!" He set his jaw and stared the man into movement.

The man raised an open hand to Sammy and started back the way he had come. “Sorry fella, I didn’t know I was doin’ any harm.”

“Move! I don’t want to see you again!” Sammy issued his final threat to the retreating man. He watched the man leave the parking lot, cross the street and disappear into the neighborhood. He didn’t like the feeling that remained with the man’s departure. No conclusion had been reached in the matter. He walked to the corner of the bus and watched across the street to see if he could pick out anything more in the darkness. He heard Jean’s footsteps on the bus, then the door opened as she worked the lever. She reached the bottom step and was looking in the same direction as Sammy.

“Who was that?” She had only been aware of the man’s presence when she had heard Sammy’s first challenge.

“I don’t know Jean, but I don’t like it. That man was after something, no question.”

He looked up at her. “Go get August and Henry and tell them to come out here. Have Josh stay with the team." As she departed, he issued final instructions. "Tell Henry I don't like this one damn bit!"

She made her way to the grandstand entrance as Sammy divided his watchful eyes between her and the darkness across the street. Inside she followed Sammy's instructions and soon Henry and August were trotting through the parking lot. "Sammy, what's goin'on?"

"Some guy was sneakin' around the bus, lookin' it over. He didn't look like no citizen to me." Sammy looked at Henry, "Even with my .45 in plain sight he was a cool customer."

"What did he say?" Henry asked as he accepted Sammy's testimony.

"He said he drove a bus for a livin' and just wanted to look at this new one. If he was a bus driver, then I'm a Sunday school teacher." Sammy spat on the ground to punctuate his pronouncement.

"Did he look like police?" Henry sought.

"Don't think so. I've never seen a cop be that cool." Sammy's anger was still there.

"Good job Sammy, you did exactly right! August, you stay out here with Sammy and cover each other's backs. Sammy, tell Auggie what he looked like. I'm gun-a get this show on the road tonight." Henry ran back to the park and disappeared through the entrance. As he ran, Sammy's words about "never seen a cop be that cool" circled his mind.

Upon reaching the dugout, he cornered Father and grasped his attention from the game. "We're gun-a leave after the game tonight!" Henry's demeanor left no room for questions, but Father Mike allowed few men to issue him orders.

"What are you talkin' about, we're not going to drive again tonight. These players are so tired they can't…" Henry grabbed Father Mike's arm with a strong grip, which in itself communicated a great deal more than words.

"Sammy just found someone snooping around the bus and this guy wasn't playin' hide and seek! We've got to move tonight and re-establish ourselves in Helena, with a different security set-up. We got some serious attention being paid to us!" As Henry went to draw Josh aside, Father rubbed his face in disgust at this whole business.

The team lost the second game of the double header and Father Mike made arrangements to move the team that night, against the protests of the local hospitality. He thanked them and asked that they call ahead to Helena to let them know the team was arriving early. Nobody found it easy to argue with a priest, so the plans were changed.

The beginning of the bus ride was spiked with individual complaints, but Henry paid no attention to the minor problems of the ball players. He had to get away from the discovered location and set up a tighter defense at the new location. Jean would no longer stay on the bus during the games. If this, or anything like it occurred in Helena, he would have to react with a departure plan from that moment. Who the man was became a crucial element in all his considerations.

Thursday, August 2, 1945

The ride to Helena was taxing on everyone. Rest was the main resource sought by all on board, including Walt Chambers. Henry stayed awake with him during the drive and kept him supplied with coffee, purchased before the concession stand had closed in Billings. As a result, the whole bus welcomed the two stops along the side of the road, mandated by the liquid flowing through Walt. Jean was treated like royalty on those stops. Each man insured the gentlemanly thing was done to provide her privacy. Jean's thoughts were more to the point. She was just glad the bus stopped.

Thanks to the phone call, a harried group of welcomers were on hand in Helena, after just putting the finishing touches on the high school gym facilities. Their discovery of a woman in the party sent them back for further arrangements. This time Jean was housed in a classroom located in the main hall, just outside the gym doors. Henry didn't like her vulnerability in that classroom, so he moved his cot next to the gym doors. The two green bags were stationed with August and Josh and the other bags and suitcases were put in with Jean. The routine of the day was broken by the need to keep one of the men posted outside.

Henry suspected the stranger in Billings, was a detective, or FBI agent. But Sammy's words of impression left the door open to other possibilities. Henry knew someone was closing in, but who?

There was no game on Thursday night and Henry could not keep the players in the gym. He sent his three men to patrol their activities while they were in town. He and Jean stayed at the gym with Father Mike and Walt. They played cards to pass the time. No long conversations were welcome, just the friendly banter of talk over a deck of cards. Tomorrow would bring a weekend of baseball and Henry could have a little more control over the team.

Walt and Jean teamed-up and cleaned-up in cards.

Saturday, August 4, 1945

The round robin tournament had started on Friday evening. The heat of August was too much for the fans and players alike, so a full night of baseball was planned for each of the three days. Friday's games were well attended. The Colorado team notched another win. John Houser was back playing and the team seemed to be well rested and in good spirits. Father was glad things had stayed together. The nearness of the four men's departure was off set by the appearance of the strange man in Billings. Father Mike was determined to keep Jean from going any farther with the quartet. She could be in trouble with the law, as it was, but fleeing the country would not be viewed as the actions of an innocent person.

The Colorado team was scheduled for the second game on Saturday evening. They scattered around the ballpark and as the first game reached the halfway point, Father Mike collected everyone in the locker room, under the stands, to get them dressed and ready for the game. The team emerged from the player's tunnel before the first game had ended. John Houser was carrying his baseball shoes and spotted Jean sitting alone in the bleachers. He climbed to the row in front of her, sat down to one side to put on his shoes. He asked how she was doing.

"I'm ok." She smiled back at him. "How's your ankle?"

He flexed his right ankle in the air and pronounced it, "Good as new."

After lacing up his shoes, he leaned both elbows back on the bench to Jean's side.

He looked up at Jean and asked. "Can I ask you something personal?"

"You can ask." Jean replied, leaving all options open.

"I look at these guys you're with and, to me, they ain't nobody from Washington. They resemble a bunch of two-bit hoods. The fact that at least two of them carry guns lets me know something screwy is goin' on. But for the life of me, I can't fit you in with this bunch. Can you tell me why?" He waited for her to absorb his personal question and then began to think she wasn't going to answer.

"Those four men are just lost souls. I'm one too. I guess that's why we're in the same 'bunch' as you call it. I'm not a part of them, I just happen to know one of them. Henry's looking for a new start in life and so am

I. We're just spending too much time looking for it together."

He kept looking at her. "Are you in some kind of trouble?"

"Look John, I've made up my mind. In a couple of days I'm headed west and these fellows are going their way. So let's leave it at that, OK?" She got up and started to move to a different location. John caught hold of the cuff of her jeans to get one more thing said.

"If you need help, just let me know. OK?"

She looked at him and smiled again, then she looked at his hold on her cuff. He got the message and let her go.

As the second game got underway, Colorado had drawn the visitor's card and batted first. The first three and a half innings passed without a score. The opponent was the local team from Helena. They had some talent and the game was close. Father Mike had his young high school lefthander pitching and hits were hard to come by for Helena. With two out, John Houser readied himself at third base as he did on every pitch. The batter got around fast on the curve ball and cracked a solid line drive down the third base line. John made a lunge for it, but it was just out of his reach. From his belly, he kept his eyes on the flight of the ball and saw it land just inches into foul territory. For a second, everyone relaxed after seeing the results, but the third base umpire was pointing to fair territory indicating it was a fair ball. The batter had slowed to a trot, anticipating a return to the batter's box, when he saw the umpire and with the yelling of his first base coach, started at a full run again. The left fielder, who had given up on the ball when he saw it hit foul, responded to the yells from his teammates and began the pursuit again. By the time he retrieved the ball and got it into the relay man, the runner was standing safely on second.

The Marine in John exploded at the umpire. The umpire stood with his arms folded across his chest and waited for the on-coming player. When John got to within two feet, the Ump held up the open palm of one hand. No further was the order. John's disciplined background made him stop at that imaginary boundary, but his mouth kept running. He was incensed at the Umpire for calling a clearly foul ball, fair.

By the time Father Mike reached the scene, he had heard John say about everything that could be said and he figured he was too late to keep him from being thrown out of the game. He skirted himself between John and the Umpire and immediately felt John break the Umpire's imaginary line and do everything but climb over Father Mike's back. Colorado's good-natured catcher, Buck Hutchins, arrived with the home plate Umpire. Buck was the owner of the voice Jean had heard from behind the curtain that day Heaven was defined for him. He grabbed John and along with Doc, got him back to his position. Once there, the two talked to him using all the baseball logic available to cool him down.

Father had seen the ball from the third base dugout, which was not a good vantage point to judge from, but he took up John's argument in less painted language, to no avail of course.

The Umpire just stood with his arms folded and finally brought the hearing to a close by saying "I called the ball fair."

The home plate Umpire issued warnings to get back to the game and avoid any official action from being taken on the field. Father Mike walked over to John and quickly advised him, "Son, that's baseball. Now forget about it and start from here."

The local crowd loved the turn of events and gave the Colorado team as much static as social standards would allow. This was baseball too, allowing an opportunity for the people in the stands to spout off and relieve their pent-up frustrations within the controlled environment of the game. Things were just starting to settle down as a new batter came to the plate. John had not taken Father's advise and was still grumbling under his breath when, on the next pitch, the batter pulled another hot ball down third. John wasn't ready. The ball took a short hop and went under his glove and through his legs for an error. The crowd went wild as the runner from second rounded third and scored their first run.

John had a cold stare fixed on the third base umpire. The next batter struck out and ended the fun for the crowd that inning. As John walked across the third base line toward the dugout, the Umpire spoke to him, "Your name John Houser?"

John was caught off guard by the personal note and the fury within him faltered a bit and he responded, "Yeah, what do you want now?"

"John, I'm Agent Raymond Castle of the FBI. When you come out the next inning, tell your first baseman not to give you any warm-up tosses. I have some questions for you." The Umpire turned and walked casually back to his position.

John couldn't believe what he had just heard. He wanted the Umpire to repeat what he had said, just so he could make sure it was real. He walked the rest of the way to the dugout, caught in a dumbfounded world between fury and astonishment. He struck out when he was at bat. John followed the Umpire's instructions as he went to third base in the bottom of the inning.

The Agent/Umpire walked to the base and began to talk without looking at John. "You have some strangers on the bus with the team that maybe don't belong there?"

John didn't look at the Umpire, but scrapped half circles with his cleats in the dirt in front of him. "Yeah, I think so."

"How many are there?" The Umpire asked.

John paused trying to decide how to count Jean in the deal. "There are four of them."

"How 'bout a girl?"

"Yeah, there's a girl, but I don't think she is a part of them." John followed his instincts to protect Jean.

"Have you seen weapons on them?"

"At least two of them have .45's."

"Who else on the team knows about them?" The Umpire was running short on time.

"I don't know. I just started figuring this out today. What did they do?" John was trying to make sense of it all.

"Not now John. I'm goin' to be around the rest of your games. I will contact you if I need more information. Don't do anything. Just watch and listen.

Do you understand?" It was time to resume the ball game.

With military presence, John replied with a quiet, "Yes sir."

Agent Castle now had confirmation of his theory. Later that night he would send word to Jack Frazier that he had found the fugitives. But, well-intended agency people fumbled the message, plus Sunday was not a good day to locate the agents in charge. It would take two more days for Jack Frazier to mobilize his personnel and move them north to the heart of Montana. In the mean time, Raymond Castle enlisted the aid of the local police and Montana State Police. Agent Castle was instructed to keep gathering information and develop a plan to take the fugitives with the least amount of danger to the team or other civilians. Frazier said the first three agents to assist him would be there on Monday with the remaining force being assembled by Wednesday.

Raymond could see on the map the next stop was Great Falls. If Canada was were they were headed, this would be the jumping off place. He thought he could get enough law enforcement personnel together to stop them by Tuesday, but he knew any team he assembled for the task would lack continuity. Until a reasonable force was in place, any confrontation would have potentially disastrous results.

John kept notice of the four men and their activities, recounting their habits and patterns during a day. He could formulate a rough routine they would follow and could pass that on to the Agent.

Sunday, August 5, 1945

Father Sullivan conducted mass for the players that Sunday morning. The Protestants on the team always attended the services and participated in everything but the Communion Celebration. Jean attended for the first time.

After mass and breakfast, Father was seated in the grand stands of the Helena gym, reading a letter. Feeling the need to talk, Henry walked up the few bleachers and sat next to him. "Am I bothering you Father?"

Not looking up, Father knew it was Henry, “No, no not a-tall. What do ya have on your mind?”

“Is that a letter from family?” Henry asked, trying to assess the degree of his intrusion.

“Yes it tis, it’s from my brother Tom.” Father explained as he leaned the face of the letter toward Henry to show him the signature.

Noting the U.S. Navy stationery, Henry asked, “Is he in the Navy?”

“Yes, he joined the Chaplain Service when the war started. He’s been in the Pacific now for, let me see, three years I think it is. He hasn’t set foot back in the States in all that time.” Mike Sullivan displayed the pride at having a brother like Tom Sullivan.

“What’s he say about the war over there?” Henry asked.

“Well he says the Kamikazes are real and the worst thing goin’ on now. He was aboard the Franklin, one of our big carriers, when it was hit and burned so bad it nearly sunk. He said it was an immense tragedy, which is beginning to be a common sight in the Navy now.

He's been transferred to the battleship Missouri and thinks they will be ducking more Kamikazes for a long time to come. When the landings on Japan come, he says he might be sent ashore with the Marines, but in any case, he's afraid he will be needed no matter were they put him. He says here, he wonders what the Missouri has in store for its fate in this war."

"I'll tell ya son, that's nasty business over there." Father said as he folded the letter.

"How can he get so much information through the censors, I thought they watched that stuff pretty close?" Henry was surprised to hear actual war news from a letter.

"There are certain avenues of communication that are still sacred, like from a Priest in the conflict to his Church. The Chaplain General's office handles this mail personally and makes sure it is delivered intact and in confidence." Father Mike explained.

"Gee, has it been rough on you with him over there?" Henry had put himself in the place of having a brother in the war.

"Personally, yes. I don't want anything to happen to Tom. But I know his faith and my faith remain strong enough to accept God's plan for us, whatever it may be." He looked Henry in the eye, including him as part of his personal unknown fate.

Henry nodded with his lips pressed together, as he absorbed the meaning of the look he had received. "I wanted to let you know, it's only a matter of time and we'll be gone. I don't want anybody hurt."

"I pray all the time for that very thing, Henry." Father kept his stance.

Henry got up to leave, then turned back to Father Mike. "How come you didn't go over seas like your brother?" It was just curiosity.

"No doubt, there is a need over there for people to carry the faith, but I've seen what war can do to the people back here. People who have to go through their daily lives never knowing what day will bring them that awful telegram about their son, or husband. There's plenty of work to be done here too, Henry. No one goes untouched." Father nodded a polite gesture to Henry.

Henry walked away thinking about Father's last words. Had the war touched him? Then he thought about his decision to pull the robbery because of the coming of the end of the war. Maybe the war had been an influence on him all along, but he never felt it. Priests and pastors work in the minds and souls of people every day, that's their job. Maybe Father Mike knew something Henry didn't.

At the ball game that night, the tall young right-hander had pitched the entire game for the Colorado team. It was now the bottom of the ninth, with the Billings team at bat. During the game, John had his spotty conversations with the third base "Umpire". Agent Castles had prevailed upon the tournament organizers to get on the field again. Everything had been handled under strict confidentiality, so he would not lose control. John was eager to do more to get the four guys, but Agent Castle kept insisting he remain in the background and let the FBI handle it.

The Colorado team led 7 to 6 in the bottom of the ninth after fighting off a determined Billings team over the last two innings. The young right-hander on the mound was Gary Bell. Soon to be 18, his talent for throwing a baseball was well in advance of his emotions to react to the results. But he and his left-handed mate, Steve Masters, had gained valuable lessons in life and in baseball while on this tour. All their teammates were like big brothers and never had a crossword been aimed in their direction.

Gary walked the first batter on four straight pitches. He couldn't find the plate on the second batter either. Father Sullivan watched from the dugout knowing the Billings players were now going to wait on the young man to throw strikes before any attempts to swing at a pitch. Father called time out and walked to the mound. He saw John, Doc and Mike Thompson, the shortstop; all start to come to the mound too. He waved them back to their positions. When he got to the mound he noticed the young man's face was flushed with frustration. "Gary, have you heard from your mother lately?"

Gary looked at him wondering if this was a trick question. "My mom?" he asked, trying to make sure that was the question.

“Yes, has she written to ya lately?” Father pressed on with a healthy smile.

“Yes, we got mail yesterday and I got a letter from her.”

“Is everyone doin’ fine at home?” Father asked as if they were standing on a street corner somewhere.

“Yes, every things fine.” The youth replied “Good!” Father patted him on the shoulder. “That’s the important thing ya know?”

He raised his eyebrows and gave a quick smile. Then he turned back to the dugout. Gary nodded as he watched Father go.

The home plate Umpire announced, “Play ball!” and Gary addressed the pitching rubber from the stretch position. Before he got the next sign from Buck, he looked into the dugout. Father was standing there very relaxed. Gary threw the next pitch and it was a ball. Three more pitches gave up the third straight walk. The bases were now loaded with nobody out. The winning run was on second. Gary continued to struggle. The fourth batter came up and stood at ease in the box. Gary threw two more balls.

In the dugout, Walt tugged at Father's sleeve, "You're way past the time of getin' him outta there. What are you doin' to him?"

Father just raised his hand to Walt, in a quick brushing-off motion and continued his calm outlook from the dugout. The chatter from the Colorado fielders was constant and supported the young pitcher with no sign of disillusionment. The next pitch was a ball.

Gary took the ball thrown back to him by Buck and stepped back off the mound. He looked again at the dugout and saw Father's supporting nod. Then he looked around the infield and there were his teammates reading themselves for the next pitch. Realizing those people were there to support his effort, he felt the embrace of brotherhood. His frustration vanished.

He felt the strength of purpose and the confidence of the men around him. He took his place again on the mound. He noticed the batter's stance at the plate, as if he were going to take a "Ruthian" swing at the next pitch. This humored Gary. The batter looked ridiculous to him. He suddenly felt superior to the batter's purposeless gesture. He took the sign from Buck and started his delivery. He was going to give the batter the biggest, juiciest pitch he had, right down the center of the plate. He could take advantage of the batter's mind-set now. The ball felt good leaving his hand and he knew he had accomplished something before the ball got to the batter.

The batter had set in an exaggerated stance to swing for the fences as an intimidation factor, but now he saw the ball coming slow and straight to his hitting zone and his fraction-of-a-second response was to hit the ball. And that is what he did. The crack announced to the whole park that he had gotten "all" of the ball. It was a wonderful line drive headed straight for John Houser at third.

In a fraction of a second, the screaming line drive was in John's mitt for the first out. John's right foot reached for and found the third base, as he griped the ball in his glove with his right hand. The "Umpire" yelled the second out with John's force on the third base runner who had not reacted to getting back to the bag. The second base runner had started running with the swing of the bat and now was in no-man's land and he stood there helpless as John threw the ball to Doc to force him at second for the third out. A triple play had ended the game.

The Colorado team went wild and ran toward the young pitcher. The crowd spent a few seconds in silence as they collectively processed what had occurred. Then the elation of seeing a triple play swept everyone into applause for the rare baseball play they were now a part of. All of the emotion, the joy, the heartbreak, the laughter, the worry; all of these things and more are invested in a game. And the game gives back more that it takes. This is baseball.

Before John left his position at third to join his celebrating teammates, he turned to Agent Castle and smiled through a friendly barb, "You finally called one right!" The Agent smiled back but said nothing as he enjoyed this little time frame in a baseball game that transcended into a life experience. He would never forget the third baseman's conclusion of the moment with the embracing warmth of humor.

Father Mike didn't move from his position on the dugout steps. He knew the young right-hander had gone through a 'right of passage' in the game of baseball and the process of life itself. He turned to Walt, now ready to listen to what Walt had to say about how to manage the team. Walt saw the smile of satisfaction of Father's face and spoke as a wise old baseball fan. "Father, if you tell me you planned that, I'm gona personally find another Priest to hear your confession!" With an exchange of smiles, the two veterans of the diamond secured the event in their hearts.

Chapter 11

Monday, August 6, 1945

The team had the luxury of sleeping-in and starting late for Great Falls. The glow from last night's victory still registered on the faces of the players. The trip to Great Falls was going to be short. After two games at the most northern point of their tour, they would double-back and face the longest leg of the trip as they headed south and west into Idaho. This would begin the return loop of their journey. Father, Walt and now John harbored personal thoughts about what the next thirty-six hours would bring. Henry could feel the nearness of Canada and for him, the hours dragged.

Henry's analysis of the progress of the authorities hunt for him had been based on the news reports and his own observations of lack of activity in or around the team. He knew there was a chance of law enforcement emerging at an unknown moment, but that was just a part of what he inherited with his actions of July 20th. The man in the darkness could be dealt with, if he and his men stayed alert and smart. So, as he closed nearer his planned exit from the tour, he believed the FBI was scattered and did not know where he was. This was kept as the basis of his planning.

Agent Castle was getting frustrated with the time it was taking to get personnel into the Helena area. Had he been able to argue successfully for his initial theory, the fugitives might now already have been brought into custody. He was not in a position to issue any "I told you so's" to his superiors. It was not a career-building thing to do. So he was left with too short of time and too long of distance to gather a successfully functioning body of enforcers. He knew Great Falls was the key. An overwhelming force here could make all the difference in making the arrests without getting innocent people hurt. Two agents arrived on this day and Raymond elected to move on to Great Falls with what he had, including the help of the local and Montana State authorities. He would have to develop his plan on the fly.

Arriving at Great Falls High School, the players were relaxed and at ease, knowing they had the rest of the day and most of tomorrow, off. Soon after arrival, word started spreading from their hosts about an announcement on the radio by President Truman. Something about a large bomb being dropped on a city in Japan. The word atomic was used, but no one really understood what that meant. A radio was set up in the gym and most everyone sat around it listening to the various accounts, which were all derived from the President's broadcast. All attempts to develop the story were hindered and all broadcasts seemed to be alike. The lack of new information prompted Buck to turn the dial, locating one station playing the latest swing music. Never shy and a good dancer, Buck grabbed Jean's hand and pulled her out in front of the radio. Her initial protests were overcome by the sound of that music and the fun of dancing. For a catcher, Buck could swing.

Mike Thompson was the only other player who could match Buck's talent on the dance floor. He and Buck would cut in, as the music would command this opportunity to dance with a girl. Jean loved to dance and had the energy to go from song to song. The entertainment value kept everybody around the radio and the dancing three-some. Jean begged out of the engagement when her energy reached its limits, but the radio remained the focal point of the evening. Jean sat in the stands with Henry and talked. Henry talked of his plans.

The music and dancing with Buck and Mike had brought something back to Jean. It reminded her of a life she had enjoyed for so long. A life less complicated. California was now confirmed in her mind. She interrupted Henry in his narrative. "Henry. I think this is as far as I go."

There was a long pause between them as Henry absorbed what she had said.

Henry accepted it and asked. "Do you need any money?"

"No, I've still got my money. I'll be O.K." Jean was comfortable in her decision.

"Are you leaving tomorrow?" He asked.

"Haven't made all my plans yet, but I think it will be Wednesday. Besides, I'm beginning to like baseball." She smiled.

Henry tried to sum up their few months together. "Jean, it's been wonderful. Being around you has been very important to me. Maybe too much so for what is best for you. I regret the circumstances surrounding us, but I don't regret us. I only hope that being with me won't bring you trouble."

"Oh, it probably will. I haven't been able to side-step trouble my entire life. Right now I'm not thinking about that. Without my family, what comes my way is mine to deal with. I think I'm up to it." The mention of her family brought back the careless frame of mind, which was the reason for her being here in the first place. The bitterness toward her family was still alive. "Well, thanks for the ride, Henry." She stood up to go see if there was any more news on the radio, but looked back at Henry. "It's been a roller coaster ride alright. I just didn't know the coaster was going to be on fire during the ride!" She smiled. He smiled back and nodded a complete agreement.

Tuesday, August 7, 1945

Morning came with a renewed interest in what had happened in Japan the day before. One of the players was sent out to get several copies of newspapers and when he returned, Jean was one of the first to get a copy. She took it over to Henry's cot and there the two studied the account of the bombing of a city called Hiroshima. The article said it was one bomb dropped by one plane and literally obliterated the city. This was unbelievable. Where did this bomb come from? Wild accounts in rumors had for a long while spoke of a giant bomb that could destroy cities, but that was all fiction. Was this real, or part of that fiction?

With the President saying it was real and all accounts reporting factual information of the destroying of Hiroshima, all believed in the authenticity of this new bomb. If all the United States had to do was fly one airplane over any city, blow it apart with one bomb; then there could be only one conclusion, the war would end. On September 1, 1939, at 4:30 in the morning, Hitler had officially begun World War II by invading Poland. Now, almost six years later, the entire war was going to end.

Father Mike was walking near-by and Henry called to him while pointing at the paper, "Father, it looks like brother Tom is gun-a be sittin on that ship, with nothin' to do!"

"With God's help Henry, I hope he gets bored silly!" Father smiled back.

Jean excused herself from Henry and hurried to catch up with Father Mike. "Excuse me Father, do you have a moment?"

"Certainly, young lady, what is it that I can do for you?"

"I've been reading lately about the war. With the end so near, I'm not so sure what it was all about. I spent all these years ignoring what was going on, now I think I made the wrong choice."

Father looked around as if trying to make a decision of putting her off, or trying to tackle this huge question. "Sit down my dear, let's see if I can help. So you don't know too much about what happened these last four years?"

"I'm sorry to say, I don't." There was a sincere quest in her voice.

"Well, let me see. I guess the best way to explain it is greed. If you look back over the eons of history, as it involves humans, you will find greed to be the basis for almost every war. I'm sorry to say, religion is probably the second reason. Imagine, killing in the name of God! In this century, imperialistic designs by several countries on neighbors with lesser militaristic power has gone unchecked, just as it has for 3,000 years. You look at Great Britain and her empire, the Dutch, France, even the United States. You will see how the quest for the material wealth of a nation has made it acceptable to hold people prisoners in their own land." He looked at Jean and could see she was following with interest.

"So it started again with three new-comers to the imperialistic game. Germany, Japan and Italy had leaders who thought they should be a part of this grab for other's wealth. With quite different leadership in each of the three, they found a common bond in their desires. They formed an alliance and started on their conquests. Now, since all of the world was already divided up, in order for these three to be successful, they had to confront existing powers and tear their desired share away from someone else."

"There are dates which define this war, as to when it started and when it will end, for that matter, but the truth is, this war is probably a result of centuries of wars, which lead directly or indirectly to the next. You remember Italy's invasion of Ethiopia, Germany's aid to Franco in the Spanish Civil War and Japan's invasion of Manchuria and China. All of these little wars took place in the thirties, while the rest of the world watched. A sort of approval by non-intervention."

"One thing led to another and the land grab got more serious and soon, the three Axis powers started believing they could take anything. Their military could overpower any force in the way. And they were almost right. In the early years of the war, no one could stop them. They conquered country after country until a huge part of the globe was in their hands. In 1940, the United States was neutral and

Russia had a peace agreement with Japan and Germany. England stood alone against the three greatest aggressive powers in the world. No matter, the details now, but by whatever miracle God saw fit to employ, England succeeded in its lone vigil against the greatest evil the world has yet come across."

"Of course you know about Pearl Harbor. This is where the mistakes by the Axis powers began. Japan attacked America, Germany invaded Russia and Italy invaded Egypt. In each case, the attacking power bit off more than it could chew. America entered the war and started gearing up our great industrial might for war. Russia turned on Germany and overwhelmed them on the vast open territory west of Moscow. The British turned on Italy in the deserts of North Africa, pushing them and the German's off the continent. We, along with the Brits, French, Poles, Free Czechs, Russia and a host of other nations, compressed the Nazi war machine into a burned out cinder in Berlin. Now it looks like we've got Japan ready to quit."

"Now, it hasn't been easy Jean. Last count I heard, maybe a half million of our boys have been killed in the four short years we've been in this. Some people claim 25 million Russian's died in their war against the Nazis. Then, of course, there is the slaughter of millions upon millions of innocents, including this awful business we are now hearing about the six million Jews being exterminated."

"So, it's now time to start counting the dead and investing time, money and effort to rebuild the world. I would say, for the rest of recorded history, man is going to look back at this time in horrified amazement at the extent of killing that was done. It should sadden everyone to know this greatest of all tragedies has taken place."

"But for right now, Jean, we will leave the counting and the judgments of the war to other people and other times. Now is the time for us to be thankful that it is all coming to an end."

"We have lost a great deal in human lives and futures. Who can tell what great minds were lost during the killing. What great benefit to mankind was not allowed to materialize, because the one person who would have originated its birth, is now just a number in an endless list of victims."

"And what of their children and their children's children, who will never be?"

"Why did it happen? How could God allow this to happen? Man can speculate on these questions for eternity, but only God knows for sure. The thing for us to do is to remember what has happened and make sure future generations know it did happen. It is the only way we can lend services to making sure this never occurs again."

Such was the thinking of that day. A quiet anxiety hung beneath everyone's elation, as they cautiously thought about the possibility of life without war. The game that night took back seat for the players. The purpose of more than a decade was being realized.

Henry's plans were charged and ready. His timing was excellent. When the war ended, he would be in Canada.

That afternoon, John Houser prepared to go to the locker room to take a shower. As he approached the locker room door, the door suddenly swung his way and the progress in both directions was stopped. Realizing someone was attempting to come out, John prepared to apologize for his part in the bad timing. Coming on through the door was Sammy Keller. Sammy had a scowl and was upset by the stupid door incident. He stared darts at John.

Sammy stepped through the door and closed it behind him, blocking John's path.

John said nothing and did not attempt to move past the antagonist. Instead the two stood looking at each other in a contest of wills. Each man's dislike for the other began to manifest in the stand off.

Sammy spoke first. "I hear you're some kind-a war hero."

"I was there." John's reply said more than Sammy understood.

"Well I don't think much of war heroes. I got no use for them." Sammy was pushing with his mouth.

"You got your .45 on you?" John leaped far ahead of Sammy.

Sammy quickly replaced his surprise with anger. "What if I don't?"

"Then I would be shocked. I don't think you would talk to me like that without your gun. A coward like you always hides behind a gun."

Sammy exploded. In one movement he drew the .45 from his pants and shoved John against the wall with the .45 pressed into his neck. Sammy was so furious he couldn't speak.

So John spoke. "See what I mean?"

Sammy had drawn the gun with a rage to kill, but now he could not go forward and did not know how to back off. He kept John pined to the wall. John did nothing but look past the gun and into Sammy's eyes. Sammy had never seen a man do that to him before. He felt the stronger will of his adversary.

Father Mike came around the corner and from five feet away took in the horrible scene. "For God's sake man, what are you doin'?"

Sammy never turned his gaze away from John.

"Hello Father." John said with as light a tone as he could put past the gun at his throat.

"Sammy here, wanted to show me his .45."

Sammy saw a way out. He relaxed the pressure he held with the gun. His left hand turned loose of the wad of shirt it had held. "That's right Father." He pulled the gun away from John's neck and held it up to display to the Priest. "See, the safety is still on. We wouldn't want to have any accidents." Sammy retuned the gun to his pants, then mockingly used his hands to brush John's shirt as if he were tidying up. "You got-a be careful around guns, Marine, you just never know what's gona happen." Sammy brushed his way past Father Mike and turned the corner.

Appalled, Father Mike asked if John was O.K.

"Yeah, I'm O.K. Ya know Father, your timing is ***immaculate***." John was relieved to have the incident done.

Father wouldn't let it go that easy, "But I'm not at all sure about yours." He looked to see that Sammy wasn't coming back and then followed John into the locker room.

"John, you know about these men?" Father said as he caught up with John.

"Yeah, they're some grease balls pullin' this scam on us to get outta the country."

"Who else knows?" Father was assessing the extent of the danger.

"Oh, I suppose everyone knows they carry guns, but I'm not so sure they know why or what they're up to."

"When did you find out?" Father pressed.

"Over the weekend, I kinda put two and two together." John fabricated for the sake of Agent Castle's request.

"John, don't provoke that man again, or any of them. I think they are going to be gone soon and I don't want anyone getting hurt on my watch."

"Aye, aye, Father. It's your ball game." John started preparing for his shower.

Father walked out of the locker room and as he closed the door, he leaned back against it. He lifted his eyes up as beads of sweat ran down his forehead. "Lord, I know combat is a terrible thing, but right now I think I know what's comin' in second! Keep one eye on us if ya can!" Then he blessed himself and reached for his hanky to dry his face.

Both Henry and Agent Castle had been busy during the day. Henry gave instructions to his three men, as soon as it got dark, Sammy was to locate a good car in the parking lot and commandeer it for their run. The bags and luggage would remain locked on the bus, with Jean holding the key in the Grand Stands. Josh would be with Jean. August would be with Sammy.

When August brought word of Sammy's success, Josh and Henry would slip away and the four would make a dash for the Canadian border, ninety miles away.

Raymond still didn't have the people he needed to put a good, sound plan into effect, so he stationed two troopers with two deputies about four miles north of town, which would act as the first road-block and pursuit team, as needed. Two agents and two deputies would be at the ballpark, observing the parking lot in plain clothes. Raymond would be in the top of the grand stands with binoculars and a two-way radio to direct his meager force. His final card was an arrangement through the State Department for the Canadian Province of Alberta, to have a Home Guard unit and Royal Canadian Mounted Police Officers at the border to enforce a road-block there.

For both Raymond and Henry, tonight would be the culmination of their respective abilities to command.

Everything was routine as the team arrived at the ballpark. To Henry it seemed like time was not moving, as the expected preliminaries were the same as any other game night.

The game started. Walt, Father Mike and Henry were the only ones in the dugout. The relief players had all been sent to the bullpen, down the right field line. R.M.V. was the home team tonight as a courtesy gesture by the Great Falls team. Sammy and August were in the parking lot awaiting the time to begin their search. Josh and Jean were in the stands. Henry would nervously step to the top of the dugout and look into the stands for any sign of problems, or perchance, police. Each time his eyes ended the survey with Josh and Jean.

Dusk was coming and Henry thought Sammy should be starting his search. The field lights came on as an official prelude to the coming of darkness. Henry stepped up and looked through the stands. For a moment, his eyes caught a shadowy figure who stood out even in the dim light of the recessed area in which he sat. Henry's thoughts stayed with the man as he continued his gaze across the stands, ending again with Josh and Jean. He sat down and blew a breath of air to calm his nerves. He kept thinking about the shadow. The note of familiarity kept ringing somewhere in his memory. Then the chill struck him as he remembered Tuffs's bodyguard that night in the bar.

He stepped back up to look for the man, but no one was there. Henry searched the rest of the stands in particular for him, but did not see anything that brought back the image. Josh and Jean were still there. Henry sat back down wondering if he was creating something out of nothing. In any case, the memory heightened his sense of care.

Agent Castle had been observing Sammy and August from his perch high in the back of the stands.

He had watched Sammy walk through the lot, looking into cars. He knew what was going on. He kept his team up-dated on the movements through the 'walkie-talkie'. He felt like a neon sign with this cumbersome device, but it was the best available way to communicate. He had a good location and felt he wouldn't be seen.

Then he spotted something different in the lot. Another man was moving among the rows of cars, in a crouch and carrying something. This was not a member of either group, a complete surprise to Raymond. He put the binoculars on him and could see in the dim light from the field, that he was carrying a rifle. It looked like the big automatic used in combat. This was an assault weapon and it meant big bullets were going to be flying soon. He got on the two-way to his agents in the parking lot and told them of this new development. He told them where to find the man and ordered a flanking movement by all four to stop him.

Sammy found the car and signaled August before he got in to start it.

It was now time.

August disappeared into the ballpark.

Henry gave another look into the stands and thought the time for action should have been here already. He anxiously gave Sammy the benefit of allowing him to carry out his assignment. He sat down again. The Colorado team was in the field. There was a play made on a local runner at second base and the Great Falls player's spikes came up into Doc's chest. Teammates rushed to the scene where Doc and the opponent were nose to nose in angry exchanges. Father started out onto the field, but Henry grabbed his arm and said, "Stay here!"

Father resigned himself for the greater safety of the team.

The argument continued on the field until the four umpires could get between the parties of disagreement. The milling around and final accusations were put down by the umpiring crew and order was restored. Doc and the offending runner stood on either side of second base, with an umpire standing firmly between them. Everyone else had retuned to their stations to start the game again.

Henry started drifting into thought again and now he felt enough time had passed. He stood up and looked into the stands. This time he started with Josh and Jean. They weren't there. He quickly looked back and forth, but did not see them. Something was wrong. Adrenaline shot through his system as he pulled his .45 and in a voice desperate with purpose, ordered: "Walt, Father, lets go, something's gone wrong!" He motioned with his gun for them to precede him toward the parking lot. By all visual and vocal signals, this was a real crisis, so they responded immediately.

As they ran into the parking lot they heard a car screech out onto the pavement of the street and roar off out of sight. Jean was standing beside the bus, pointing at the car. "It's them Henry, they took the bags!"

At that time, not far away, two loud rifle shots rang out. Henry was shocked to realize he had abandoned caution in his hast. He saw men struggling at the point where the shots were fired. Several men had a hold of one big man and he was fighting them for control of the rifle and his freedom. Henry knew it was Tuffs Bellenger's shadow now.

"Everyone on the bus, right now!" He shouted and shoved at Walt and Father and pushed Jean ahead of him as he climbed the stairs. Shots rang out again from the scuffle and Walt didn't need any other prompting to get the bus started and moving. Henry stood beside him and pointed the way with his gun.

On the field, John Houser heard the reports of the automatic rifle and recognized them from his days on Guadalcanal. He looked into the dugout and saw it was empty. He started sprinting toward the dugout as Steve finished his delivery of the latest pitch. The hitter smacked a line drive that was going to intersect John's route across the diamond. At shortstop, Mike Thompson moved to make a play on the ball, but saw John cutting in front, so he relaxed to let John make the play. John felt the presence of the ball and ducked and continued on his primary mission. The ball screamed onward to a now unprepared Mike. He was barely able to throw up a forearm to deflect the ball from his face, but the acrobatics left him on his back in the dirt, wondering, "What the hell happened?"

John's call to Doc brought him running from second and soon everyone but Mike was running off the field. Mike sat there and watched as the world went nuts.

John reached the parking lot in time to see the bus disappear around the corner, headed north. The struggle in the parking lot was barely under control as Agent Castle came running and yelling into his two-way for the road blocking force to abandon their position and take up pursuit of the car, with three men in it, last seen heading east. Castle ran to the scuffle and yelled for help from the players. Soon, everyone in the ballpark had given up places in the stands to see what all the excitement was about in the lot.

To Agent Castle, he had seen the flight of the three dangerous men in the car and they were to be the first target. He had not seen the bus leave, but had now to get control of the stranger before any one here got hurt.

In the car speeding east, Sammy, Josh and August were laughing and slapping each other on the shoulders. “We did it! We did it!” was their victory cry. Josh yelled from the back seat, “I didn’t think we could do it Sammy, but it happened just like you said!”

Sammy said, “I told you! I told you, ole Henry could be had and we took him!” He handed Josh a pint of whiskey he had secured for this moment. Josh sat between the two big green G.I. bags and took a pull on the bottle.

August took the bottle from a gasping Josh and he too took a big pull. “I tell you vat, who da hell vants ta go ta Canada, anyvay?”

They all laughed again as Sammy took the bottle. “Boys, I got plenty of whiskey in my suitcase and we’re gona celebrate all the way to Chicago!” He toasted them and tipped the bottle to his lips. They were surprised to see Sammy take that drink, but the moment was indeed a celebration.

Josh jumped in with the obvious, “Sammy, I didn’t know you drank!”

“Yeah, there’s a lot you don’t know kid! I been on da wagon for eight years, but I can’t think of a better time ta fall off than tonight!" Laughter came easier and easier.

Walt, Father, Jean and Henry were on the bus headed north. Four police cars came at them from the north, with lights flashing and sirens screaming. Walt glanced at Henry for instructions, but Henry just watched the on-coming cruisers. They all watched as the cars sped bye, one at a time and continued out of sight to the south. The lawmen had been schooled from the beginning to expect a car and had been given notice that that car was now headed east of town. In the confusion of the parking lot, no word had gone out about the bus, so it continued on in the darkness, by itself.

The parking lot was still a mass of confusion. The big man was down and the lawmen now had him cuffed. The two deputies had been injured in the struggle, so the two FBI agents were having players help them keep the man down. The city police were soon on the scene and able to take control of the prisoner, finally releasing the FBI agents to join the pursuit. Raymond told the agent with the other two-way to get his car and head east to take charge of the chase for the three men in the stolen car. Raymond took the other agent and sought John out in the crowd. "John, what happened to Henry?"

"He took Father Mike and Walt on the bus and they're headed north!" John relayed what he had seen. He didn't know Jean was on the bus.

"O.K., you stay here and tell any police officers who show up to follow me after that bus." He and agent Lassiter ran for their car to start the chase.

As far as John was concerned, a Marine went where the action was. He wasn't going to stand around and point the way for someone else. He cornered a likely group of local men and asked if any of them had a car to take him on the chase. Like a flash fire, everyone caught the fever. People were running for their cars, some not really understanding why, just understanding there was some excitement to see. Doc and the other players held John long enough to find out what was going on. They too started flagging down cars and jumping in to go save Father and Walt.

As Agents Castle and Lassiter sped north, they could see a long stream of headlights following them.

Raymond calmly said. “If this isn’t the damnedest mess I have ever seen. We’ve got the roadblock from the north now chasing the car that was supposed to go north, to the east! The bus that was supposed to stay in the parking lot is now running free to the north! And behind us, we’ve got an army of sightseers on our ass thinking this all is just a part of the ball game!”

He looked at Agent Lassiter and giving a sarcastic chuckle, “Frazier is gona have my butt for this!”

The eastbound car had gotten a good jump on the pursuit; even though the three were unaware a pursuit even existed. They had left the parking lot before the ruckus started, so they had no idea the lot was full of FBI and police. They had taken the information Henry had given them, read the articles themselves and concluded the same as he had, the authorities didn’t know where they were. Based on this, Sammy had sparked the idea of a mutiny; not that the idea had ever been very far from his mind. With nobody chasing them, thanks to Henry’s bus idea, the timing was perfect to break away and head for the hideouts of Chicago. In Chicago they would be among their element and able to control their lives. Canada never appealed to any of them. The crossing of Montana, North Dakota, Minnesota and Wisconsin didn't seem to be much of a problem when nobody knew where they were.

The drinking went on as the miles elapsed. Josh turned his attention to the two green bags. He wanted to liven up the party again, so he opened the top of one of the bags and grabbed a hand full of wrapped bundles and tossed them up front. As the currency landed on the two in the front seat, the laughter started again. Then August said as he examined the bundles, "Hey, dese are da tens and twenties. Throw up some of dose big bills."

Josh opened the second bag and grabbed a hand full of bundled hundreds and tossed them. Then he dug deeper to secure more bills, grabbed a hand full and threw them. But this paper was not bundled and it reflected the light differently. The laughter slowly stuttered to a halt as the three men looked at the "different money". They picked up the individual pieces and looked closely at them. Sammy said softly, "Newspaper." They all saw it now. Newspaper cut into the size of U.S. currency.

Sammy locked up the brakes as his rage took hold. The car skidded for seventy yards, with Sammy's anger at the wheel. Finally the right tires caught the side of the pavement and spun the car backwards into the ditch. It came to an abrupt halt as the rear-end embedded into a bank of earth.

"What the hell is goin' on?" Sammy screamed as he got out and swung the back door of the sedan open. He drug a bag out on the ground and around in front of the headlights. He started pulling handful after handful of cut newspaper out of the bag. Only a few bundles of twenties had resided at the top of the bag, to keep the deeper secret. August and Josh brought the other bag around and the same results were found. They only had a fraction of the thousands of dollars in real currency. They stared in amazement at the newspaper bills scattered all over the ditch. Sammy drew his .45 and took two steps toward Great Falls. He started firing and yelling, "Damn you Henry, you double crossing son-of-a-bitch, I'll kill you!" He emptied the clip willing the bullets to reach the intended mark.

Josh stood back and remembered Jean was the one with the newspapers and scissors. He thought it best to keep this to himself. He and August were glad the drunken, angry man had emptied his pistol. The car was hopelessly stuck in the ditch and the right rear tire was blown. Steam was winding its way out from under the hood and the headlights lit the way to nowhere.

Sammy went to the back of the car and kicked on the trunk until it gave way. He fumbled through the luggage and found another bottle. He walked to the dirt embankment, sat down and started some serious drinking.

In a stupor, Josh and August looked at each other, then the car, then Sammy. Neither felt like a drink now, so they sat down on the bank and tried to sort out reality from the events of the past five minutes.

Henry walked to the back of the bus where up on the luggage carrier was the large white canvas bag he had bought in Casper. It was now bulging with its contents. He pulled the bag down and opened it on the seat. It was full of green bills of currency. Jean had taken the paper bands off of each original bundle so more bills could be packed into this bag and also to prevent the visual rectangular impression the bundles would have made pressing against the bag. Henry had used Sammy's own words to make this insurance policy. In Omaha, Sammy had told him he ought to know he couldn't trust anyone in this business. So he didn't. He pulled the rope closed at the throat of the bag, leaving it on the seat.

The hour and a half ride went with little talk. Henry was up front watching each mile pass. Occasionally, he would walk to the back and look behind them for any sign of car lights; so far, nothing. As the border came closer, Henry began to feel the stress of the most harrowing part of his journey coming to an end. He expected to get through the border by Walt telling any Canadian authorities about a simple bus tour. He was almost home.

Soon, the structures at the border crossing came into view. An office/residence to the left, then the island booths came into the headlights. Walt was steering for the right lane next to the middle booth, when he saw the path was blocked. He got on the brakes and slowed the bus to a crawl as he squinted to define the problem in the headlights. He stopped about thirty yards from the booth as they saw what awaited them.

There were at least seven Home Guard Defense soldiers, with fixed bayonets and their rifles aimed at the bus. The bright red tunics of four Royal Canadian Mounted Police Officers stood behind the kneeling row of Home Guards. The R.C.M.P. had pistols drawn.

Henry was bent over, beside Walt, taking in the same scene. He looked left, then right and saw the ground was not suitable for the bus to bypass the Canadians. Even if it were, how could they outrun the bullets once they had flanked the station? He knew the Canadians would not fire into U.S. territory without just cause, so he stared exploring other options.

Walt contributed: "Looks like the 'Good Neighbor' policy is workin' well."

What Henry wanted was for Walt to turn the bus around and backtrack the way they had come. Out of sight of the Canadians, he would turn left or right to find away across the border elsewhere, even if it meant a foolish attempt to cross on foot and try to evade horse and motor vehicles lugging the heavy bag. Desperation had retuned for the final performance. He instructed Walt to turn the bus around. Walt started by turning the wheel to the right and moving the back of the bus toward the right ditch. Almost there, he stopped, turning the wheels to the left to move the bus forward across the road. He expected to repeat these maneuvers a couple more times in order to get the bus pointed back south. As he completed his first move forward he was sitting at a 45-degree angle across the highway, the front of the bus pointed northwest, toward the superintendent's residence. The Canadians were still in their defensive positions to the right of the bus. Their rifles pointed directly at the bus's door.

Walt looked to the south as he started to turn the wheel for the next reverse move, when all his actions came to a halt. “Henry.” He addressed the man who was giving the orders.

“Yeah?” Henry responded as he studied the Canadians to make sure they were not coming across the border to initiate an arrest.

“How many rounds do you have in that gun of yours?” Walt asked deadpan.

“Nine, why?” Henry replied in curiosity.

“I think you’re gona need more than that. Looky yonder.” Walt pointed south.

Henry pivoted and looked between Walt and the steering wheel, to the sight Walt had already discovered.

There was a string of car lights for as far as could be seen, all advancing on the bus.

“Crap!” Henry said as the back door idea slammed shut. “Okay Walt, leave the bus where it is and get down so someone doesn’t take a pot shot at you.”

"That's the best idea you've had young man!" Walt was relieved of his driving duties and an imagined "bull's eye" on his body.

Henry, Jean, Father Mike and Walt sat in the isle of the bus while the headlights started stopping about thirty yards from the bus. As each car came in, a large semi-circle formed as the drivers tried to find a vantage point to see the action. In the middle of the formation sat Agents Castle and Lassiter. Raymond slowly shook his head in amazement at the spectacle.

East of Great Falls, the pursuit was closing fast on the grounded vehicle. Surprised by the headlights from the ditch, the cars came to screeching halts to investigate the abnormality. Officers piled out on the opposite side and with spotlights flashing and weapons drawn. They called for the men they saw in the ditch to get their hands up.

Josh immediately broke, running into the nearby darkness. August didn't try to run. He knew he had aunts who could out run him, so he never considered it an option. He stood up with his hands in the air. Sammy went into shock at the sight of the police. He never expected this, either. Just as John had predicted, without his gun, the coward in Sammy unfolded. He stayed huddled in the ditch, scared to expose himself to the guns of the law. The police advanced on him with flashlights and took no chances in forcefully imposing the cuffs on him.

The police at the scene radioed back to Great Falls about the capture of two men, with a third man "in the bush". They knew it would take morning for it to be sound enough and safe enough to go after Josh. They had to keep the force assembled there until they could get Josh. This didn't allow for any relief to travel in support of Agents Castle and Lassiter.

Castle and Lassiter had their hands full. John and other members of the baseball teams found Raymond and asked if they wanted help in storming the bus. Raymond had a better idea. He pronounced each of the players deputized on the spot and ordered them to spread around the parameter and keep the crowd back. Highly disappointed in not receiving orders to charge, the players resigned themselves to the less glamorous duty of crowd control. The Agents got shotguns and a bullhorn from the trunk and secured positions behind the open 'wings' of their car doors. Raymond talked to the person on the bus he thought was Henry. He gave him instructions for surrendering; telling Henry it was only a matter of time before the inevitable. He considered Henry a dangerous man, with a belief that he had at least one killing on this spree. Raymond was determined not to get anyone else hurt. He could wait for this thing to end on its own. The bus just sat there, idling.

Without badges or weapons to enforce their orders, the spectators paid little attention to the men in baseball uniforms. They were intent upon seeing a real live police drama and they stayed where they could get the best view. They settled in, as an audience at the movies would do, displaying the patience necessary to outlast the standoff.

Wednesday, August 8, 1945

The early morning hours ticked by and nobody had moved. Everyone was waiting for the light of day to bring this thing to a close. Father and Henry had talked quietly through the darkness, while Jean and Walt sat near by. No one thought about sleep. Henry would raise his head once in a while to see if anyone was advancing on the bus. If someone had, they could have ended it rather unceremoniously. Henry would not have resisted. He knew it was over; he just couldn't yet bring himself to walk down off the bus. Besides, in the darkness lighted by all of the headlights, someone might get edgy seeing him suddenly appear and fire off some ill-fated rounds.

The hours passed. In his latest glance to the south he could see more car lights coming. There were hundreds of people out there with more on the way as news of the event spread around the area. People in a nearby town got out of their beds and put together pots of coffee and sandwiches to distribute to the spectators. It was like a Sunday picnic in the dark. The two agents were irritated at the inconvenient presence of the crowd, but did appreciate the coffee and sandwiches as they waited.

"So what are ya thinkin' Henry?" Father asked.

"I think it's gun-a get light here pretty quick." Henry avoided Father's meaning.

"Then what?" Father pressed on. "They're out there waiting for you to end this thing. You're the only one that can do it peacefully. You know that don't you Henry?"

Henry's thoughts leaped past the question. "I just wanted to start my life over. I wanted a life like those people out there have. I wanted all the things that have made me what I am ta be erased, so I could become the kind of guy I really think I am."

"And you were goin' to make this miraculous change with a bundle of money? Is that what you think it takes?" Father was beginning to see into Henry.

"Yeah, I guess that was the idea. With money, people don't question you, they don't look at you and wonder who you are and whether you're good enough. If you got money, they just fall into line, no questions asked and you are who you say you are. I've seen it happen that way." Henry stared ahead as he pictured the people he had seen with money.

The sun was starting to come up.

"Henry, money doesn't change people. It only changes the way other people think about you. If the money disappears, they'll change the way they think again. No Henry, it's not the money; it's what's inside of you. With faith in God and your own will power, you can make changes to your life. But don't look to what people think as proof of what kind of person you are. The most important person to define who you are is you. Once you know for sure, what other people think or say just doesn't matter."

"Right." Henry didn't understand it all. "How am I supposed to know who I am if I don't know who I am?"

Father gave a little chuckle at the nonsense statement Henry had just uttered. The chuckle brought a grudging smile from Henry. "The way you do it is with help. You find people that are important to you; you ask for their help and listen to what they say. You work with them and your faith to find the right way for you. That's why people like me have a job in this world. Don't think you're the only one who ever felt this way. Too many times people think they have to solve their problems all by themselves. Left alone, you can lose perspective on real life and make the wrong choices. Following your faith in God and looking to others is the way all problems can be dealt with. You may not like all the answers, but you will find a way to live with them as they are."

Henry looked at Father Mike as the sunrise was giving a small amount of light to his face. "Don't you think it's a little too late for me, now?"

"No, it's not too late. If you let this thing continue and somebody gets hurt, then it's goin' to be near impossible for you to get turned around. If you end this now, you can start now to make the changes you want to make."

"Well, in any case, I'm down to one choice..." Henry was cut short by a loud roar.

He and Father both, could not grasp what the noise was. The sunrise had brought light enough to see clearly now as both rose to their knees and looked out of the bus windows. It was a collective roar of hundreds of voices, like the sound that greeted a winning home run in the bottom of the ninth.

They saw the crowd rushing the bus. It was very startling, except that the bus seemed not to be the target of their surge. All the eyes of the people could be seen looking up above the bus, not at it. Then bits of paper began to float down from above the bus. The paper was completely out of place. What was it and where was it coming from. Henry and Father now noticed movement at the back of the bus. It was Jean. She had taken the white bag and shoved its open end out of a window, pushing the contents out of the bag. The large bills were spilling into the morning wind.

The angle at which the bus had been parked, caused a southerly morning wind to pick up the bills and swirl them above the bus and in the direction of the Canadians. The crowd was caught by the magic of money dancing free in the air and everyone was overcome by the urge to chase it. It was not out of greed that they moved, but out of the attractive nuisance created by Jean. The two Agents and the ball players were helpless. The Agents lowered their weapons and watched. Gunfire was out of the question now. Agent Castle said, “Well I’ll be damned! Lassiter, how am I supposed to explain this in a report? After we get this guy into custody, we’ve got to take up a ‘collection’ from these good people!”

After Jean had emptied the bag, she punched it out of the window and came running down the isle. She hurdled Walt and side stepped Father and as she started past Henry he reached up and grabbed her by the belt ring of her jeans. He arrested her progress and with a twist of his body, brought her back and down into his lap. “Whoa, whoa! Where ya goin’?”

At being stopped in her rush, she broke into tears. She had had enough of the problems the money was causing. She sobbed to Henry. “The money’s gone now Henry. This whole thing was about the money and look at what it’s done! Well it’s gone now!” Her energy was spent.

Henry looked at Father. Then he kissed Jean on the forehead and said, “Look kid, I’m sorry you were drug into this. I’ve always been the happiest around you.”

He nodded to Father to take her, then motioned for Walt to come forward. He released the clip of ammunition and let it fall harmlessly to the floor. He pulled the chamber open to make sure there was no round still remaining in the gun, then he handed the gun to Walt. “Here, take care of this.”

Eager to get the gun out of Henry’s hands, but not too enthused about being the one to be seen carrying it, Walt crawled forward and pulled the lever to open the bus door. He tossed the gun out onto the pavement.

Henry extended his hand to Father Mike saying, “I never wanted anyone hurt.”

“I know son.” Father Mike shook his hand.

Henry crawled past Walt and Walt put his hand up to stop him momentarily, “Don’t do this again!”

Henry smiled at the good hearted man, “Not likely, Walt. Not likely!”

Then he moved toward the stairwell and was quickly out of sight. He went down the stairs in a crouch, still not wanting to be a target. The scene out side the bus was a mad house. The crowd had the bus surrounded on three sides as they chased the wonderful vision. He looked down at the gun Walt had thrown out. He stepped over it and into the crowd.

Not knowing the correct timing for his little group of three to emerge from the bus, Father continued to comfort Jean and let the regaining of her composure set the time for him. Her sobs had subsided and she was wiping her eyes with his hanky. He asked. "Are ya ready ta go lass?"

She said, "I only wanted to help him be the kind of person I know he is. I don't think I did anything but mess it up."

"Jean, me darlin' girl, you did more for that boy than you'll ever know. You shared a dream with him. A moment shared is a moment given life. He'll remember you for who you are and he'll be a better man having known a person like you." With that he helped her to her feet and the three walked to the stairwell. Jean, Father Mike and Walt stood in the stairwell surveying the frenzy of the crowd.

At the southwest corner of the office building, hidden by the building's corner, was a lone figure. It was Henry. He was looking back at the scene marveling at the fact he had just walked through it unnoticed by anyone. He saw the three figures standing on the bus and gave a silent "thank you" to them. He disappeared behind the building.

THE END

EPILOGUE

Eldon Appleby found he had been promoted into the position he had always desired. He was then charged with the responsibility of finding and arresting himself. This was never foreseen in all his schemes to retaliate against the Railroad. His intent had been to slip quietly away with his new "retirement" funds. But things went terribly wrong. He never retrieved the fifteen thousand dollars from the creamery.

When he heard the three fugitives were in custody in Montana, he went to his brother-in-laws empty house, sat down at the kitchen table and wrote the following:

"On the soul of my dear wife, I never intended for anyone to get hurt. I am responsible for guiding those four young men into the robbery on July 20th. My reasons were based on greed and revenge. I can now see how wrong I had been. Captain Paully's death was a result of my misguided mind and hands. I didn't expect to see him in the Yard that night, but when I did, I lost control and all the years of hate came to me. In my unforgivable anger, I shot the man to death. It was by my hand and my deed that he died and had nothing to do with the four young men in the Yard that night. I regret everything. As a result, I do not expect to be in the eternal company of my dearly departed wife.

As it is my duty to bring the murderer of Captain Paully to justice, I will do so now. I have found myself guilty of his murder and have imposed my sentence."

He shot himself once in the head with the same gun he used to kill the Captain.

The creamery was torn down in 1949. One section of the crew was assigned the task of salvaging the metal from the building. As one young employee was cutting four-inch pipe away from its concrete, encrusted base, he noticed something strange inside the pipe. His fellow employees thought it highly unusual to see him walk off the job that day, without a word to anyone, never to return. They said it was as if he didn't need a job anymore.

On September 2, 1945, Father Tom Sullivan stood high up on the starboard wing bridge of the Battleship U.S.S. Missouri, which was at anchor in Tokyo Bay. Along with nearly the entire U.S. Naval Fleet, the Missouri was not there to bombard the mainland of Japan to soften up a landing zone for an invading force. The "Mighty Mo", as her crew affectionately called her, was selected to host the signing of the formal surrender documents between the Allies and the Empire of Japan.

Father Tom looked down on all the "Brass" assembled below him and watched as General Douglas MacArthur led the proceedings. Father Tom saw the formal documents being so attentively signed and resigned by all representatives of the warring parties and he thought, "What a waste". Millions of people lost their lives in brutal, inhumane acts of violence and it all comes down to a formal "tea party" to put the finishing touches on the worse catastrophe the human world has known. There was still plenty of work for he and other men of God to do in this world.

Josh, August and Sammy went to trial together, in Federal Court. They received convictions for the robbery and kidnapping and a list of other related crimes connected with the events from July 20th to August 8th, 1945. They were found innocent on the murder charge as the jury declared the killing to be a separate incident from the robbery. Eldon Appleby's last letter had saved three lives in this courtroom.

Josh and August were sentenced to twenty years in Leavenworth Federal Penitentiary for their parts in the crimes. They were eligible for parole after 12 years. They made parole in the 15th year. August used the trade he had learned in prison to support himself the rest of his working life. His skill as a baker surprised him. He married and never again returned to the wrong side of the law.

Josh went back to Detroit and soon fell back into old habits. He was shot to death in 1964 as he was making a money drop on behalf of the criminal organization he belonged to.

Because of his violent history, Sammy was given a thirty-year sentence to be served in the Atlanta Federal

Prison. He never had a parole hearing. Without a gun, Sammy had turned to the protection of a gang of inmates. He had been assigned duties as their collector of debts.

In 1956 he was stabbed to death while trying to collect a debt of cigarettes owed to members of the gang. No one came to his aid. He never had smoked.

A Federal Grand Jury brought Jean Lester up on charges of aiding and abetting a fugitive from justice and her hearing was held in front of a Federal Judge in Kansas City. Her father attended each day, but she never saw her mother during this time. Nobody, called to testify to the Grand Jury, could give any just cause of the charges alleged against her. Even the three convicted in the case, had a sudden loss of memory about Jean on the trip. They knew they were headed for prison and other inmates don't take kindly to "Rats". It would be especially tough on them to "Rat-out" a woman in exchange for shorter time. So the three had nothing to contribute in Jean's hearing.

The presiding Judge felt logically, that Jean had in some fashion violated a law or two along her travels with the fugitives, but in absence of any testimony to that effect, he dissolved the Grand Jury and ordered her released.

Her father arranged to have her live with his sister in Dayton, Ohio. She got a job at an airfield working for an annual air show. While working there, she met a young test pilot who had been decorated as a P-51 fighter pilot during the Second World War. He was a good-looking adventurer by the name of Turner Moore. For the first time, Jean knew she was in love. They were married in 1948. Turner became very supportive in her reconciliation with her Mother and sisters. They had three sons, the oldest following in his father's footsteps as an Air Force Pilot. In 1970 he was shot down while flying a mission over North Viet Nam, spending two years as a prisoner of war. Jean was haunted by the memory of the little article she had read about Ho Chi Minh, in 1945.

Sunday, August 8, 1965

Father Michael Sullivan completed his morning mass at his Denver Church and waited to greet his parishioners as they filed out of the Church. George Avery and his wife Alice found their way to Father Mike. Father reached out and shook George's hand saying, "I missed you at mass last week George, were you ill?"

"No, no Father far from it." George explained, "I was on a fishin' trip up in the Canadian Rockies. It was the kind of Church I would like to attend every week."

"Ah, me too!" Father joked with him.

At that, the man reached into his suit pocket and retrieved a business card. He pressed it into Father's hand and said, "You do it Father. Take some time to go fishin'. You get a-hold of these people and they will treat you like royalty. It was the best trip I have ever been on!"

Father thanked him and said good day as other hands reached for his hand in George's place. After the last hand had been shook and the last pat on the back, Father walked through the Church to his office. He was going to prepare for the next mass, when he discovered the card George had given him, still in his left hand. He held it up to read.

HIDDEN SUNDOWN TOURS

Hunting, Fishing, Sightseeing, in the Canadian Rockies

Please Contact

Hank or Pauline Lester

Father thought as he studied the card. “Lester? I know that name. Ah yes, but it was a Jean Lester.” The memory of those summer days in ‘45 came back in very detailed form. “Hank Lester? Could it be her brother? No, she had no brothers.” Then the possibility occurred to him. “Hank Lester…Henry Lester…ah…Henry Lapointe. Could it be one in the same? Well I’ll be!” He thought for a moment about the young man with the gun. Then spoke to himself “If ya are one in the same, I believe you’ve been in God’s hands these past twenty years. I can think of no better hands to leave ya in.” With that he dropped the card into the wastebasket.

He got up to leave the room and mumbled to himself, “A fishin’ trip? Naw, I couldn’t do that, what with getten’ up early every mornin’ and eating fried fish, fried potatos, eggs and bacon, then spendin’ the day pullin’ in large, wild trout, or sittin’ under a tree on the bank to take a nap. Then spending the evenin’s over an open fire cookin’ the day’s catch, spinning yarns about the ones that got away. And oh, sleepin’ in that cool mountain air…! No, it wouldn’t do, it just wouldn’t do.” His heavy sigh brushed the thought aside.

About the Author

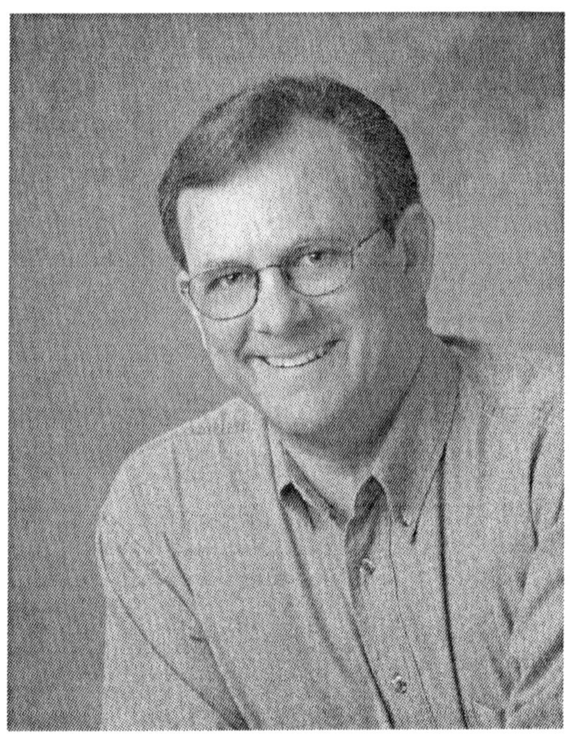

This is the author's first attempt at anything close to writing for public consumption. Yet, the story he tells is original and entertaining, affording the reader many facets to peer into life and observe the differences between people. If we were all made alike, there would be no place for story telling. Born and raised on the western plains of Kansas, the author spent his childhood as a shy reserved boy who would walk the streets of his hometown, WaKeeney, with his eyes riveted on the pavement carrying his steps. The fear of meeting other people's eyes and fumbling the social graces defined his shyness. But he watched people from behind closed lips and learned what made them laugh, what made them cry, what made them hope, and what made them dream.

The people of greatest influence on the author were people from the two generations before him, the people who actually lived the twin human challenges of the Great Depression and the Second World War. From his quiet stance in life, he would gather a harvest of thoughts from these witnesses to a world he never saw. The importance of what they said cannot be lost to the driving forces of today's life. They were and are too valuable a gift to this world to let their passing be the end of what they did here.

Printed in the United States
1269000001B/8